It was him—the sea bum

"I want to talk to you," he said.

Summer jerked her elbow away. "I've got a business to run."

"Why did you leave my boat?" he asked, his voice a low rasp.

"You were asleep."

"You should have said something."

"Like what? What could I—"

"I've been looking all over for you. For more than two years."

Summer tried not to think about the mole on his shoulder. She'd fingered it, kissed it, tasted it with her tongue. The idea seemed ludicrous now.

Dear Reader,

Evelyn A. Crowe's legion of fans will be delighted to learn that she has penned our Women Who Dare title for November. In *Reunited,* gutsy investigative reporter Sydney Tanner learns way more than she bargained for about rising young congressman J. D. Fowler. Generational family feuds, a long-ago murder and a touch of blackmail are only a few of the surprises in store for Sydney—and you—as the significance of the heroine's discoveries begins to shape this riveting tale.

Popular Superromance author Sharon Brondos has contributed our final Woman Who Dare title for 1993. In *Doc Wyoming,* taciturn sheriff Hal Blane wants nothing to do with a citified female doctor. But Dixie Sheldon becomes involved with Blane's infamous family in spite of herself, and her "sentence" in Wyoming is commuted to a romance of the American West.

More Women Who Dare titles will be coming your way in 1994. Patricia Chandler and Tracy Hughes have two great, daring stories lined up for you in the spring. And watch for titles by Vicki Lewis Thompson, Margaret Chittenden and Margot Dalton this month and next as we begin to draw the curtain on '93!

Marsha Zinberg,
Senior Editor

No Turning Back

Anne Laurence

Harlequin Books

TORONTO • NEW YORK • LONDON
AMSTERDAM • PARIS • SYDNEY • HAMBURG
STOCKHOLM • ATHENS • TOKYO • MILAN
MADRID • WARSAW • BUDAPEST • AUCKLAND

ISBN 0-373-70573-5

NO TURNING BACK

Copyright © 1993 by Sally Pfisterer.

ABOUT THE AUTHOR

It took Anne Laurence forty-three years to figure out what she wanted to be when she grew up—a romance writer! From the start of her career with Harlequin, Anne has gravitated to the Superromance series, which she feels is the best vehicle for the intense, dramatic stories she likes to tell.

Anne also loves to read romance novels, but not while she's writing. "I'm a single-minded person," she says, "and I prefer to concentrate on one thing at a time." We're all betting that her single-minded concentration will continue to help her create unique and compelling stories like *No Turning Back*.

Books by Anne Laurence

HARLEQUIN SUPERROMANCE
394—ALWAYS SAY YES
539—REMEMBER WHEN

For Larry

PROLOGUE

OFF THE WEST COAST of Florida, the Gulf of Mexico stretched, a calm blue. At high noon in mid-August, it shimmered like shot silk under bright skies. Standing in the water, Summer experienced the ocean as a vast skirt, flowing out from her waist, on out... on out....

Out there, it looked so peaceful. Inside her, memories came to her in her mother's voice.

Don't you see how beautiful you are? You can be anything you want to be. A model. A rich man's wife. A movie star. Be it, Summer! Be it, for God's sake!

Summer O'Malley had been raised along these warm, changeable waters. Here the gulf gently cradled the string of keys that ran the length of the western coastline. Summer knew the limit for walking out into the sea. She knew the depth for comfortable laps. Being a strong swimmer, she'd honed her body in this long crescent cove, and she was aware of the variables that could suddenly threaten a person.

On out. On out. Wasn't that the way to do it? No matter how strong she was, she simply had to swim out as far as she could. To the point of exhaustion. To the point where exhaustion made the decision. To the point that she couldn't get back, no matter how supple and strong her body was.

My God, Summer. It's not just your face and your coloring. I mean, who do you know with strawberry blond hair? Or cornflower blue eyes? Or tawny skin that never gets sunburned? You have a body other girls would die for. Of your friends, who has legs like yours? Huh? Use 'em! For God's sake, use those legs to walk out of Fiesta Key. You've got a body that won't quit. Use it! It's your ticket out of this backwater.

Her mother had been a hard teacher. And Summer had been a hard, rebellious student. Even now, at twenty-five, resistance still knotted inside her. Her mother's death two weeks earlier in a car accident didn't change any of that. If anything, the shock had fueled Summer's anger. Even if they'd recently reached an uneasy truce, they hadn't settled their differences.

Summer had never felt so sharply the residue of her parents' bitterness. Her father's rages and early abandonment... Her mother's continual harangues.... In combination with grief and Summer's own built-in resentment, the residual anger seemed overwhelming.

With a graceful, arching dive, Summer began to swim. The restless water grew deeper. Far ahead, a single boat wallowed in the sea. A listing cabin cruiser in bad shape.

Summer's internal rhythms took over. She stretched out. She pulled back.

No, her mother hadn't begun to understand her. Summer had always seen herself as an ordinary person who wanted a normal life. She just happened to have an extraordinary appearance.

Vaguely, Summer thought she should go back. She could feel the physical strain now. Her muscles told her she was way out. She should fix Poppy's lunch. Off and on, she'd been staying with her grandfather, comforting him. She should go back. The sky, even the water, struck her as white, white, white.

The cramp in her thigh was the first really clear warning. She had to be way out. She hadn't realized it, but she could hardly breathe now. Her intuition hinted at that point of no choice.

Flipping over in the water, she saw that the beach along her grandfather's old resort property was a long way off. But the bright white, the bright sudden pain, the unusual sensations in her well-toned body were what stunned her.

Had she done it?

She hadn't planned to. Not really. But had she done it? She'd sapped her strength. Her laboring breath confused her.

"Hey! You! Are you in trouble?"

Feeling something she'd never experienced but that she recognized nonetheless, Summer peered across the water to the derelict cruiser. *Spare a Dime*. Sarasota, Florida.

At last she felt the fear.

"Help!"

Was that her own voice?

No! She hadn't meant to do it!

She saw the man who'd called to her from the cruiser jumping into the water. After that, only impressions flitted through her mind. It seemed like forever until he reached for her upper arm. He cussed at her. As they gripped each other, she had a chance to look at him.

The stubble of a black beard. Long black hair plastered against his head. Deeply tanned skin. Broad shoulders, slippery with seawater.

A bum from the derelict boat.

He was as mad as hell. But he was also powerful. Summer clung to him, even knowing she had to release him to let him help her.

Forcing herself, she relaxed her grip. Still in his embrace, she trusted him. She focused on treading water, on keeping her balance against him. She squinted to reduce the blinding white light. She saw his eyes from inches away.

Green eyes. Not unlike the gulf on some days. They resembled mottled jade, ancient and patinaed and... rare treasure.

Although they still struggled, still had to swim to his waiting cruiser, Summer sensed that she'd been rescued. She felt the stranger who held her gathering his own strength. He was gaining control over both the situation and something inside himself.

He watched her as closely as she watched him. Because of their extreme circumstances, she knew that he was as fundamentally aware of her as she was of him.

The stranger switched his embrace to a lifesaving hold that she'd also been taught. Summer felt her urge to survive crossing a fine line. As he tugged her in a steady rhythm toward his old cruiser, other life urges shocked Summer's already-shocked system. Again she was starkly aware of this man as a man, and she yearned to forget the past. She longed to feel something besides anger and grief. She needed human comfort.

This man was a sea bum. She sensed he was attracted to her the way she was to him. With this man, this one particular man... Well, Summer thought uncharacteristically, what could another abandonment of convention mean to someone who'd so obviously already dropped out? How could some more time, as brief as it would be, spent in his capable embrace, compromise a man who was so apparently at rock-bottom?

In any case, the way she was feeling, there seemed to be no turning back.

CHAPTER ONE

EVERY SO OFTEN, when Summer met the jade green gaze of her child, she thought of the biological father—of "that afternoon" two and a half years ago. The connections played catch-up at odd moments. Like now, at the checkout in the supermarket. Summer's neediest hours, her wildest fantasy, her most irresponsible behavior had resulted in the miracle of a lifetime—in Carrie Miller O'Malley, now just shy of twenty months old.

And while Summer thought of Carrie's daddy every day, his identity remained unknown to her. To those closest to her, Summer had simply gone off the deep end. She'd done something drastic in those dark days after her mother's death.

Which was true, even to Summer. "That day" remained an episode she never discussed. It was certainly something she couldn't justify. Both her grandfather and her best friend, Dee, steered clear of the subject. They accepted Carrie O'Malley for the charming creature she was—for the creature who had redeemed her mother from bitterness and anger.

Of course, in the checkout aisle leading to the beeping register and groaning belt, that charming creature developed a dozen hands. Especially when Summer had to hurry.

"Carrie," Summer admonished her softly, exchanging a knowing smile with the matronly cashier. "It won't be long, now, sweetie."

"Cookie."

"Yeah, your best word," Summer admitted. "What would you do without that one?"

Because an older couple was also watching their little tussle, Summer shared more smiles.

"She's so cute," the checkout lady said.

"Yeah, well, she has her moments. And the grocery store, well, I'm sure you know what I mean."

As the woman filled the last bag, Summer tucked Carrie's upside-down tulip-shaped hat onto the child's head.

"No."

Again Summer's smile included her small audience. "Another very essential word."

"Cookie."

Plucking up the familiar tiny red boxes in their cellophane wrap, Summer filled the greedy hands. To Carrie, everything delectable was cookies, and she grinned charmingly.

"Cookies."

"Actually, it's raisins."

With final nods to their audience, Summer pushed the cart toward the automatic door. The Laurel and Hardy routine her daughter instigated was always a crowd-pleaser.

Summer tugged at her baseball cap. She pulled it down tightly, near the rims of her sunglasses. Even in her usual shorts and T-shirts and sandals, even with baseball caps and sunglasses, she attracted attention. She just always had. Her reticence didn't seem to faze anyone else. People simply wanted to look at her. She wondered which would come first—getting used to it or growing old.

Leaving the store, she pushed the cart into the heat. Inland, the January day sizzled.

Trudging through the busy lot, Summer checked her watch. Even with her new, more convenient minivan, she found herself under pressure. The growing catering business she shared with Dee kept them busy. Only at the rear doors of the van did Summer pause long enough to open the small box of raisins in her child's grasp.

When Carrie dipped her head, fishing out her first raisin with chubby fingers, Summer tweaked a soft, escaping strawberry blond curl. In everything but hair color, Carrie resembled her father, or what Summer remembered of the child's father. It had been a long time since she had seen him.

In fact, things stood as they did by Summer's choice. She knew how to search for Carrie's father, and that she didn't do so made her feel the familiar guilt. *Spare a Dime.* Sarasota, Florida. She'd never looked for the boat. She'd never told him about Carrie.

Summer's thoughts were interrupted by the sound of a souped-up hot rod screeching to a halt beside her.

"Hey, baby. How about it?"

In the past—before Carrie—Summer would have bristled. The would-be Lothario, hanging out the window of his car, drooling, would have gotten a sharp reply. Since Carrie, however, Summer had developed an easier style. She'd lightened up.

"Yeah," she replied, pushing her cart to the van's back-seat door. "How about it? At least ninety degrees in the shade, don't you think?"

Good-naturedly, the guy rapped the door of his noisy car with a knuckle. He grinned at her. "Have a nice day, lady."

When he rolled off, Summer smiled to herself. "Maybe the world isn't *too* bad," she said to Carrie, lifting the child into her car seat.

Although Carrie disliked the transfer from the grocery cart to the car seat, she didn't protest too much. She was tired. Nap time was just ahead, and she went back to choosing another raisin as Summer buckled her in.

"Be sure to chew, chew, chew," Summer warned.

Carrie nodded.

Finally on their way, Summer glanced at her watch again. She reached for the air-conditioning switch. As usual, the traffic slowed her down. Getting back on to the string of keys paralleling the coast of the mainland would be another hassle.

Still, she liked living at her grandfather's old resort on the beach. She'd been there since she'd discovered her pregnancy, and frankly, she'd needed the financial backup. She'd been in night school then, holding down two waitressing jobs.

Of course, now they had no choice except to leave. Poppy had sold the resort, and soon they'd have to vacate. In this case, Poppy needed her. Perhaps for the first time in his seventy-odd years, Fred Miller actually needed someone else, and Summer would be there for him, just as he'd stuck to her like glue ever since she could remember.

At the southernmost tip of the major key just south of Sarasota, Summer got hung up at the bridge leading to the next key, the one where her grandfather had lived for more than fifty years. The old bridge split at the middle, arching above the water to allow boat traffic to pass.

A bell rang, and waiting cars began to line up in the shimmering heat. Summer glimpsed her dozing daughter in the rearview mirror. The bright red raisin box drooped in Carrie's chunky fingers. Just enough sleep, Summer thought, to revive the toddler while she unloaded Poppy's groceries and checked the pot of chicken soup. Even with her mix of charm and contrariness, Carrie was an easy and adaptable baby.

At last the bell stopped clanging and the bridge locked into place. Thank goodness for air conditioning, Summer thought. Her back-seat passenger still dozed.

Just down the narrow road, Summer reached the Flamingo Resort. She pulled into the lot surrounding the office. Typically, old resorts lining the beaches had their offices along the roads. Behind that were guest quarters, the beach, and then the main attraction, the gulf.

The Flamingo Resort was in good shape. Its dozen individual stucco bungalows were painted, like the office building, in flamingo pink with bright green-and-white trim. A forties-style resort, it retained its original flavor, even its original plumbing. The Flamingo Resort, once alive with guests and a holiday mood, was now closed and quiet.

As she got out of the van, Summer's gaze ran automatically to the cove. She felt especially close to "him" today—to Carrie's father. When that happened, Summer had to admit it. She regularly watched for him. And though his derelict cruiser had broken down in that very cove, she hadn't seen it since that day.

For all the mystery and even the magic of that afternoon, "he" remained some sort of derelict himself. A sea bum, her grandfather would have called him—someone so attracted to saltwater and freedom that he couldn't function in the real world. No matter how magical the child they had produced, Summer knew enough of him to stay out of his life for as long as she could.

One day she'd make a stab at finding him. She owed it to him. She owed it to Carrie. But for now, Carrie didn't miss what she didn't know. For now "he" existed as a fantasy Summer indulged too often. Reluctantly, Summer admitted even the final truth. She was afraid of the tender, dangerous stranger who had fathered her child. The man who had made her feel so—

"Need some help?"

Summer pivoted from the open door of her van. Her tall lanky grandfather hovered in the doorway of the main building, which housed the resort office, his rooms, the kitchens and the small dining-bar combo. Once again, the silent premises struck Summer as sad. She knew that behind his curmudgeonly exterior, Poppy was also sad.

"It's just your groceries," Summer managed to say. "Got much?"

"Not too bad. Why don't you let me . . . ?"

"Naw, naw." He already moved toward her. "You get Boop."

Poppy had been calling Carrie "Boop" since he'd decided she looked like Betty Boop, with her big green eyes. Unfortunately, almost everyone else had fallen into the habit. Even Summer.

So Summer went to get Boop.

Poppy fiddled with the rear doors of the unfamiliar van. "Damned contraption," he muttered.

Summer squelched an offer to help. She respected his independence. To see him feeling defeated and unwell hurt her.

"Was Irma here?" Summer asked, glancing over her shoulder.

He entered his small private kitchen after her, a grocery bag on each arm. "Yeah. Just left. Not much for her to do. I keep telling her not to come out, but the woman has one helluva mind of her own."

Although Summer thought the pot was calling the kettle black, she didn't say so. For as long as Summer could remember, Poppy and the woman who ran his resort office had been squaring off toe to toe. And while Summer stayed out of it, Irma McGinty was Poppy's equal at clever retorts.

After stirring her pot of chicken soup, Summer tasted it from the old wooden spoon. Poppy unloaded groceries, and Carrie awoke in her high chair. Because they often ate dinner together, baby equipment cluttered Poppy's quarters, just as it did in the first bungalow, where Summer lived.

"How's my little Boop?" Poppy asked, chucking his favorite person under the chin. "Got some raisins, hmm?"

Carrie grinned. Picking out one of the raisins from where she'd dumped them on the tray of her high chair, she stretched toward her great-grandfather.

He munched the raisin with an exaggerated expression. "Good, huh?" Apparently feeling Summer's eyes on him, Poppy turned to her. "You don't have to cook for me, you know."

"I know I don't."

"Especially not today."

"Yeah, well, I'll go back as soon as Carrie has a nap. I brought the bookwork with me, and Dee's overseeing the preparation."

"This party's gonna be that fancy, eh?"

"Our fanciest yet. There'll be a lot of people there. Calder Parks is a big deal in Sarasota. He has all kinds of connections to the opera and to the museums. If we do well, we might drum up some business. The kind of business we want to do. Fancy catering for fancy people."

"Saw that fancy outfit in the van."

Summer turned back to her pot of simmering soup. She and Dee aimed for a classy yet fanciful operation. For something different. Dining In, as their catering service was called, set the tone with gourmet delights and lots of ribbon and flowers.

Dozens of candles, rented starched linens, bright silver and tons of pressed-glass settings—everything had been selected for a touch of formality but mostly for freshness. And that included the natty tuxes that either of them wore, depending on who oversaw the main buffet table. Tonight it was Summer's turn to run the show. Dee would man the support systems in the kitchen.

Naturally, to take center stage, even at a buffet table, challenged Summer. She didn't mind the hard work involved in a business that fed the public. Nor did the demanding hours and untenable schedules bother her much. Even the bookkeeping wasn't bad. And that the display had to be perfect wasn't it, either. It was the show they had to put on. To appear in a white, fully rigged-out tux and spiky white heels invariably drew every eye. To Summer, that was anathema.

But dammit, Summer was also determined to do business. If doing business meant doing something a little different, like parading around in a long-tailed, snow white tux, she'd do it. She wouldn't like it, but she'd do it.

Looking back at Poppy where he dawdled with Carrie over the last of the raisins, Summer forced the topic he always avoided. "The real estate agent called me today."

He glanced at her sideways.

Oh, God, it hurt. But it had to be done. They had to leave Fiesta Key. That Poppy had been made reasonably comfortable, at least financially, by the sale of his property didn't count. He lived frugally, no matter what the amount in his bank account.

Summer plunged ahead. "She, the agent I mean, has some more houses for me to see."

He shrugged.

"They're all on the mainland. There's just nothing out here, not with beachfront that—"

"That doesn't cost an arm and a leg. Time was, you know, when I could have had any of it for a song. And now..."

And now, Summer thought, feeling his frustration, we have to leave not only the Flamingo Resort but the beach.

"So are you still up to baby-sitting tonight?" she asked.

"Of course I'm up to sitting Boop. Hell's bells, all I gotta do is walk over to the bungalow and watch TV until you get back."

"We have a midnight deadline, and that includes cleanup. Anything beyond that goes into overtime, so I shouldn't be later than twelve forty-five."

"I'm telling you it don't matter. Don't sleep much nowadays, anyway. And besides," he added, turning slightly away, "Irma claims she's coming over for a while."

"Ir...?" Summer barely kept her surprise to herself. Poppy had a crawful. He'd also deal with Irma McGinty. He'd been dealing with the bristly spinster for years.

RYDER CRAIG OBSERVED the party from its edges. He knew that part of doing business in big real estate was doing the social scene. Tonight's event was a typical mix of family, friends, business associates and employees from Calder Parks Development.

Ryder simply preferred a few buddies, cold beer and fishing boats.

"Hey, Ry."

Thinking himself very funny, Artie Berry, a fellow employee at Calder Parks Development, oozed up to Ryder. Like everyone else, Artie was having a good time. A talented pair of bartenders and a friendly if elegant ambience had their effect.

"Nice digs, huh?" Artie asked, swaying into Ryder's space.

"Very nice."

"But then, I guess you're used to it. Can't be too different in Palm Beach at your old ancestral lair."

Artie wasn't being anything but his friendly self fortified by a few drinks.

Ryder's lips twitched. "I haven't been to Palm Beach in years, but yeah, it was a lot like this."

"Black sheep, eh?"

Ryder dropped his gaze to the glass of tomato juice in his hand. "Something like that."

"Yeah, well, if you're gonna be a black sheep, it's better you don't get it plastered all over the Florida papers. Notoriety only makes it worse, you know."

Ryder demurred silently. Artie appeared somewhat contrite.

"Of course that was about five years ago, wasn't it? And you're really a great guy, Ry." Because Ryder remained quiet, Artie pushed ahead readily over his gaffe. "Of course it helps to be the apple of old man Parks's eye." Artie's gaze returned to the roomful of people, to the doors opening on to the crowded patio.

Yeah, Ryder thought, the house reminded him of the winter home of the New York-based Craigs. Tradition. Wealth. Social graces. The ocean washing beyond torch-lit pools and terraces.

And then, Calder Parks himself served as a reminder. Calder had been a friend of Ryder's father. Two years ago, when Calder had offered Ryder a position, Ryder had felt not only the genuineness of the man's offer but their connections to the past. Since then, he and Calder had gained a real respect for each other.

"Hey, Ry," Artie whispered, jabbing his elbow into Ryder's side and speaking from the corner of his mouth. "Have you seen the gal in the white tux?"

"The white tux?"

"Yeah, yeah. She's on the patio. Behind the buffet. She's with the catering company, somebody said. Man, you should go out and have a canapé. You know what I mean?"

Artie lifted his eyebrows up and down. Ryder chuckled. He didn't think anyone made a better party drunk than Artie. In the morning, the fairly straight guy wouldn't remember his hours as Mr. Hyde.

Ryder felt tempted to stroll out to the patio. But then nothing could ever compare to the fantasy woman in his head. A woman rising from the ocean like some lush sea goddess, burned his memory, to the exclusion of all other women. A lady in a mere white tux could hardly make him forget.

"No," he said. "I think I'll go on home."

"Go? The old man won't like it."

"He won't care."

"Yeah, I guess. You and old Calder are buddies."

Ryder smiled. As he spoke of "his buddy," Calder Parks strode toward him, full of the energy that was his trademark.

"Ry. Artie," he said, smiling broadly. For all his silvered hair, tanned skin, expensive suits, money and ambition, Calder Parks was a likable guy. "This is a great party. Why don't you two get out there? Have some fun. Rub some elbows." He winked at Ryder. "Make some bucks."

Ryder smiled back. "I was just thinking I'd call it a night."

"But for pete's sake, it's only...what is it?" Calder groped for his watch. "Well, it's too early to turn in."

"Yeah," Artie concurred, sauntering off in the direction of the bar. "It's only the cusp of the evening."

Calder laughed. "Only the cusp, Ry. You can't go at the cusp. Really," he said, sobering. Grasping Ryder's elbow, he coaxed him in the direction of the dining room. "In fact, I gotta talk to you."

On through the dining room, Ryder found himself in the kitchen with Calder Parks and a dozen other people. Although the large kitchen was a beehive of activity, that didn't deter Calder. Passing the center of the hubbub, he nearly pushed Ryder up against a wall.

"Look, Ry. You know how I feel about you."

Yeah, Ryder thought. Calder had had one drink too many. Their feelings for each other were both mutual and true, but Calder had never pulled anything like this.

"Look, Ry," the man said, oblivious to repeating himself, "all my friends are here tonight. Everyone that my wife and I care about. It's a great party. A grand evening. And it's more than just business, Ry."

"I know that."

"Why don't you let me tell everybody . . . ?"

Ryder's heart jerked into overdrive. He didn't know what to say.

"Look, Ry, you know how I feel about you and how well you've done with my company. I gotta admire you, Ry. So why don't you let me tell everyone that you plan to stay with Calder Parks Development, that you'll step in for me one of these days. You're like a son to me, you know. Especially after everything you've been through."

Ryder was at a loss. But even knowing that he should, he just couldn't give Calder the kind of commitment the man wanted.

On the verge of edging them into something that wouldn't embarrass the older man—into something that would make tomorrow easier—Ryder glimpsed a woman in a white tux. She stood stock-still, not three feet away from him.

His mind went blank.

It was crazy. Calder's miscalculation. The steamy, overly bright kitchen. A million people, coming and going in black tux pants, white pleated shirts, cummerbunds and tidy black bow ties.

Ryder lost all sense of finesse. His eyes were riveted to the beauty in the white tux. It was his sea goddess. God, she was still the most glorious creature he'd ever seen. Damn, if he didn't even know her name. But it was her. *His sea goddess*.

Indeed, her gaze galvanized his. Cornflower blue eyes seemed as cold as the North Sea.

CHAPTER TWO

SUMMER COULDN'T seem to move. It was the sea bum. The sea bum in dark, graceful evening attire.

Somehow, somehow, she had to move. She had to remember why she'd returned to the kitchen. She searched the milling mass for Dee. But Dee was oblivious, working over a tray of cheese sticks.

A sudden hard hold on Summer's arm forced her to look into the man's jade green stare. Oh, Lord. Carrie's gaze. Only this time it didn't dance with charm.

"I want to talk to you," he said.

She jerked her elbow away. "I've got a business to run."

He seemed to recall, then, where they were. The older man he'd been talking to, her client, Calder Parks, had left the room.

Still, the bum's gaze drilled into hers. "I want to talk."

"Well, I don't."

Summer kept her voice calm, as level as his. Hardly anyone would notice they spoke. Not in the organized hysteria of the kitchen. She turned away. He reached for her elbow.

"You can take a minute," he said.

Finally Dee looked up. Her hands went still. Her familiar brown gaze measured Summer's, then switched to the unknown male. That was all it took. Dee knew who he was.

Summer sent her friend a reassuring look. "Five minutes," she mouthed, holding up a hand.

Dee nodded back.

Summer led the way to a rear porch. They'd piled the plastic containers for transporting cold stuff there, and the porch was a quiet contrast to the kitchen.

Summer could hear the ocean around the other side of the house. On this side, the night was dark. A single weak porch light illuminated lawn furniture and plants.

Stiffening, Summer pivoted to face the large dark stranger.

"Why did you leave my boat?" he asked, his voice a low rasp.

"You were asleep."

"You should have said something."

"What should I have said?"

"I've been looking all over for you."

"I'm not hard to find."

"The hell you aren't. You for damn sure don't live in Sarasota. Or on the keys. What's your name?"

"Summer O'Malley."

"You aren't married, are you?"

"No."

Her steady replies to his rapid-fire questions took the edge off his temper. He relaxed his broad shoulders. Summer tried not to think about the mole on the one smooth firm shoulder. She'd fingered it, kissed it, tasted it with her tongue, and the memory burned her cheeks.

The idea seemed ludicrous now.

Now she was drowning. Here again was the most amazing male she'd ever encountered. She dismissed the remembered tenderness whispering through her mind. That was only fantasy. She'd known all along the fantasy would trip her up when it got its chance, and its chance had come. She didn't dare look at his hands. His hands could weave warm magic.

At last, Summer found her best weapon against the fantasy that he represented. What they'd shared had been no more than a one-night stand. Aside from Carrie—

Summer's scurrying thoughts hit a wall. *Carrie.* She swallowed hard. She'd never been so frightened. Until now, she hadn't imagined— The "bum" was perfectly capable of caring for a child. At least financially. Probably better than she was. If he knew Carrie was his child, he might sue for custody—and win.

Here was a new ball game.

"Look," he said, obviously reading her turmoil, if not reading precisely.

"No, you look," she snapped back. "Calder Parks hired me to run this party, and I'm doing a poor job of it out here on this porch."

"I just want to—"

"To what? You don't owe me anything. As far as I'm concerned, neither of us owes the other anything."

"I just want to talk to you. I want to talk about—"

"Well, I don't want to talk."

Oh, God, she sounded like a bitch.

His jade green eyes looked coldly at her. "So what we had was an afternoon of sex, was it?"

Summer mustered every reserve. *Carrie,* she told herself. "Yes," she managed to say.

"That's all it was? Sex?"

"Yes."

"Geez, but you're a tough..."

Obviously giving up, he turned toward the door. "Just in case a name might mean something to you," he said, pausing, "which I doubt—" his eyes glittered with bitterness "—I'm Ryder Craig. So nice to have *known* you, Ms. O'Malley."

His tone, his expression, defined disgust. Summer stiffened against a shudder. She wouldn't break down now. She'd almost made it. It was almost over.

Actually, it *was* over. As soon as she preceded him through the door, he stepped past her, showing his broad back as he walked off.

Summer sensed a spell of the shakes coming on. Her gaze ran to Dee's. But when Dee would have left her post, Summer shook her head. They had a business to run. The worst was over. Summer could be sure Ryder Craig had left both the party and her life. She'd disgusted him. Even more painfully, she could now put a name to her fierce and tender lover. To the father of her child.

IRMA MCGINTY SAT in the office at the Flamingo Resort. Ramrod-straight, behind her desk. Not a strand of her steel gray hair, which was the color of her steel gray glasses, was out of place. Nor did the knitting needles in her fingers do anything but click efficiently.

When Irma had first heard that Fred Miller had been rushed to the hospital, she'd been eating the last of some birthday cake her lady friends had surprised her with. The cake had marked her sixty-fourth birthday. Irma had been eating it alone.

Of course she'd rushed to the hospital. She'd also worried, along with Summer, about the problem that had brought Fred down. That problem was obvious. Fred didn't want to leave the Flamingo Resort. Although he was too hardheaded to admit it, he was getting too old for the twenty-four-hour-a-day routine it took to run such a place.

To Irma's mind, the interest in developing Fiesta Key—the property buy-outs that had included the whole key—had been a lucky break. To Fred, the incident had been both something he couldn't pass up and an anxiety that had landed him in the hospital.

Irma sighed.

Anyway, when Fred had finally sold the resort, her feelings had, very unexpectedly, ganged up on her. Out of that unlikely morass, she'd arrived at a single plain point. She was in love with Fred Miller. She had been for years. Her spinster's heart had recognized its bottom line. It was time. Way past time. She had to either fish or cut bait.

She'd decided to fish.

In the worn office, in the overcast morning light, her knitting needles flashed dully. Salmon-colored yarn threaded through her fingers, flowing out as a great salmon-colored sheet. Irma was knitting a sweater for Fred. It was her first attempt both at knitting and at catching a man, but Irma McGinty was in hot pursuit. Well, her idea of hot pursuit.

"Irma?"

Fred entered the tidy space.

Irma knit.

"What the hell are you doin' here? I told you not to come out."

"The phone still rings."

"I can get the phone."

"People call, wanting to know how you are."

"I can tell 'em how I am."

"You can't just drop a whole clientele as if they hadn't been your friends down through the years."

"Hell's bells! I have no intention of dropping my friends."

"Flora Dicks said you hung up on her the other day."

Fred's large, rawboned frame radiated frustration. "The hell with Flora Dicks. She's a busybody."

"I'll answer the phone," Irma said, claiming the point.

Glimpsing Fred's angry expression, she reconsidered. She wasn't interested in winning points. This transitional period in Fred's life was hard for him. If anyone knew this man, she did. They'd simply fallen into a pattern that had been reinforced over years and years. Indeed, thinking of the wasted time, Irma forced her shoulders to relax, her hands to be still.

"How did Summer's party go last night?"

Irma knew Fred's favorite subjects, and she would trade on anything. From what she'd gleaned from her clique of female friends, man-catching wasn't bound by scruples.

And her backing off worked. Fred's broad, if now bony, shoulders also let down. "She did fine, I think. By the time she came in, she didn't have much to say."

"That's not like her."

"What's more, I saw her only for a minute before she left this mornin'. I don't know about these hours. Late last night, up first thing this mornin'."

"Once her new business is on its feet, I'm sure it'll get better."

He shrugged.

Irma advanced. "And Carrie?"

"Oh, Summer always packs Carrie along. Wherever Summer goes, Carrie goes. Unless it's late, like last night."

"It's good that Summer's little business is so flexible. I'm sure a lot of young mothers would like to keep their babies with them. Babies aren't babies for long."

"Yeah, well." Fred turned to go.

"Fred?"

He peered over his shoulder.

"Will you let me measure this against your back?"

"What the hell is it?"

"I'm knitting a sweater."

"For me?"

"Yes."

"Don't look like a sweater."

Irma ignored the little flame he lit. "Well, it's going to be a sweater, and I'm making it for you."

"What in hell? It's too damned hot for sweaters."

"Sweaters are always handy for evenings."

Muttering something, he came toward her, nonetheless. Irma's heart pounded. Even more unlikely, she felt a little standoffish. In all their years together, she'd never touched Fred, nor had he touched her.

"What do you want me to do?" he asked, standing over her.

She got up on unsteady legs. "Just turn around." She hoped her crisp tone hid her shaky feelings.

Again he was obedient. Irma couldn't believe it.

Because she was much shorter than he, Fred's back loomed above her. In his day, he'd been an attractive man, big and strong and always independent. He'd never been one for the ladies, and that had been a shame. Well, not exactly a shame....

"Well?" he said, twisting himself to shoot a glance at her.

Irma switched into gear. Smoothing the rough salmon-colored square over his back, she measured for a fit she didn't know how to gauge.

She was nearly overwhelmed. Fred was just out of the hospital and still a bit bony. Irma felt torn—torn by a sudden rush of tender feelings that surprised her.

"Well?" came as an impatient interruption.

She shook herself. "It should do," she said equally brusquely. Brusqueness was the norm. So was Fred's quick exit.

THE MORNING was overcast, but Ryder couldn't seem to concentrate on anything except ignoring the view. Or rather, what he thought of when he looked at the view. With a coveted office at Calder Parks Development, which was located in downtown Sarasota, he had a grand view to the west, out to Sarasota Bay, to St. Armands and then to the gulf. Always to the gulf.

Although it wasn't unusual for the view to distract him, normally he disciplined himself. He seldom looked. He seldom yearned. He didn't allow himself to. He finally had his life under control, and that was the way he wanted it. That was the way he needed it.

It was just the restlessness. And the boredom. He detested the paperwork on the desk in front of him.

He hated the polite veneer, the deep-down cunning it took to be successful in big-time business.

Still, he preferred big-time business to having no purpose at all. He'd proved that in the two-plus years he'd spent bumming around on his boat. Those two dreadful years following his trial. Indeed, the threat of chucking the ordered life he now lived, of going back to bumming around, had never been so strong since the trial.

And he damn well knew the reason.

He'd seen her again.

He'd searched for her for so long he'd thought he'd never find her. And then there she was, only to turn into something other than what he'd believed her to be.

That day, when his boat had broken down off that little dab of a key, he'd been at his lowest point. And then he'd spied her. Glancing across the flat, bright blue water at high noon, he'd watched her struggling. But only after he'd pulled them both into his old cruiser had he read her pain.

He'd wanted to comfort her. He'd started out comforting her, and then...well, it had happened. Oh, he hated that expression "it happened." It connoted some kind of inability, either to think or to take responsibility. But at the time, it had been an uncontrollable occurrence. It had seemed meant to be and magical. At the time, desire had been not merely imperative, but right.

Ryder gave it up. He got up. He paced to the window, his attention focusing inward rather than on the view.

Since he'd seen her again last night, a new light had begun to dawn. The real person did not necessarily equate with the fantasy he'd nursed for over two years. Last night, his gift from the sea had seemed a cold bitch in a hot white tux. Either desire had blinded him to who she was in the first case, or...

But the contrast was too extreme, wasn't it? It didn't make sense. For him to have found her nothing short of perfect in the one instance and then nothing short of the opposite in the next didn't jibe.

On that day, she'd seemed so vulnerable. But he'd been vulnerable, too. The worst was that while she'd irritated him last night with her attitude, he'd still desired her. Or at least he wanted his sea goddess back. Ha! The term was laughable. And so was the fantasy. She'd taught him that, all right.

A tap at his office door brought Ryder back to the view, back to the purpose of his life, back to the business at hand.

Calder Parks peered at him. "Busy?"

Ryder smiled. "Yeah, I'm standing here in the window closing a deal."

Calder came in, shutting the door behind him. "I also nail some of my best deals standing in windows."

Yeah, Ryder thought, Calder was a prince.

The prince, however, looked a little uneasy, and uneasiness was unusual for the outgoing, hardworking Calder Parks. Waiting, Ryder watched his boss settle on one of the comfortable chairs.

Calder floundered even more uncharacteristically. "I want to apologize for last night. I know I had a little too much to drink, and I also know that's no excuse, but this morning... well, this morning it hit me on the head. In suggesting that you make some sort of public pledge to take over here, I was way out of line."

Ryder couldn't reply.

Calder chuckled. "Yeah, I had a lot to drink last night. It's just that…well, you gotta know that as far as you're concerned, the sky's the limit with me."

"Calder, I—"

"No, no, now that I've started, you gotta let me finish. I've never had children, and your father and I were so close that I've always felt close to you, too. And to Vance. But none of that has anything to do with it, really. I mean, I'm not so far gone as to leave the business I've built to someone out of sentiment. It's just that you've done so well here, Ry. You've put the past behind you and done so well."

Ryder didn't think he could have felt worse. Even so, he just couldn't say the words Calder wanted to hear. Not yet.

"Look," Calder said softly. "I didn't mean to put you on the spot, and that's all I'm trying to tell you."

"You've been great to me, Calder," Ryder finally managed to say. "You have to know that when I started looking for a job, everyone was out to lunch."

"Now, now, let's not get into that. That's behind you. Anyway, sooner or later, we all need a second chance."

"Still, you've got to let me thank you. Besides, I can never allow myself to forget."

"Well…" Calder hesitated, obviously not quite sure how to continue. He and Ryder seldom discussed the time before they had established their newer connections of business and friendship.

Calder cleared his throat. "Like I say, I've always felt close to you because of your dad and me being close. Well, as close as businessmen get. We met through the real estate business, you know, through the same circles we traveled in New York and Palm Beach and then in Sarasota. Somehow the social stuff, the charity work, gets intertwined, and that's how my wife and I became friends with your dad and mother.''

This mention of long-past relationships with his parents made Ryder even more uncomfortable. Obviously Calder sensed that, too. Still, they'd never gotten into this aspect of what Calder knew about Ryder's boyhood. Evidently the time had come, and Calder went on.

''The way I see it—I mean, the way you were as a kid and then even as a young man fresh out of college—well, I didn't approve of your mother's talking badly about you all those years. I've never raised kids of my own, but it was clear that she treated you and Vance differently. That she played favorites.''

Ryder's chuckle sounded sour. ''It was right that she preferred Vance. Vance always did what she wanted. He still does. He was good in school. He's good at the business our family left us.''

''No more good than you were and are.''

''Yeah, but Vance really wanted to do what Mother wanted him to do. Vance looked forward to joining the real estate firm with my dad. I always wanted something different. Mother said I was rebellious and wild. And I was. Worse yet, I couldn't have said exactly what I *did* want, even then. In some ways, I still can't.''

Calder hedged again. ''Well, all I know is that you've finally done beautifully here. No one could expect more. Your dad would be proud of you, too. He loved you, Ry, despite the long hours he put into his business.''

Avoiding further embarrassing sentiments, Calder got up from his chair and joined Ryder at the window. He pumped his hand. He smiled and seemed a little misty-eyed.

They were fine again.

As Ryder watched his mentor leave his office, he felt threatened again, on the brink of disaster.

He couldn't get his sea goddess out of his mind. Not after having seen her again. And while being on fire was to tempt the devil, he wanted Summer O'Malley. Just as he'd wanted her the first time he'd seen her. Summer O'Malley, sitting on his boat, covering her lush body with her arms, looking like a half-drowned, desperate goddess from the sea, was a permanent picture in his mind.

When he'd called the number for Dining In that morning, he'd gotten a crisp message on an answering machine. Her tone had made it easy for him. He wouldn't call her again.

Besides, she wasn't who he'd thought she was.

Walking to his desk, he sat down, and meaning to pick up a contract that needed checking, he picked up the phone instead.

He redialed her number.

THE OVERCAST MORNING did nothing to dampen Dee's spirits. Summer had met Dee Rosenblum in night school. When Summer had first suggested the idea of starting a catering business together, Dee had been equally excited. Now that their dream had begun to materialize, Dee saw the sky as the limit. Their party at the home of Calder Parks the night before, as well as two phone calls they'd received that morning, more than hinted at the success they hoped for.

The single difference between Dee's enthusiasm and Summer's remained one of style. Since unlocking the kitchen at the rear of the church, near Dee's home on the mainland, Dee hadn't stopped chattering. For now, she and Summer rented the kitchen, a basic facility that served as an economical step in attaining their next goal—a kitchen of their own.

"Really, Summer," Dee said, peering at her over the piles of asparagus tips, new potatoes, tomatoes and peppers that would go into a vegetable salad with a raspberry vinaigrette.

They were doing the prep work for that evening's sit-down dinner. Bookings for parties on successive evenings were unusual, and they felt lucky this would be a smaller one than the one last night.

"Really, Summer," Dee reiterated, again on track after rewashing a pepper, "I think you should always work from the buffet. You did great last night. It wasn't as scary as you thought it would be. I mean, aside from that obnoxious little guy... What was his name?"

"Artie Berry, I think. But actually, he wasn't all that bad, either. Only a pest. There's always a pest."

"Face it, Summer, you look better in a tux than I do. Even if you are more reluctant."

"*More* reluctant? Is there a reluctant bone in your body?"

"Still, if you look better in a tux, then you should—"

"Point taken." Summer brushed off the subject.

Screeching noises from the next room elicited little reaction from either Dee or Summer.

Dee merely heaved a sigh. "Whose turn is it?"

Summer had already wiped her hands on a towel. "Mine."

Rounding a corner, Summer found what she expected. A shiny tile floor, with chairs and tables lining the periphery, was lit by old metal lights. In the middle of the space, stood Carrie, the source of the screeching.

Jeffy Rosenblum, who was five to Carrie's almost-twenty months, hung over her, holding her ball above his head.

"Okay," Summer said, smiling. "What's up? Besides the ball, Jeffy."

A contemplative child with big brown eyes like his mom's, Jeffy was unusually reasonable. "*She*," he said accusingly, "wants to have everything. She wants her ball, but she wants my trucks and cars, too. So I took her ball to show her how it feels."

"Wait a minute, wait a minute." Summer looked at her child.

Carrie was watching the unfolding event with a grin on her face. She loved upsetting Jeffy's more orderly world.

"She's taking your cars, then?" Summer's searching gaze answered her own question. Some of Jeffy's cars and trucks were nicely lined up along an imaginary road. Others had been secreted away in a messy pile in a corner.

"I don't get her," Jeffy said stoutly.

Summer smiled. "Frankly, I don't get her all the time, either. Maybe she needs to be a little older, and then we'll understand her."

"Yeah, I hope she gets better by then," he said, eyeing "her" with doubt.

Oh, goodness, Summer thought. Parenting. Jeffy had lots of cars and trucks, and sharing was a virtue. And yet, his things belonged to him. She'd certainly brought enough toys for Carrie to play with, and Carrie's ball was a brand-new favorite. Poor Jeffy was applying the civilized behavior he was learning in kindergarten. Carrie didn't know rules from her chunky elbows. Jeffy was placid and fair. Carrie was a pirate.

"Okay," Summer finally said, heaving a sigh. Years of well-meant decisions loomed ahead of her. "Sorry about your cars, Jeffy. We'll take time out. Carrie, bring your ball into the kitchen."

Summer expected to hear "No!"

But Carrie didn't seem to mind. "Baw," she said instead, taking the ball from Jeffy's grasp and jauntily waddling toward exile.

In the kitchen, Summer asked Dee, who was sure to have overheard, if she'd done the right thing.

"It's quiet. That's what counts."

Summer didn't know how quiet it was. Or ever would be again. She and Dee rolled grapes in blue cheese and nuts. They'd be served, frozen, as an hors d'oeuvre. Carrie followed her ball around, under the worktable and between their legs.

"So," Dee said, "aren't you gonna tell me?"

Summer didn't look up from her busy fingers. She both had and hadn't expected this prod. Dee was always considerate, but also invariably straight.

"Carrie looks just like him," Summer admitted, getting to the point.

"I have to say I was floored when I saw him. It's no wonder. If you're gonna go off the deep end, he's the kind to do it with. So what's next?"

"That's the question. I'm not sure what to do. I've always thought I'd look for him when the time was ripe...when I thought Carrie—"

"The time's ripe."

"Yes, and he has his rights, too. It's just that I don't think he...I mean, I don't know if he can appreciate..."

"What're you saying. He's not a monster. He has a right to know. A right to choose. Those are forfeits you made when you took the chance you did. I mean, you had to know the guy was a good guy if you—"

"No, I didn't even know his name."

"Wow," Dee whispered, wide-eyed.

"Yeah, it's pretty shocking. But at the time, I thought—"

"At the time, you weren't thinking. That's the whole point. Lord knows your mother was never easy. Not that I even knew her. It's just that from what you've told me, she must have been really hard on you. Taking out her bitterness with her own life by trying to live yours wasn't healthy for you. And then, for her to die like that...I mean, so suddenly in that accident and without having made up with you. Well, aside from the grief, you must have been confused."

"You don't need to make excuses for me, Dee. I'm glad you've always understood and never pushed me about how Carrie came along. But, well, I can't be sorry about Carrie. I can never be sorry."

Dee's gaze followed Summer's to where Carrie edged around the door, just enough to steal a peek at Jeffy who was making car noises in the next room.

"I've made a lot of mistakes," Summer admitted. "My quitting high school, my three-month marriage when I was eighteen, my giving in to impulse when my mother died. But Carrie isn't a mistake.''

''I understand that. The question is, what do you do now? You obviously didn't tell him last night.''

''There was no way to tell him in that mess. And then he seemed so different last night. He was so intense, so demanding. Right away, he jumped on my case with a whole list of questions. He wasn't the man who...''

''So you think he's a creep, huh? I guess creeps can come in great packaging, but it sure breaks my bubble. He's nothing short of gorgeous, although he's not exactly drop-dead handsome. More like the outdoors type.''

''You have to remember, though,'' Summer said, voicing her worst fear, ''he's obviously got what it takes to have custody of Carrie. That's what really scared me. More and more, courts are ruling in favor of fathers And while I'm getting it together now, it's clear I don't have what he has.''

''Yeah, with the job he's obviously got, with the clothes he had on, he could probably hire some super-whiz-bang lawyer.''

''All I can think about are the worst things that can happen. I hardly got any sleep last night.''

Apparently Dee didn't know how to encourage Summer. She moved the covered tray of grapes into the freezer. Getting ready for the next round, Summer wiped up.

''Why don't you let me take this party tonight on my own?'' Dee finally said, offering the best she could offer—space.

"No. I won't let this ruin what we've got started. We've worked too long and hard, Dee. Anyway, I want to be there tonight. I want to do this, too."

Seeing Summer's determination, Dee gave her a hug before going back to business. The muscle of their operation, Jean Vasquez, an energetic widow, swept in, picking up the support chores. Dee would remain with Jean while Summer took Carrie home for a nap. Summer had the book work to do. If they were lucky, she'd also have more calls on her answering machine.

But on the way out to Fiesta Key, and especially once she saw the ocean again, Summer resumed thinking. Although she didn't need to check for his cruiser anymore, the puzzle he now represented didn't seem to fit together.

The polished man in the tux, the one who'd treated her so coldly, was hardly the unshaven guy who'd rescued not only her body but her soul beneath the noonday sun. Although a sense of the familiar knit the two men together—just as did the same jade green stare—the polished veneer didn't quite suit either man.

Ryder Craig. How could she have not even known his name? It seemed so impossible now. But on that day, he'd been wonderful to her. There'd been an innate trust between them. All along, that trust had encouraged her to believe she'd look for him one day.

The best thing about that afternoon, however, was that it had acted as a catalyst. That afternoon had made this more successful day possible. It had literally saved her.

That's what a goner I was. Summer shuddered.

That day may have been a fantasy. It was looking more and more as if it had been. But in her heart, Summer simply could not regret it.

She hated the expression "Oh, it just happened." She'd never used it. She knew it hadn't just happened. She'd made a decision—under pressure for sure, but a decision nonetheless. She'd never regret that. When she tucked Carrie in for a nap, Summer recognized that all over again.

Back in the makeshift office in the bungalow's small living room, Summer concentrated on what had to be accomplished. She also heard the second message on her answering machine.

"This is Ryder Craig. It's just before noon. Summer, we need to talk. Call me at this number."

Even as he gave his number, and then recited a second private one, Summer acknowledged that her only choice was to see him again. The only way she could decide whether he was safe for Carrie was to try once more. Just because she'd seen the worst of him last night didn't mean he couldn't be a good second parent—a parent Carrie had a right to.

CHAPTER THREE

EVERY TIME he saw her, her beauty struck him like a sledgehammer.

When Ryder had first heard her voice returning his call, he hadn't believed it. She'd agreed to meet him. To see her walking toward him now, even at the crowded juice bar, elicited the same response.

Her fluttery sundress, in a pale yellow, hinted at curves beneath while also showing a good bit of tawny skin. Still, she was more aloof than alluring. She'd tightly pulled her strawberry blond hair into a neat upsweep, and her lovely features and carriage also revealed her control.

It was, however, the large and very dark pair of sunglasses she wore that best gave evidence of her attitude. Ryder saw them as the barrier they were supposed to be and was irritated. For some reason he couldn't explain, he felt she had no right to separate herself from him. *That* day, their mutual trust had been elemental.

Still, her not trusting him now was as apparent as her beauty. Oh, yes, he was conscious that others in the bar watched her. And that rankled, too. She and he had agreed that the juice bar, located near his office, would be a good place to meet. At the time it had seemed neutral ground. Now he saw it was too public.

The open-air restaurant was lively and charming. The shady interior was cluttered with small white tables and chairs, and overhead orange-and-white awnings billowed, then snapped in a fairly stiff breeze. The day was sunny and perfect, their situation tense.

After brief formal greetings, Summer agreed to a glass of freshly squeezed Florida orange juice. The long list of possibilities, of odd combinations of exotic juices, got scant attention. While she settled at a table, Ryder fetched their colorfully decorated drinks.

As he rejoined her, he glanced at a nearby table. A mother seemed oblivious to the ongoing tussle between her young sons. Flipping through a magazine, the woman sipped her lime-colored juice as the pair of boys wrestled across their chairs.

Still, Ryder focused easily on his companion. She sat across from him, cool and collected, picture perfect. Since they'd spoken only yesterday, late in the afternoon, he hadn't considered what he'd say to her. Simply being with her had seemed imperative.

But now that push had come to shove . . . well, what he could see of the expression on her beautiful face looked guarded.

"I'm glad you agreed to meet me," he said, sounding unoriginal, even to himself. "So you shop in the area?" *Worse yet.*

"I do most of the marketing for our catering service, and that takes me all over. We're always looking for the freshest, the most prime. Fruits, vegetables, fish, whatever. I was driving in, anyway."

He wished he could see behind the glasses. While her mouth drove him nuts, he needed to read what she felt. He needed to look into those bright blue eyes again.

Everything about her was extraordinary. Lush. Voluptuous. And yet, she didn't seem to trade on her appearance. Rather the opposite. She downplayed her flamboyant looks—at least, today she did.

"I, uh, work nearby." *Dammit, Ry, where's your brain?*

"So you said."

This is not my sea goddess.

Hell, he couldn't see behind the glasses, and the damned kids tumbled around their chairs. Hoping to have some effect, he sent them a hard look.

Surprisingly, it was his companion who bristled. "Don't you like children?"

"I don't know anything about children." *What had he said now?* Even the sunglasses didn't hide her cold reaction. Her lush lips tightened.

"I mean," he said, "it's not that I don't like kids. It's just that I've never been around kids. I have two nephews I've only seen as babies."

That didn't cut it, either. Here was the opposite of his soft, willing, vulnerable gift from the sea.

"I realize," he blurted out, "that we don't know each other. I mean, other than..." He was sounding absurd. "I'm saying that it's hard to know where to start. In fact, I was hoping we could start over. Not that our start..."

She simply stared at him.

He stumbled on. "Mainly, I want to apologize. For the night before last. At Calder Parks's party. It was a shock to see you. Not that you didn't look extraordinary."

Again, he could tell he'd misstepped. Badly. Perhaps she was defensive about her looks.

He backtracked. "I've been searching for you. Especially at the start. I spent a lot of weekends driving on the keys. I focused on Fiesta Key, but..."

"I'm not surprised you didn't find me."

When she spoke, it was reluctantly. Because he directed an open, interested look at her, she relented.

"My grandfather owns a resort on Fiesta Key. At the time, I wasn't actually living with him, but my mother had just died, and I was there a lot. Of course the resort itself was closed for mourning."

In Ryder's mind, some of the pieces began to fall into place. Admittedly she'd been desperate that day. "I see. You say you weren't living with your grandfather at the time. Does that mean you are now?"

"I have a bungalow there, but we're looking for something else. My grandfather's sold his resort."

"Yeah, I've heard about that. That little key is up for development, isn't it?" At her nod, he went on. "I take it your catering service is just getting off the ground."

Again she nodded.

"I'm sure it'll do well. It seems like a classy operation."

"Thank you."

For a minute, it seemed as if it might be getting better. But then the little rascals rammed into Ryder, jarring his grapefruit juice enough to spill some of it on his suit pants. That the mother remained ignorant, and the boys did, too, irritated him.

Dismissing the spilled juice, he felt a tightening of his lips nevertheless. Since Summer watched, he forged ahead.

"Look, I know this is awkward. But just because we started off the way we did..." She stiffened, and he plunged ahead. "I'd like for us to see each other."

She seemed put off by his suggestion. Or maybe by the noisy brats.

"I can't see you," she said.

"But why?"

When Summer O'Malley got to her feet, he did the same.

"You've made your apology, and I accept it. Let's just leave it at that."

Before he could think of the next inane thing to say, she turned and walked away from him. He stood by the table, watching the sway of her lithe body and light skirts. Just like every other red-blooded male in the place.

Along with a thousand other emotions, jealousy crackled inside him. He reached overload. He couldn't figure what had happened.

Forget the fantasy, man. The sea goddess has exited stage right.

SUMMER BOILED. As if her minivan wasn't hot enough. The way he'd looked at those two little boys!

Not that they hadn't been obnoxious. And not that the juice bar in itself hadn't been a mistake. They should have met someplace quiet. But would that have made a difference? She doubted it. Maybe she'd gotten lucky. At least he'd admitted to not knowing about kids.

And then there was all that embarrassing stuff about how they'd met. She'd never thought of it as embarrassing before. She'd been too mesmerized by the fantasy. To share the embarrassment with him...

Well, she'd learned a lot about Ryder Craig. Enough to protect Carrie from him.

And yet...

Well, dammit, she had to be sure. She'd have only one chance at this very important decision, and she'd cool off before making it. Everything in her resisted considering it at all. And yet...

By the time Summer reached Fiesta Key, the air-conditioning was having its effect. Anyway, it was always better on the keys. Especially on Fiesta Key. Fiesta Key was home. Having known little of her father, who had left her and her mother when Summer had been small, Summer had lived with her mother in the same bungalow she now shared with Carrie.

Since she'd had Carrie, though, Summer had been able to make peace with her mother's memory. Summer now saw that her mother had been desperate. When she'd been abandoned by her young husband, she'd been forced, like Summer, to return to Poppy because of finances. Summer's mother had then grown hard and determined—determined to make Summer live out the dreams that had never come true for her.

Additionally, Summer's mother had never gotten along with Poppy. She had pushed for too much. Poppy lived frugally. It had been a never-ending squabble.

In the end, Summer had rebelled. Her mother's insistence that Summer use her budding beauty to get what Summer hadn't wanted had thrown Summer not merely into misery and anger but into making a string of mistakes. Those mistakes had culminated in her flirtation with suicide, then in her subsequent rescue by Ryder Craig.

And that had brought Carrie.

Indeed, Carrie had healed Summer. Her baby had gotten Summer back on track. Carrie had demonstrated what was important.

Irrationally, Summer felt all of that was now threatened by Ryder Craig's reappearance in her life. He represented her worst hour in her messy past. She feared that just as she'd attained a hard-won stability, it might fall through. Or that he might wrest it from her again.

Worst of all, he represented something off the deep end—something she wasn't sure she could resist now, any more than she had the last time. There was a sense of the irresistible about him. She'd proved that in spades.

Finally on the little key, Summer let the surroundings soothe her. In an area where development had been rampant for over two decades, Fiesta Key had been left behind. The major landowner on the key had lived at his retreat for more than fifty years. Only along the beach had a string of resorts been built. Then, at the landowner's recent death, everything had changed. His property had been sold to a developer and the rest had become inevitable.

One after another, the small, family-owned resorts had been gobbled up. The prices had been beyond refusing. Poppy had said goodbye to friends and families that had been like his own family. Then, he'd had his minor breakdown. A warning, the doctors had said.

Pulling into the parking lot at the Flamingo Resort, Summer bypassed the still-quiet office. Maneuvering down the driveway toward the gulf, she entered the circle of pink and green and white bungalows. At their center, a large bed of palms and sea grapes rustled in the sun and wind.

Summer and Carrie occupied bungalow number one. The porch across the front, overhung by a slowly revolving fan, was the largest space in the small unit, and expecting that Carrie would be napping, Summer entered quietly.

Although she was ready to talk to Poppy about their necessary move, she found him asleep on her two-man couch. The shortness of the couch emphasized his length. In his sleep, his anxiety was clearly reflected on his face. Her heart wrenched.

He stirred.

"Hi," she said softly, when he focused on her.

"I must have fallen asleep." The basketball game on the nearby TV rumbled as an undertone. "You just get here?"

"Just now."

"Boop's asleep."

Summer smiled. "So I gather. Otherwise you wouldn't be. When Boop's awake, no one sleeps." Putting down her purse and sunglasses, Summer kicked off her sandals. "When I pulled in, I saw Irma's car up at the office."

"Oh, Gawd," he mumbled, reaching to switch off the television. "I can't seem to get the damned woman to stay home."

Sitting down beside him, Summer patted Poppy's knee. For as long as she could remember, she and Poppy had been tight. Their life with her mother hadn't been happy, and the two of them had endured it by knowing they had each other. In tears and rages, Summer had gone to Poppy. Even if he hadn't said much, or been able to fix much, he'd always been there.

Now she took her turn at being there for him.

"You know," she said, picking her way around his native recalcitrance, "Irma's life has been tied to the Flamingo Resort for so long that she isn't any more sure of what to do than you or I. And then, she only wants to help. Nobody was more faithful at the hospital than—"

"Hell's bells, I know that." Poppy got up and shook his shoulders.

Summer's gaze followed him to the front door. "I'm just saying you should be more patient with her. You have the patience for me and for Boop."

"We'll see," he muttered. "It'd be easier, though, if she wasn't there every time I turn around."

After watching her grandfather leave, Summer got down to brass tacks. She realized she'd missed another opportunity to discuss the house she had to find for them, but she also promised herself to push the matter soon.

Anyway, she had to get to work. Carrie would wake up, and before then, Summer wanted a start on her afternoon routine of bookkeeping and phone calls. Going back to her room on tiptoe, she stripped out of the sundress she'd worn to meet Ryder Craig. She also kept him from encroaching on her thoughts.

Always dressing comfortably at home, she got into a skimpy white tank top and short white shorts. After letting down her hair, she went, barefoot, to her desk in the living room.

Aside from the desk and couch and TV, there wasn't a space for anything but a table and lamp. All of Carrie's things packed her room, while Summer's bedroom also bulged at the seams. The tiny kitchen had proven useless for Summer's experimental cooking. Only constant picking up and a pale color scheme made the place bearable. Still, any thoughts of a house just for herself and Carrie were also out of the question. She had to stick by Poppy.

And then, just as she got going, she heard Carrie waking up. Putting her daughter in white ruffly rompers, Summer allowed Carrie to wander back and forth from where she worked at the desk to the baby's room. As usual, Carrie dragged out toy after colorful toy, padding on pink feet and chattering nonstop. Only the occasional no punctuated the burble.

Summer did notice, however, when a car pulled up beside her minivan, out on the driveway circling the palms and sea grapes. Even in the waning late-afternoon sunlight, the sporty car gleamed like a red candy apple dressed out in chrome. An expensive apple.

Summer's heart started an automatic thud, thud, deep in her chest. Knowing it was already too late to change into something less revealing, she remembered the important point. Ryder Craig. Indeed, Ryder Craig, now in jeans and a navy blue polo shirt, extricated himself from the small vehicle. Readjusting the mirrored sunglasses he wore, he looked around.

"Oh, my gosh." Summer could see him putting two and two together. She was at home.

And Carrie—Carrie was in her room.

When he knocked, Summer got up from the desk. She couldn't act as if they weren't there. The decision she'd been struggling with had been taken from her.

He would now know he had a daughter. Both relieved and frightened—and hardly able to breathe—Summer opened the door.

But her visitor's mirrored sunglasses put her off. She even bristled a bit. A touch of anger eased the guilt of not having told him about Carrie sooner. And while his gaze was obscured and she could read little aside from coolness, she could tell that those jade green eyes behind the sunglasses scanned her body up and down.

She felt vulnerable. No shoes. Long bare legs. Her bottom easing out from the cuffs of her white short-shorts. Her full breasts evident beneath the skimpy top. She lifted her chin. If he was a gentleman, he would've called first.

But he wasn't a gentleman. Even for all the trappings he'd acquired, he remained the sea bum. A smart-assed sea bum behind mirrored glasses. The polite veneer of earlier in the afternoon at the juice bar had vanished.

"So this is where you live," he said.

"Yes." She kept the door close to her side. If she matched his coolness, maybe he wouldn't stay. Maybe she could steal a little more time. That way, she'd be on better ground when she told him.

But no, he planted himself there, on the screened porch just outside the door. The soft whip of the ceiling fan stirred his hair. "The place has great style. It's too bad these old resorts are going by the wayside. I think people are more comfortable in them. They're user-friendly."

Summer realized that here was a man who'd know something of their predicament. He'd mentioned being in major real estate development. Still, her mind buzzed with stealing time—with what to say for her own best advantage where Carrie was concerned.

Although Carrie's room was quiet, Summer knew her daughter couldn't have fallen asleep again. This was a temporary lull.

"Listen," he said more softly, stripping off the mirrored glasses so she could make contact with those green eyes. "I think we got off on the wrong foot this morning. But then," he added, a cryptic smile on his lips, "when haven't we gotten off on the wrong foot?"

Summer looked down at the threshold beneath her bare toes. A softer, more amiable Ryder Craig was impossible to resist. This Ryder Craig was unfair. Here was the one she remembered from that day on his cruiser.

"Anyway," he said when she didn't reply, "I couldn't seem to leave it as it stood."

"I see."

"Could I, uh, come in?"

Summer felt like a helpless animal. What could she do? Moving back, she let him step into the small space of her living room, the floor of which was strewn with bright toys.

He was thrown off balance. While she closed the door, he simply stood there.

"Do you baby-sit?" he asked.

"No, I—"

"You don't live with someone?"

"No. I mean, not like you think. I—"

"Were you married?"

"Once. When I was eighteen, but—"

"Oh."

"You see, it's not what you think. Not at all what you think. In fact . . . well, why don't you sit down."

At first she thought he wouldn't. But then he moved to the two-seater couch. There wasn't anything to sit on but that or the desk chair.

Summer remained standing. She noticed when he got hooked into studying her again. This time, without the glasses. It was far better with the glasses. His eyes made her blood heat. Desire had always been ready between them. She lived with the proof.

Of course, it had to get worse. Summer had to pay the piper. Carrie came in on chubby feet, a brightly colored ball clasped in front of her round belly. To Carrie, nothing better than company existed. She grinned her pirate's grin. "Baw," she said, showing off.

Unfortunately, neither adult had even that much to say.

Ryder Craig's gaze was riveted to the face of his child. His eyes coursed over her tiny features. He studied her cheery gaze, her slightly slanty smile, her dimpled chin.

Yes, she had to be his. It was so obvious. In that moment, Summer knew she was paying for two and a half years of silence. Worse, she'd pay more.

His voice finally sounded with a dawning recognition. "My God in heav—"

"Baw," Carrie insisted, her attention locked to this very unusual guest.

When Ryder remained frozen, she nudged the ball in his direction, her effort ending in the usual result. With a hollow sound, the ball bounced wide of where Ryder sat. Probably reflexively, he snagged it, glancing at it as if it were something he'd never seen the likes of before.

He was in shock. His eyes drifted to Summer's. "Ball?" he repeated to check his understanding.

Summer nodded.

Oh, God, he looked so stunned. This was the worst emotional beating she'd ever endured.

Ryder peered back at where Carrie stood, still grinning. Summer saw the child was less sure now. But not much. Carrie was accustomed to winning people over.

"Ball," Ryder finally managed to say, bending from his seated position on the couch to roll it back in her direction.

Of course that was all it took. Carrie screeched in delight, then grabbed at the ball as it rolled by her. When she missed it, it tumbled into the short bedroom hallway behind her. Giggling happily, she trundled after it.

Looking back at Ryder, Summer felt her own guilty flush.

"Sh-she's mine." He was on his feet like a shot. "My God, weren't you going to tell me?"

"Yes."

"When? When she was eighteen?"

"No. I had every intention of telling you soon."

"Soon? Like that night on Calder's porch? Or this morning over juice?"

Summer could understand his bitterness. That he had no doubt Carrie was his was obvious.

"I'm sorry," Summer said softly. She wasn't afraid of him. She remembered his gentleness too well to ever be afraid of him. But her guilt. It debilitated her. She hadn't realized what she'd deprived him of.

"I'm sorry," she said again. "I just couldn't seem to tell you."

"You couldn't seem to tell me? What about the day you found out you were pregnant? Couldn't you have tried to find me then? Or how about the day she was born? Didn't you think that, just maybe, I should know? How many birthdays has she had? Let's see. I can't even count the months I'm so—"

"One birthday. And yes, I thought about you then. But I didn't think—"

"What? You didn't think that a child would matter to me? You thought I was what? Some kind of—well, I guess we both know the words we could use. But this is *a baby*... God dammit," he said, his voice dwindling to a whisper.

The tension in the little room was so fierce that Summer couldn't think. Next, Carrie's sudden cries startled her so badly that she jumped. The baby stood just in the hallway, her ball in her hands. Both Summer and Ryder jerked around to look at her.

"It's all right," she said to him. "She's not used to... well, to arguments." Summer already had the child in her arms. She raised her voice over Carrie's continuing wails. "We live here alone, you know."

Ryder's shock and anger now turned into something else. Summer felt sorry for him. He looked stricken.

"It's all right," she said, wanting to comfort him, too. "Really, kids cry. And Carrie cries with the same verve she does everything else. Here, let's all sit down on the couch. All right, Boop?" she asked Carrie soothingly. "We'll all sit down, and you can see that everything's just fine."

She peered over the strawberry blond curls on her daughter's head—to Ryder. He gingerly sank onto the couch, as far away from them as he could get.

"When she cries," she explained, "she's so loud that it can seem kind of scary. But most of the time she's happy as a clam."

He seemed to doubt every word Summer said. He observed Carrie as if she'd landed from another planet. Summer chuckled. She couldn't help it. He looked so earnest.

It was awful.

She felt giddy.

For comfort, Summer sought the soft, sweet-smelling flesh of her baby. She cuddled her close. As always, Summer took strength from Carrie.

Carrie also calmed down, shutting off her tears if not her hiccups. Through watery leaf-green eyes, she peered at her father while keeping two fingers in her mouth.

He stared back.

"When will the hiccups go away?" he finally asked.

"Soon. They're almost gone already."

"*Hick.*" Carrie was always contrary.

With a long brown finger, Ryder reached out to stroke Carrie's plump arm. "I'm sorry, honey," he said to her. "I didn't mean to make you cry."

Summer's heart wrenched. She thought she might be the next one to burst into tears.

Fortunately, Ryder had apparently had his fill. When he got to his feet, Summer followed him to the door where she hefted Carrie to a hip. Carrie still watched with wide green eyes. Her fingers drooped from her rosebud lips. Her hiccups faded.

Ryder hovered over them for a moment, looking from Summer to her child. "I'd better go," he said. "I'll call you."

Summer couldn't blame him. If she was confused, he had to be reeling.

Then he did the most tender thing imaginable. She felt as if she'd returned to her fantasy lover on his listing cruiser. He bent and kissed Carrie on the cheek. The next deeper pass of his lips weighed on Summer's mouth.

"I've never regretted that day for a minute," he whispered, his green eyes filling her view. "I still don't. I hope you don't, either."

With that, he closed the door and Summer let Carrie slide to the floor. She simply had to sit down. Sit down and get a hold on herself. On her tears. On her regret. On the abrupt, long-buried suggestion of desire.

CHAPTER FOUR

STRUGGLING FOR equilibrium, Ryder walked to his car. The last light of day turned the animated sheet of nearby gulf water to purest mother-of-pearl. Pearl essence softened the coconut palms and sea grapes, the circle of old resort bungalows and yes, even his red Mercedes 300SL.

He was in shock.

He had a right to be.

Even as he reached to open his car door, he stopped and started walking back toward the house. He was running on emotion, but he couldn't seem to help himself. A single factor ran in his head. He had a daughter.

The screened porch of Summer O'Malley's little house seemed quiet and closed to him. Even so, he mounted the steps and, standing under the gentle whip of the overhead fan, knocked at the door.

She appeared, still barefoot and scrubbing back her red-blond hair from her forehead. She looked vulnerable, even as she met his eyes with a budding stubbornness.

"I..." He, too, dealt with frustration. "I need to talk to you. Can I come in?"

She remained grudgingly in place, fixing him with her blue gaze. But then she relented.

Almost sighing with relief, Ryder stepped back into the small cluttered room while Summer closed the door. Carrie had disappeared, but he could hear her somewhere nearby. The bungalow offered no privacy.

Since his reluctant hostess remained aloof, Ryder stopped in the middle of the scattered toys. His words exploded from him, equally as unreal as the rest. "We'll get married."

Summer surprised him by relaxing her shoulders. "Sit down," she said even more softly.

Ryder sank onto the edge of the couch. He felt confused. But Summer held the lion's share of his attention. Rubbing her hands together, she picked her way through the colorful array with the ease of experience.

"Look," she said, "I probably know what you're feeling better than you think I do. I, at least, had time to get used to the idea of Carrie. Really, in hindsight, I admit that—particularly where you're concerned—I should have done some things differently."

When Ryder would have seconded that wholeheartedly, Summer plunged ahead.

"Of course I've felt the consequences of . . . well, of what we did. . . . And believe me I'm not complaining. I even admit to my part in what . . . in what happened."

Again, she glanced away, then back. Ryder admired the way she kept drawing up the courage to go on. He also waited as patiently as he could.

"Let's face it," she said, pinning him with cornflower blue eyes, "what we did was stupid. We totally ignored both the risks and the consequences. Like I say, I've been living with those consequences. I had to decide against an abortion—which wasn't a difficult decision in my case. But then, I had to consider adoption and how, or even *if* I could take care of her. I realized I had to grow up. I had to put someone else first, and now you're probably feeling a lot of that... well, just out of the blue, really. But I've also learned that making rash decisions isn't the way to do this. You need time for this to sink in. You need—"

"I don't want an illegitimate child running around without my name," he blurted out.

Again, she surprised him, this time with a cryptic smile. "Do you think I like that?"

He entrenched himself in silence.

She began to pace again—not nervously, but more as a contemplative glide, as a release, as a bit of space in which to think and form her words. "The truth is, people seldom marry anymore simply because they have a child. If I could choose, I'd give Carrie a traditional family and home life. But I can't give her that. I can only give her my best effort, my love and my prayers. The fact is that two wrongs don't make a right, and they won't in this case, either. The bottom line is that we're strangers who made a very bad mistake."

The bottom line for Ryder was that all the while he admitted her truths, all the while he admired her courage, he disliked every word she said. What they'd had that day had seemed above truth and consequences and, well, even above this one more screwup in his life.

But no, that wasn't the worst, either. Relegating that day, his child, to one more screwup was repugnant. Besides, he didn't feel like that about the circumstances. Nor, he could tell with great gratitude, did Summer O'Malley regard the situation with anything but hard truth, with admirable love and with courage.

She was smiling at him again. Just a wisp of a dry smile. "So," she said, "as much as I appreciate your offer of marriage, I respectfully decline."

But Ryder couldn't manage a smile. Although his emotions ranged wide and wild, he felt no humor. Still, he, too, relaxed his shoulders. He'd take his cue from Summer. He'd think. He'd do his best by the situation he'd created. He would also grow up.

Unable to continue looking at her because desire also tugged at him, he dropped his gaze to where his hands knotted between the spread of his knees. "So," he murmured, more to himself, "where do we go from here?"

Her tone sharpened. "*We* don't have to go anywhere from here. As I'm sure you can see, your daughter wants for nothing. She's the center of my life, and she'll have everyth—"

"I'm sorry. Anyone can tell you love her. I know you're doing your best—"

"Even if it isn't enough?" she finished for him— tartly.

He stared at her. He didn't know how they'd gotten off on that tangent, but he didn't want to scrap with her. Anything but.

Still, he kept his mind from his most immediate emotions, those that centered on her and him, and he refocused on...well, on Carrie. On their daughter. Surely it was sinking in and he could think better now. "I guess what I'm trying to ask is how much you'll let me be involved."

She remained stiff, caution as clear in her eyes as in her stance. "That's up to you."

"Well, that's the only thing I do know. I want to be involved. I want to support her. And don't think I'm making any judgments about what you're doing for her. Believe me, I neither have the right nor do I have any complaints. From what little I've experienced, I'm damned impressed."

Good. She relented again. Just a little.

"As I told you," she said, "I'd reconciled myself to contacting you one day. I think Carrie has a right to know you and, well, I guess you have your right to her, too." She stared at her hands—rubbed them together at this hard admission. Then she met his gaze. "Still, I'll have to feel comfortable about you, about when and how often you see her."

"I understand that."

"I think the best thing is to take it one step at a time. It would be good for you to see Carrie here. At least for a while. Good for her, you know."

"Yeah, I see."

"Short visits would be best."

"Uh-huh."

"Supervised."

"Right."

Visions of a threesome arose in Ryder's mind. But just barely.

"Most important," she was saying, "is that we see each other as strangers."

"What?"

"Well, I mean, after all, we are. Strangers, that is. And while I'm perfectly willing to be as cordial and helpful as I can be where Carrie is concerned—because that's what's best for Carrie—I have to say that..."

Ryder held his breath. He didn't like the word *strangers*. He didn't like what she was getting at.

She continued, anyway. "I'm going to be very blunt with you this one time. Just to clear the air and to set things straight. I know what you must think of me, but there will be no more of *that*."

"Of *that?*" Part of Ryder played dumb. She knew it and he knew it, and she began to pace again. She looked so damned beautiful. But she was also intelligent and caring. An amazing combination.

And he hated the word *strangers*.

"That day," she said, forcing firmness into her voice and slender frame. "That was something that's totally out of character for me."

"Yes, I remember. You said your mother had just died, and—"

"But that's not the point." She faced him, stock-still. "If I'm going to let you see Carrie *willingly,* I'll have to feel comfortable. You said you understood that."

"And I do, but—"

"No, no buts. The facts are that you and I are strangers, that we made a mistake and that we're not going to make that mistake again. Not ever. This is something we'll have to agree on, or we won't be able to—"

"All right." Ryder heard the stiffness in his voice. He even got to his feet and matched her tough stance with one of his own. "And since we're putting our cards on the table, I, too, have something to say."

"Okay," she murmured, unrelenting.

"I want to be the first to tell you that I don't have such a great reputation." He noted the sudden doubt flooding into her eyes, and he did as little as possible to stem it. "I don't know if you'd recall, but about five years ago I was in the papers. I was tried for murder, and though I was acquitted, a thing like that is never lived down. The fact is, I was innocent, but my name has never been completely cleared. I—"

Ryder might have gotten past Carrie's delighted "Hi!" as she entered the room, but the phone rang at the same time, and that couldn't be ignored.

Summer reached toward the desk. "I'm sorry, I don't have the answering machine on, and—"

"I know. You're building a new business. Go ahead, pick it up."

Squelching the same old resentments, Ryder sank back down onto the edge of the couch. He rubbed his face, then, elbows to his thighs, he dropped his hands between his lax knees. He didn't want to look at Summer's lush bottom, barely contained in the tight white shorts.

Her body was long and lithe, perfection. She had received him sweetly, given him . . .

Geez, he intoned as an inward warning. *That's way off base, buddy.*

Forcing himself, he zeroed in on her end of the phone conversation. "Yes, the other night at the home of Calder Parks . . . well, thank you. I'm glad you enjoyed it."

The tiniest nudge at Ryder's knee reminded him that he and Summer weren't the only people in the small room. Lifting his eyes from the floor, he was caught in his daughter's twinkly green gaze.

"Hi," he said softly.

Grinning brightly, Carrie shoved the ball-shaped toy she carried into his hands. An odd contraption, it had pierced holes of different sizes and shapes. Inside, circles and triangles and squares rattled around.

Before he could react, Carrie swiped back the ball and opened it. The plastic forms tumbled onto the carpet, and she bent to retrieve them, placing them, one by one, along the tops of his thighs.

Again, Ryder heard snatches of Summer's ongoing phone conversation. "Yes, we've done a wedding, but it was fairly small. You say your caterer, what, mixed up the bookings?"

At the sound and feel of the first form clunking into the ball on his lap, Ryder refocused on his daughter.

She seemed to expect something from him, and his automatic "Good" pleased her no end. One by one, she went on fitting the shapes into the right holes. Each time he watched her chubby fingers, studied the expression of concentration on her sweet babyish features. Each time he experienced her deep pleasure, both at her success and at his murmured "Good girl."

"Well," Summer was saying somewhat breathlessly, "that's quite a wedding. And quite a menu. And the date is—when did you say?"

Ryder looked back at Carrie. Her task completed, she swept away the toy, consigning it to the litter on the floor. Then she looked boldly up at him. Stretching, she pushed a chunky finger into the cleft in his chin.

He chuckled. "Yeah, and I see you have one, too."

Her finger touched her nose. "'Ose," she pronounced.

"Right. Nose."

"Eye."

"A big green eye."

"Teef."

She went on to point out other features, naming each one, and he understood every word she said. But his mind buzzed with other revelations.

Oh, Carrie definitely had Summer's coloring—the same strawberry blond hair and creamy, tawny skin. But in the basics, Carrie resembled him. In her slanty smile, he thought. In her dimpled chin. In her mannerisms, he saw his brother, Vance. Even more wrenchingly, he saw his father. And then, of course, it hit him. Carrie O'Malley represented the next generation of Craigs.

Ryder's heart faltered. Nearly five years had passed since he'd seen any of his family, but he still felt deep remorse.

He heard Summer closing a catering date.

He saw Carrie reach her pink pointing finger to explore the cleft in his chin.

He fought the lump in his throat.

He smiled at the delight in the child's eyes.

"Chin," he managed to say.

"'In," she repeated, giggling and stumbling backward for her mommy, who had just hung up the phone, to catch.

His eyes met Summer's. "My God," he whispered, "she's beautiful."

Summer swept Carrie up and hugged her. "And what's more," she said, smiling genuinely this time, "she's smart. We emphasize smart around here, don't we, Boop? Smart, and caring, and polite, and busy, and..."

Summer's eyes engaged Ryder's, warm with the last of her smile.

"We aren't strangers," he said impulsively.

Her gaze held his. Her smile vanished. With deliberate motions, she set Carrie down and opened the door as an indication for Ryder to leave. "Listen," she announced, "I've already made too many mistakes in my life, and I'm not making any more if I can help it."

He paused in the doorway. "We're not strangers," he repeated.

"I want to feel good about your coming here," she said as a warning.

"We're not strangers," he said again softly. His final truth he imparted over a shoulder on stepping off the porch and hearing the screen door slap behind him. "We've had a baby together, lady. That's as intimate as it gets."

SUMMER BURST into Poppy's kitchen with Carrie on one hip and a diaper bag swinging from her opposite shoulder.

Fred, who sat at the kitchen table reading the newspaper, glanced up unsurprised.

"I owe you one for this," Summer said, putting down her burdens.

"Hell's bells, I've told you a million times I don't mind keeping Boop."

"Yeah, well, last-minute stuff like this is above and beyond the call of duty."

Carrie waddled toward her great-grandfather, her grin the most ready for him.

"You're no trouble, are you, Boop?" he murmured, picking her up to sit next to him on the old plastic banquette.

"What time is it?" Summer asked, checking the clock and answering her own question. "It's only six, but it feels like midnight."

When she slowed down, then even hesitated, Poppy stared at her.

She hiked a shoulder. "You've gotta know how grateful I am to you. For how you handled this...well, my pregnancy, and—"

"Hell's bells," he huffed, going back to his paper. "We don't need to go into that."

Forcing a nonchalance she didn't feel, Summer spread some plastic stacking cups on the table for Carrie's eager fingers.

Poppy disliked "discussing things." Especially emotions. He was of the old school. For him, families stuck together no matter what. And they didn't wear their feelings on their sleeves or hang out their dirty linen in public.

Still, Summer had no choice but to go on.

"Today, I mean, over the past couple of days, I've seen him again. I mean, Carrie's father."

Although Poppy sent Summer a guarded glance, he didn't reply. To the reticent Fred, Carrie's father and the circumstances of Carrie's arrival were also out of conversational bounds.

"His name...well, his name is Ryder Craig, and, as it turns out, he's not the sea bum I thought he was. He's established in a real estate firm, and he's single. He's also interested in seeing Carrie." Since Poppy only grunted, Summer continued. "I ran into him again by accident. The other night at that fancy party. You know the one."

He nodded grudgingly.

"Well, about an hour and a half ago, he showed up at my bungalow and he found out about Carrie. He was in shock, of course. But he's also very certain about wanting to see her again, and I've decided to let him."

"You've gotta be careful about these things, you know."

Although Poppy would never tell Summer what to do, he'd voice his opinions, and especially his reservations.

But then again, Summer didn't question that. She, too, had her reservations. Hers simply differed from Poppy's. She wasn't so much unsure about the safety of letting Ryder Craig into their lives as she was about her own emotional safety in doing so.

Still, she didn't have time to think about that. Nor would she discuss that aspect with her grandfather. Not ever. That would embarrass them both.

The single necessity was to be very straight with Poppy. In general, Poppy trusted her and her decisions. That's why he wasn't setting up more than a token resistance to letting this man in their lives.

"H-he told me he thought we should get married. You know, to give Carrie a name."

Poppy jerked to attention. "Well, that says something for him."

Summer smiled ruefully. "It's out of the question. I told him so."

Obviously Poppy's old-fashioned heart urged him to tell her she was crazy, but he didn't.

Summer headed on toward the worst. "He also told me something I think you should know."

"Oh?"

"He said he was involved in a trial some years back. About five years ago. He said he was tried for murder and that although he was innocent, his name was never cleared. I think he would've told me more, but

I got this phone call from this woman . . . Well, what I'm saying is that I don't remember anything about any trial. I must have been about twenty, and I've never done much except skim the papers. But you. I thought you might recall . . ."

"Let's see," he murmured, looking at Carrie, then back at Summer. "About five years ago. And his name's Ryder Craig."

Summer saw again that her grandfather was, despite his recent hospital stay and his ongoing resistance to the changes in his life, as sharp as a tack.

"Yeah," he finally said, "I remember some of it. The Craigs are a big-deal New York family, but because they winter in Palm Beach, we got some of the news here, too. As I recollect, he was supposed to have murdered a girlfriend or someone like that. He, uh, was let off, but there wasn't too much sympathy for him. The woman who testified against him was taken apart on the witness stand by his high-powered lawyer, and it left a bad taste in everyone's mouth. Some doubts, too."

Summer didn't know what to think, much less what to say. What her grandfather had told her so opposed what she knew of Ryder Craig, especially of him on that day . . . But no. She wouldn't let that day of two and a half years ago color anything she learned of Ryder Craig as a real person. She had to be realistic, both for Carrie's sake and for her own.

"So it's the same Ryder Craig, is it?" Poppy asked cautiously.

"Yes, the same."

When he glanced back at his paper, she went on.

"About tonight," she said, "I told you I got this call from a woman who attended the party at Calder

Parks's. When her caterer, whom she's had lined up for her daughter's wedding for over a year, lost track of her date, she phoned her daughter and they decided to see if we could step in. Naturally I called Dee, and she thinks we can do it, but we're cutting it close with only three weeks to prepare. Besides, this'll be our first big wedding. On the other hand, we can hardly pass it up. This woman is active at the Asolo Center, and she could get us all sorts of business. So we're on the spot. I'm going to the grocery store now, and then I'll meet Dee at the church kitchen. We'll get started on the stuff we can fix and freeze in advance. We figure if we get on top of it we won't panic. Maybe.''

"I got it. And don't worry about bedtime. I'll put Carrie down here, and you can leave her till mornin'.''

"Thanks, Poppy.'' Summer bent to drop a kiss on his rough cheek.

"No problem,'' he replied, not minding her peck too much.

When Summer settled her purse on her shoulder, however, he conceded somewhat. "You know, girl. If a jury of twelve men good and true found this Ryder Craig innocent, it's gotta mean somethin'. And besides that, he told you about the trial right off the bat. That counts for somethin', too. It was the honorable thing to do.''

Summer smiled. Honor. Duty. Her Poppy was old-fashioned and sometimes a pain in the neck. But he was also bone-deep fair.

"Thanks, Poppy.'' Her last squeeze was for Carrie.

OFF THE west coast of Florida, sunsets were dazzling. Even in the winter season when the sun set early, the light lasted, blurring into vibrant colors as it gave up altogether.

By the time Summer left Poppy's quarters at the resort, pearl gray faded to light violet darkening into deepest purple. It was only a little after six, but Summer had a lot to do. And then, being busy was good. It kept her mind from going over...

"We're not strangers," he'd said.

And while she stubbornly resisted his soft utterance, her heart...

Sliding to a halt at a stoplight, Summer tossed back her hair. She didn't use sunglasses and baseball caps at night. After dark, her looks didn't inhibit her as much. Even so, when she glanced across at the noisy pickup that waited next to her van, she sensed the driver staring at her.

In this case, a barely perceptible hulk of a male driver studied her so intently that she thought his scorching gaze would bubble paint. Turning away, she tilted her chin. She'd leave no doubt that she wouldn't be tampered with.

Actually, she dismissed the guy as easily as the light changed. But at the next traffic signal, the one marking the turnoff into the supermarket lot, the bulky male in the rusted-out pickup eased up beside her van once again. When Summer felt his eyes on her, she refused to look his way.

As a typical goad, he revved his engine, but she still wasn't buying. Having experienced such unwelcome attention many times, she'd discovered that her playing ignorant usually got boring for the pursuer.

Still, the darkly clad guy was obviously determined, probably to get her to look at him. Out of the corner of her eyes, she saw that he let up on his brake

just enough to pull slightly ahead of their parallel po-
sitions. He then gunned his engine, only to jerk it into
a jolting, stopping reverse.

She wished his transmission would drop out onto
the road.

Still, she didn't peek. She knew better. Fortunately,
someone honked at him, and even as she heard him lie
on his horn in reply, the light changed and she moved
off.

Some people, she thought, turning in to the large
lot. Unfortunately, she encountered the last of the
shoppers who stopped off on their way home from
work, and the lot was full. Searching for a convenient
slot, because she anticipated the double or even triple
baskets she'd have to cart out, she drove slowly.

Also at that point, a pair of slightly lopsided headlights, probably misaligned in a fender bender, fell in
behind her. The guy driving the pickup switched his
high beams on and off and the light pierced her eyes
in her rearview mirror, causing her to squint, and to
tell this second nut in as many minutes what she
thought of him.

She searched for a slot. He followed. If, she
thought, she could find a spot, she'd get out and give
this guy a piece of her mind. But entering a pool of
light cast by one of the parking-lot lamps, she saw that
the man who now tracked her was the same guy who'd
challenged her at the stoplight.

''Nuts,'' she muttered.

When in public, Summer considered the attention
she drew as hardly more than annoying. Nor was it
really that constant. But sometimes, like this, when
there were few people around and she had a good dis-

tance to walk before she reached the nearest safe place, she did feel a tug of fear.

What guys like this might do was hard to judge. She'd definitely learned not to be friendly. And while to be cautious seemed an encroachment on her freedom, when she had to think about it, she did take the cautious route.

Even as she parked in a place that was some distance down the aisle and also the only slot she could find, she felt angry as much as anything else. She knew overreaction would be downright foolish. And so, dragging in a deep breath, she got out of the van and turned to lock it.

Sure enough, the mountain of a guy cruised up to watch her from the window of his truck. She still could only have described him generally because she refused to look at him.

Tempted, oh, so tempted, to scream at him, she kept a lid on it. She wasn't about to reduce herself to his level, and she truly believed that ignoring jerks like this was the best policy.

Lifting her chin, she made a beeline for the next aisle. She heard him rev his engine, but she kept on walking as fast as she could. She'd be damned if she'd be intimidated in this little game she'd played a dozen times since she'd turned fifteen and her body had ripened like some lush fruit.

Okay, okay, so she was mad, she thought, still striding, still holding her eyes to the brightly lit oasis ahead.

My God, it wasn't even seven o'clock yet, and there was a store full of people and even a couple of basket-pushing customers dotting the still-hot asphalt.

What did she have to be anxious about?

"I'm not afraid so much," she said under her breath. "I'm angry!"

Of course the jerk had driven around to the aisle she used. Now he flashed his lights from low to bright, dogging her as closely as he could. By the time she reached the automatic door of the grocery store, she was nothing short of furious. Gunning his engine, and with a last squeal of his tires, the jerk swung out of the lot and off into the street.

"Jerk, jerk, jerk," Summer muttered, heading for the service counter as the automatic door hissed shut behind her.

Naturally, a half-dozen commuting moms and hubbies waited to cash their checks, and by the time Summer reached the window of the service counter, the frizzy-haired woman who manned the operation seemed to be the enemy.

Summer stayed cool. She'd been shopping in the store for years and that should count for something. The woman behind the counter peered at her and smiled, completely disarming her. "Ms. O'Malley," she chirped, "can I help you?"

Now that Summer was here, facing the sanity of the workaday world, she didn't know what to say. But feeling some encouragement, she started. "I hate to do this, but..."

"You hate to do what, dear?" The woman tilted her head as if really taking the time to listen.

"Well, now, I'm feeling downright silly." Summer smiled, even blushed a little. "You see, I was in the lot, and some man in a pickup... well, he followed me, and..." She choked out a chuckle. "Golly, this sounds so stupid. I guess I was more angry than anything, and I've obviously gotten carried away."

"No, no," the woman said, grabbing the microphone. "Security, security, please," she blasted out storewide.

"Really," Summer protested, "I don't know what security can do."

"Well, we'll see. Wait just a minute. Arnold's on tonight and he's very good."

Summer stepped aside and waited for Arnold. She'd started this, and it was her own fault. She wasn't about to brush anyone off. She'd also admit her mistake. After apologizing to Arnold, she'd slink away and fill her grocery cart.

Sure enough, Arnold was Johnny-on-the-spot, and Summer found herself facing another considering expression. He caressed the rim of his Stetson, stroked his graying mustache, then asked her to explain.

She did. And it grew worse and worse. Although Arnold listened patiently, Summer could barely reach the end of her tale quickly enough. Really, what could Arnold do about a guy who'd left the premises twenty minutes earlier?

"Well, Ms. O'Malley," he drawled, once she'd finished. "You go on and get your groceries, and me and a coupla bag boys will follow you outta here once you're done."

"Oh, really," she said, "I—"

But Arnold interrupted with a signal to the service counter. "Buzz me when she's done, will ya, Harriet?"

"Sure, Arnold," the woman replied, flashing Summer another quick smile.

Summer's cheeks burned. She'd overreacted and she knew why. She'd had one heck of an afternoon—Ryder Craig had lit a fuse that had just resulted in an embarrassing fizzle.

CHAPTER FIVE

"WHAT IN the blazes are you doin' here?"

In answer to Fred's question, Irma sent him a tight glance up from her knitting. What she was doing was obvious. She was sitting by the phone in the little resort office, hoping it would ring. She badly needed an excuse for being there.

"I told you," she said, holding up for her own inspection the two lumpy strips of knitted salmon-colored yarn, "that I think someone with a civil tongue in his head should answer the phone. If and when it rings."

"Yeah," he scoffed, "*if* and *when* it rings. There're damned few calls now, and I can be as polite as anybody."

Appearing as neutral as she could, Irma fixed the one needle back into the yarn and began to knit. "I'll finish out the week," she stated.

Hovering, Fred mumbled something she didn't want to hear.

Truly, she was nearly disheartened. All morning she'd gone over the wide-ranging advice her various friends had offered. In her opinion, the best solution was to keep playing it by ear.

Glancing beyond the desk, Irma saw that he remained lurking there. Curiosity nipped at her. She wondered if he wanted to open another subject, and her heartbeat picked up.

"Is everything all right?" she asked as casually as she could.

"Yeah, yeah, everything's fine."

"You don't sound like everything's fine."

"And how in blazes would you know how I sound?"

"Because I've worked with you almost every day of my life for the past twenty-two and a half years."

"Good grief, has it been twenty-two and a half years?"

"Come next month."

"It don't seem that long."

"No, it doesn't seem like it, but it's true."

Good gracious, she wondered. Why did she sound so awkward? She was easy enough with her friends.

But then, Fred wasn't a friend. He never had been. And here she was, in love with the old coot. She considered chucking the whole bit and going home with her tail between her legs. Not that he'd notice.

"I'm walking down to Summer's bungalow," he said.

Irma looked intently at him. Something about his eyes, something about his voice, seemed forlorn. And forlorn...well, she'd never connect forlorn with Fred Miller.

"You say you're going down to Summer's bungalow? Is she all right? Is Carrie sick?"

"Naw, naw, nothin' like that. It's just that..."

Despite his hangdog expression, Irma felt a bit irritated. But before she could subdue the feeling and manage the patient response that mantrapping obviously required, he plunged ahead.

"She's got someone she wants me to meet."

"Heavens Fred. What in the world are you getting at?"

Now she'd gone and done it. He stiffened. Shot a look at her. Still, he didn't leave. "She wants me to meet Carrie's father."

"Carrie's fa . . . ?"

"Yeah, yeah, I'll be damned if I know what to do or say."

"But you don't have to do or say anything. Not anything beyond what's polite. Summer wants you there, and it's Summer's to decide what's to be done or said."

He seemed to accept her surprisingly ready advice. The give-and-take of advice was habitual for Irma and her dozen or so women friends, and she went on. "Summer's an intelligent woman who knows what she wants. And if it's that first marriage of hers you're thinking about—"

"Naw, naw, it ain't that damned marriage. She was just a kid then. She only wanted to get away from her mother. And she ain't been much interested in any other guy since. Naw, naw, it's just . . ."

"It's just, what, Fred?"

"Hell, I don't know what to *say*. I hardly want to shake the guy's hand and tell him it's about time, or somethin' like that."

"No, that doesn't sound too good. What do you think Summer expects?"

He shrugged helplessly.

"I'd think she wants everything on the up-and-up. And politeness is certainly best for Carrie," she said.

Again he shrugged.

Patience, patience. "You trust Summer. You admire what Summer's made of herself. I know I do. She'll figure it out and in the meantime, you'll do what she expects of you. It's grand that she's even included you today. She thinks a great deal of you, Fred. I mean, this can't be easy for her, either."

"Yeah, I guess you're right. I gotta at least give the guy a chance. After all, it was Summer who didn't let him know anything. What could he have done?"

Irma was so amazed that they'd had a conversation—that what she'd said to Fred had actually counted for something—that she sat and looked at him.

Gosh almighty, hope did indeed spring eternal.

To Ryder, thinking about that day—the one when he'd met and made love to Summer O'Malley—was both an indulgence and a threat. The threat, of course, was to the status quo he'd established in his life since. After all, to meet and make love to a woman, all within a single afternoon, was way out of line, and he'd considered himself beyond doing something like that again. To find that he'd do the very same thing now—if given the opportunity—was a surprise.

In the two and a half years since that day, he'd done everything he could to get himself back on track. Hell, he'd even fixed up his boat. And God knew, he certainly forced himself to go to work each day. He simply wasn't going to mess up again.

On the other hand, to indulge thoughts of that day amounted to a pleasurable fantasy he allowed himself as a reward for wearing suits and ties and making money with Calder Parks. For staying straight and respectable.

For turning his back on his dream.

Still, as Ryder guided his car out of the marina where he lived, making his way to Fiesta Key, he knew he'd indulge himself. He needed the fantasy of that day as much as he needed the lessons that day had taught him. To make love without any thought of protection and responsibility represented his lowest point.

But that day also represented his pivotal point, the point at which he'd recognized a need for change.

That August day had differed from this January one. It had been bright with sunlight, and the gulf, with a light chop and no wind, resembled a shallow, sleepy sea. Going to the side of *Spare a Dime,* he had deliberately scanned the water for the swimmer he'd noted earlier. He'd been wondering for a while if she wasn't too far out, if she didn't know that the gradual sloping depths could be deceptive. It wouldn't be the first time a swimmer had misjudged the gentle appearance of the sea.

He had been relieved, then, when she flipped over onto her back to catch her breath. Even more of a relief, she had reversed direction and headed for the beach. She appeared to be a strong swimmer, but he had to wonder...

Something felt wrong. Urgency gripped him. He could swear she was in trouble. And while he didn't want to interfere—well, he yelled.

"Hey! You! Are you in trouble?"

God, he could swear she was.

He heard "Help!"

He didn't second-guess jumping over the side of the old anchored cruiser. The woman was too far away to throw in a life preserver first. Only after his initial effort did he begin to question his immediate reaction. A strong swimmer himself, he was breathing hard by the time he reached her. Then the thought struck him that he might not be able to do either of them any good.

When she scrambled for him, clung to him, it scared the hell out of him. All those stories he'd heard about one swimmer going in to rescue another only for the first to be so desperate that...

He heard his own string of oaths. He had to get her attention. She was sinking them both.

"Let go! Let go, lady! I can't help you...if you don't let loose, dammit!"

He knew the courage it cost her, but she did let go. She went limp in his arms. Only her eyes, riveting his from inches away, told him she wasn't already a goner. But no, he also heard the gasp of her breath.

Or was that his own breath?

Afraid he was thinking less and less clearly, Ryder applied the grip he'd learned in a lifesaving class in college. It became easier then. But not much.

When they reached the boat, they grabbed the ladder. Neither could do more than gulp air. They couldn't even speak. While Ryder saw the woman trying to thank him, her coughing sounds prevented her from doing so.

They simply faced each other, one hand on the lowest rung of the ladder, the other helping them tread water. They held on, looking at each other.

He was stunned.

Oh, clearly he was dazed. The unreality of the emergency had that effect. But he also knew, without the slightest doubt, that she was the most beautiful woman he'd ever seen. Something of that had grabbed him, even out there in the water. Her kind of looks just had that impact.

Wondering what in the hell he'd do with her next, he motioned that she should precede him up the ladder and that he'd assist her from behind.

Nodding, she heaved herself up the first step. Water sluiced down her long body, glazing her lush tanned curves and the black one-piece suit. He himself was barely contained in an old pair of bikini trunks he wore on hot days. After all, who ever saw him, out by himself, anchoring and fishing and then moving on again only to drink or doze or read?

Helping her up the ladder didn't help him. Even physically depleted, he felt stirrings of desire, ready and hot and long overdue. Sea bums were loners in every sense. But that didn't make them immune. Not to the siren's call.

Pushing at the tight round of her tush, Ryder "helped" his catch over the side and onto the decking. Ah, yes, the old male hormones were still in order. More than in order.

But then he read the seriousness in her face. That beautiful face. His glorious Aphrodite assumed the aspect of queenly tragedy. Or that of a half-drowned kitten.

"Here's a towel," he said, plucking a beach towel from the fish-fighting chair in the center of the rear deck.

Forcing his thoughts back on track, Ryder wrapped his gift from the sea in the towel. In spite of the heat, she shivered. He urged her to the bench seat at the rear of the cruiser.

Oh, God, those tragic eyes.

Ryder sank down next to his Aphrodite, measuring the blue, sea-clouded gaze.

"Hey," he said softly, tilting her face for his inspection. "Y-you weren't trying to do something to yourself out there, were you?"

"No, not really," she replied. "I mean, I went into the water and the idea struck me that I could. But when it came down to it... No, I didn't intend to, and I thank you very much for swimming out. By the time you got to me... well, I was so panicked I could have drowned us both."

Ryder couldn't identify the emotions that rushed through him. She seemed so vulnerable, and he understood vulnerability. Without saying anything, he folded his arms around her, nestling his chin into her quickly drying red-gold hair.

She was exquisite.

She held herself stiffly at first, but then she relaxed. After a long stretch of silence, of listening to the water against the boat, to the boat tugging at its anchor chain in reply, she seemed to unwind. He knew he did. He had a million questions, but for now to simply hold his treasure was enough.

"I..." she finally murmured.

"Yes?"

Keeping her head on his shoulder, tucked beneath his chin, she avoided his gaze. "I can see how stupid I acted."

"We all do stupid things."

"Yes, but I'm sorry I involved you. I could have hurt us both. Badly."

He hugged her more tightly. He enjoyed hugging her. He enjoyed forgiving her. He felt close to her, and he hadn't felt close to another human being in a long time. "I'm sorry things haven't been good for you."

He knew he was coaxing her to confide even more. Her little laugh was sour. "Good for me?"

"Well, uh..."

"Yes, you're right. These last two weeks..."

Ryder waited. While he longed to hear what she had to say, he wouldn't push her. Anyway, he preferred that she open up to him voluntarily.

"My mother died in a car wreck two weeks ago. She and I had a difficult relationship, to say the least, and I... Oh, God, I feel so angry at her. I feel as if she's done this on purpose, just left me with all this unresolved stuff. We were doing better lately, but... I can't sleep. I can't eat. I feel so guilty, and yet if I saw her right now, I know I'd scream at her."

"It's the grief," he said, understanding grief, understanding difficult, if not impossible, relationships with mothers. "Grief can exaggerate what we normally handle the best way we can into... Well, we all go a little or even a lot crazy when we grieve."

"But she was my mother and I feel so bad, so guilty about how I feel about her now. About how I felt about her when she was alive."

"Yeah, I know what you're saying. Mothers, even if they love you, don't necessarily like you or approve of you. I mean, it seems kinda funny that we don't expect personality differences between us and our mothers, despite the close relationship, or the fact that we love each other."

When his Aphrodite sighed, Ryder felt great. Obviously he'd said something right.

"I was an incredibly rebellious teen," she admitted. "She'd say white. I'd do black."

"Huh, tell me about it."

When she sighed again, he felt so good about helping her that his own regret spilled out, much like her confession had.

"And as to a parent dying, especially unexpectedly like yours did in an accident... I mean, when a person can't make amends, or even say goodbye... Well, you're not alone in that one, either. I've heard that we all need a sense of closing one chapter and beginning a new one at times like that. And you can't close things off if you aren't allowed to be there, to talk, to say even the least thing."

He wondered if she heard his pain. His goal was to console her, to make sense for her, but that didn't exclude hints of his own feelings. If anything, she could have been telling him his own story.

Still, he wanted to salve *her* guilt, to ease *her* pain. He'd never wanted anything so badly in his life. For the first time, he wanted someone else's peace above his own.

"Look," he finally murmured, though he wasn't tired of holding her, "I've got a beer in a cooler. It's about all I have, but it's cold."

When she shook her head against his shoulder, when she rewrapped her arms around his waist, he thought he'd been given the world.

Open caring and underlying desire melded into one.

He nuzzled his lips into her now-warm, dry hair. He adjusted them so he could move his cheek down along the sun-heated skin of her temple.

He'd never felt so complete.

He tasted her. Her mouth and her salty skin. What's more, she tasted him.

Their kisses stunned him. They expressed their desire, their deeper needs. With kisses, they each took from the other. But they also gave to each other, sweetly, poignantly. Ryder felt himself slipping toward an uncontrollable desire they couldn't fulfill. Although it seemed they knew each other better than they knew anything, he retained enough sense to remember otherwise.

They didn't know each other.

He didn't deserve...

Getting up from where they sat on the rear bench, Ryder barely apologized for his abrupt abandonment of her.

"Sorry," he said, "But..."

He didn't want to leave her. He didn't want to put bewilderment, then embarrassment, into her lovely eyes.

Even so, he stayed away from her. He propped himself along the railing at the cruiser's side and peered out to sea.

With this woman he could forget what he was running away from. And though he yearned to forget, if even for a few hours, he continued to think of her. Taking advantage of her in her distraught state was beyond him.

"I guess I'd better take you back," he heard himself say. "So you can get some rest."

When she didn't reply, he turned to look at her. She appeared as confused as he felt, and once again he longed to comfort her. Sitting beside her, he tucked her close.

"Hey," he said softly. "I don't know your name. I'm—"

With two fingers to his lips, she stopped him from speaking. Boldly she engaged his eyes. The desire he'd tried to bank burst alive again.

"No names," she whispered.

Now Ryder shook his head, forcing his mind away from the memory of that day as he focused on looking for the turnoff for Fiesta Key. He was nearly there. He'd been invited out to the old resort area to...to what?

He glanced over to the teddy bear that sat as big as a person in the passenger seat of his car. With friendly brown eyes and a rotund furry body, the bear looked like fuzzy honey poured into a red vest.

Yes, the result of that day was as wondrous as the day itself had been, and he had to keep himself sharp for seeing Carrie again.

Daily he proved to himself that he was as good at making money and conducting an orderly life as anybody. Success. Achievement. Tradition. His family's watchwords. He continued to remind himself of their importance.

And now, with a daughter...

Well, daughters, too, required responsibility and staying on track.

He had it all sorted out. For the past few days, he'd been in touch with the Craig family lawyer. Carrie would eventually have her piece of the Craig pie. He'd also established a schedule for her support. That would be handled without embarrassing contact between him and Summer.

Additionally, his subsequent phone calls to Summer, in which he'd kept her abreast of the process, had been open if also formal. He wanted as little of the inevitable awkwardness between them as possible, and he'd be scrupulous with respect to Summer's position about seeing Carrie.

In the end, Ryder knew what he was doing. He was getting his ducks in a row. He was falling in with Summer's ground rules. Ground rules, he understood. Ground rules, as much as they smarted, were safe. He wouldn't repeat the screwups of his past.

Entering the old resort, Ryder followed the narrow lane to the circle of bungalows. He didn't mind this little call that was meant to establish future patterns.

Naturally, he had no idea what the patterns or procedures would be. And really, he didn't want to get that far ahead of himself. He'd take this astounding development in his life one step at a time.

Ryder was tugging the enormous teddy from his small car when Summer stepped off the screened porch. She came toward him in slacks and a shell pink string sweater that made her appear soft and approachable. She was barefoot, and he realized that aside from her beauty, she had a casual style resembling his own. Like him, she was a good swimmer. She was used to the ocean, and, well, he supposed he saw that she suited him.

He also noticed her habit of leading with her chin, tilting it whenever she felt angry or defensive. It was tilted now.

But most of all, the potency of that day two and a half years ago hung between them. They shared a sensual secret that permeated their encounters. As much as she didn't like to admit it and he avoided thinking about it, they weren't strangers. He still wanted her just as he had the first time, without consideration or precaution. He doubted that would ever change.

"Hi," she said, looking at him directly. Oh, she was feeling defensive. "I, uh, hope you don't mind, but I have someone here I want you to meet."

"Oh?" Did she have someone else?

"Yes, my grandfather."

Relief tugged at Ryder. "No, I don't mind meeting him. You've talked about him a lot on the phone over the past few days. He's important to you and Carrie, and I'll be glad to meet him."

"Good."

When she turned toward the house, he followed with the huge bear under one arm. He was just understanding his mistake in buying the toy when his gaze locked with that of the tall, gaunt gentleman who obviously waited to meet him. Ryder stepped forward to shake Fred Miller's hand as the older man introduced himself.

Rough-hewn rather than polished, the man had a sense of dignity about him. He regarded Ryder with a keen eye and a matching discomfort. Ryder knew this man had every reason if not to dislike him, then to give him very little space.

Still, he himself regarded Fred Miller with the respect the man deserved. If for nothing else, Fred Miller had stuck by his granddaughter and Carrie when Ryder should have been there. That Ryder had been denied the choice had nothing to do with the man whose hand he released.

"That's some big bear you have," Fred said.

"It was the biggest one they had."

"Obviously." Summer smiled, folding her arms across her chest. "Anything bigger would have to be sold with little bear houses for the backyard."

Ryder wondered if he didn't like her tough little smile best of all. Forcing his eyes away from her, he swept the room with his gaze. The small couch and desk were behind him, and a galley kitchen—just beyond a slim bar that served as a table—offered even less space.

"Maybe I should take the bear back," he suggested. "I can put it in my car before she sees it."

But it was already too late. Carrie, dressed in pink ruffles and also shoeless, burst in. A grin lit her cherubic features. Because he'd often heard that he and Vance and his father had the same smile—one that transformed their more usually sober faces to downright good-looking—Ryder again experienced her smile as a bittersweet stab to his heart.

"Hi, Carrie," he said, only to watch her smile disappear. She'd gotten a gander at the bear—surely it was the bear and not Ryder causing her reaction.

She started to wail, to positively wail, and Ryder had no idea what to do. He tried stuffing the bear behind his back, but she continued to cry. When Summer didn't rush to Carrie's rescue, but let her circle her legs instead, he felt somewhat better. Otherwise, he might have thought he'd really frightened his own child.

Summer finally scooped Carrie up as she gave Ryder another contained grin.

"It's okay, Boop," she said. "We'll let D-Daddy set it down, and then you and I can have a close look. Okay?"

Daddy.

Nearly rendered senseless, Ryder set the bear between the stools along the bar, then stepped back. Daddy. How good of Summer to admit that to Carrie, even if she had first stumbled in saying it.

But then, he recalled that this was all for Carrie's benefit. Summer had to love their daughter very much to marshal that kind of fairness.

Ryder watched as Summer moved over to the bear with Carrie on her hip. Fred also observed, and Ryder wondered if he had lost or gained ground with the man. To his mind, Fred Miller remained as remote as hell.

Fortunately, Carrie's sobs diminished into the hiccups Ryder had heard the first time he'd visited and set her off.

He felt all thumbs. But Carrie was obviously recovering.

"See?" Summer said as the pair of them knelt by the bear. "He has a nose. And eyes."

Carrie shook her head. "No," she declared stubbornly.

"Yes he does. And he has a mouth. And ears."

Carrie shook her head. She stood within the curve of Summer's arm, stolidly stating that she wouldn't go any closer to her gift. She even refused to play the name game. Finally, she went so far as to trudge out of the room.

Really, Summer's smiles at Ryder were throwing him for a loop.

"Don't worry," she said, "he'll probably be her best friend by tomorrow morning. If not sooner."

"Yeah, yeah," seconded Fred. "She's just being stubborn. She can be as stubborn as a mule."

Despite even Fred's rough attempt at smoothing things over, the atmosphere remained tense.

So Ryder made his own attempt. "Summer says you're the one who nicknamed Carrie."

"Yeah, yeah. When Summer first brought her home, she was all eyes."

Since that reminded them Ryder hadn't been there on that occasion, Ryder was glad when the older man cleared his throat, excused himself and headed for the door.

"She's gonna like the bear. She's got one she sleeps with, and as soon as she makes the connection, she'll like it. She's just being contrary. She's good at being contrary."

"I wonder how she comes by that," Summer teased, another little smile throwing Ryder further off.

With that, Ryder shook the man's hand for a final time, and he and Summer were alone.

"Really," she said, "it's nice of you to bring the bear. Carrie just has to... well, she'll be turning two soon. All the books say she's taking some big steps now. She's always been easy with people, but she's beginning to notice strangers and differences in her environment. She wants her independence. That's what the no is all about. But then, she isn't independent, and she gets frustrated."

"It sounds complicated. You say you've read books on the subject?"

"Well, yes, but the books don't always agree. Except for the generalities, I've given up on most of them."

Ryder nodded. He felt as if he needed breathing space.

But he felt other things even more clearly. Desire. He and Summer were alone in the small front room of her bungalow.

Ryder knew as distinctly as he knew anything that if he had the same opportunity he'd had that day on his boat, he'd behave no differently. If she offered herself to him, as she had, he could no more say no this time than the last.

That scared him.

Despite the memories of that day that he treasured, despite his intimate knowledge of her body and even despite the child they shared, they were, as she'd said, strangers. While he hated the term, it was accurate, and they both knew it.

Worse, Ryder remembered his rushed proposal of marriage to this woman on that first visit when he'd discovered Carrie. Now that offer seemed laughable.

Ultimately, Ryder knew this beautiful woman before him wouldn't let him see their child if he didn't recognize their true situation and follow her rules. Just in reading the way she held herself aloof from him, he saw she would insist on his keeping his distance.

He strove to remind himself of her ground rules. On the same day, when she'd laid them out, part of him had been glad. But part of him, his masculine part, was aware of her as he'd never been aware of another woman. Seeing that she still glanced away from him, he wondered if she didn't feel some of what he thought.

She moved toward the hallway, calling to the noise-maker in the next room. "Carrie, Carrie, come here for a minute."

"No!"

"That's all right," Ryder said. "Don't push her. I'm willing to give it whatever she needs. Whatever any of us needs," he amended when Summer glanced at him.

"She's usually better behaved than when you see her."

"Yeah, I had a taste of that the last time I was here. There weren't any bears around."

He was drawn to Summer's little dry smile as much as to anything else about her. He swallowed hard. "I guess I'll go. Don't worry. I'll call before I come, and when I do, I won't bring anything bigger than Carrie."

As wry as her smile was, Summer's chuckle was sweet.

Ryder left as quickly as he could. In his car, he went over his thoughts since seeing Summer again. By the time he reached the backwater marina south of Sarasota proper—where he housed and lived on his rejuvenated boat—he thought he was pretty much together.

He knew that anything with Carrie, or even with Summer, anything enduring, amounted to the impossible. He couldn't get anywhere with them without first facing his past. And above all, he couldn't face his past. Despite his present orderly life, his past remained a quagmire.

Still, early that evening, after he'd fixed himself some supper in the galley aboard *Spare a Dime,* he found himself dialing the house number in Palm Beach. Summer's tough truth about Carrie's right to him had awakened him to subsequent truths.

His brother, Vance, and Vance's wife, Brenda Jo, and their two boys should also know about Carrie. And then his mother should know, too.

Since both Calder and their family lawyer had told Ryder that Vance and their mother were in Palm Beach, opening the house for the season, Ryder wasn't surprised when Vance picked up the phone.

In recent days, Ryder had experienced one emotion on top of another. Hearing Vance's voice, he was assailed by yet other feelings. Nostalgia, longing, guilt flowed as swiftly through him as did remorse.

And anger.

Ryder felt his familiar shell closing in place.

CHAPTER SIX

SUMMER COULDN'T HELP her giggles any more than
Dee evidently could. It was late, and they were chop-
ping vegetables in the church kitchen. Pressure and
fatigue had everything to do with their mood, and the
subject didn't help.

"I mean," Summer said, "you should have seen the
look on his face. It was like he thought he'd terrified
Carrie. The bear was so big that he couldn't get it behind his back, but he kept shoving it as if he could. It
was hilarious. And then, you know how stubborn
Carrie can be. When she marched out of the room,
Ryder looked so crestfallen that I felt sorry for him."

When Dee's big brown eyes met Summer's gaze,
Dee was smiling more softly. "Actually, it sounds
kinda sweet to me. *He* sounds kinda sweet, this Ryder
Craig of yours."

Summer wasn't about to argue whether or not Ryder Craig was hers. Nor could she hide her flush from
her friend. She concentrated on the kiwi fruit, on cutting it into decorative paper-thin slices.

If anyone knew Ryder Craig was sweet . . .

That day on his boat, after he'd rescued her, he'd
been so sweet that she'd . . . Well, her memories were
a familiar routine. Once she and he had begun recovering their strength, he'd listened to her with such in-

tensity, with such total understanding, that what had followed had been natural.

He'd started comforting her, and she'd wanted his physical comfort as much as his understanding. And while it had begun as simple, human contact...

Not that he, at least, hadn't tried to resist.

He'd kissed her for a long while—as the sun and the sea and his kisses coalesced into a wonderfully sensuous whole. Then, abruptly he'd left her. He'd moved to the boat railing, to stand there and to stare out over the ocean.

Needless to say, he was an amazing-looking man. He probably stood there often, she thought, looking just like that. Contemplative. Intelligent. As sexy, as dangerous, as hell. Physically he was as perfect as he could be. And in his minuscule navy-colored swimsuit, he was almost completely revealed to her.

His rugged features were accentuated by his shadowy beard—the beard that had gently abraded the skin around her mouth. His dark hair ruffled, overly long, in the breeze like thick silk. The softer whorls over his tanned chest and along his arms and legs were equally appealing to her.

Summer's assessment ran on to his eyes. Dusty green jade. And, of course, to his attitude. Confident. He was a strange combination. He affected her with his sensitivity, with a sense that he, too, bled inside. And yet, the hard male body, the strong facade...

He was thinking—thinking about what he'd do with her. She wondered what his conclusion would be. She also feared his conclusion. His kisses had shown her what she wanted. As much as she'd shocked herself, she longed for more.

She wondered, looking at him, if she might persuade him. Oh, she realized that in her present emotional state she wasn't making any sense. She even seemed a stranger to herself.

But she also knew she wanted this man. She could trust him with her emotions. Just this one man. This one time.

When he turned from the side of the boat, she saw the change in him. Although his voice revealed his struggle, he'd moved from the sensual to the practical.

"I guess I'd better take you back. So you can get some rest."

He came toward her, having assumed a friendly attitude. Smiling at her, he sat beside her. He tucked her into the beach towel, then even cuddled her to his large, sun-warmed body.

His green eyes, as soft as his voice, met her waiting stare. "It's funny but I don't know your name. I'm—"

With two fingers, she cut off the reality of introductions. "No names," she whispered.

She saw his surprise. He was doing his best by her. But they'd lost before they'd begun. He kissed her and the urgency rekindled in his kisses. Once again he showed the need he'd been disguising for her sake.

But he remained tender, too. And sweet. For the first time in weeks, she felt at ease.

His hand encouraged her to stretch out on the plastic seat at the back of the old cruiser. He was large and heavy, and her body was unresisting, supple.

Since they were nearly nude, there were no secrets. He was hard—he had been for some time—and she wanted him all the more. She luxuriated in his desire for her. Because that desire was expressed with tenderness, she grew convinced that he wanted her for more than her body and her beauty.

Her teenage husband had wanted only her body. As she now knew, Sean had had neither sexual nor emotional maturity.

But then, who had?

But this man… She became dead sure that this man longed to connect with her soul. His needs were as fundamental as her own.

He paused, his breath heating the skin of her face and neck. His eyes plumbed her gaze. "Do you want to go below?"

She nodded.

With a swift move, he tugged her up from her supine position. He guided her down the few steps to the dimly illuminated cabin.

She was vaguely aware of the typical layout—the galley kitchen, the small appliances, the booth containing the built-in table. Next came the configuration of head and shower and closets. Beyond, a louvered door stood open to the space below the bow of the boat.

Although twin beds conformed to the V of the hull, an addition between them converted the space into a single large, nearly heart-shaped bed. Here, the portholes were propped open to the fresh air, and sunlight fell on the rumpled, pale blue sheets.

Summer dropped into the sheets as she would have into an inviting pool. They were cool and soft. Everything was surprisingly orderly for the obvious sea bum, for his old bucket of a boat.

When she looked at him again, she saw he was naked. He stood just at the side of the bed, his eyes binding her with questions.

"You sure?" was all he said.

She nodded.

Dropping to his knees on the bed, he crawled toward her. He covered her body with his, kissing her face and neck and shoulders. He stroked her until she, too, was naked and enraptured by their shared desire.

He remained sweet. But his sweetness was now hard with determination to unite them. He cherished her every inch, loving her slowly, urging her responses with quick green glances, with soft passes of his lips over hers.

She felt treasured, and when she crested and he followed, she didn't know where she left off and he began. She'd never before experienced such unity with another human soul.

But for all her earlier boldness, Summer grew shy. She turned her eyes away from him, listening to the creak of the boat, concentrating on its gentle sway.

"Hey," he whispered, coaxing her face back to his.

She saw then that he wasn't a stranger. She knew him as well as she knew herself.

"Hey," he repeated, smiling in recognition of her knowing. "You belong to me now, you know."

She wanted to deny him, but she thought he was right.

His smile transformed his somberness into an appeal to her, and she was enthralled. "I'm not claiming you as mine in the macho sense. So don't look like you're ready to mutiny." He touched her again, his thumb, his chin, stirring along her soft cheeks. "I'm sorry about the way my beard must have felt."

Summer hadn't much noticed.

"After I shave, we'll sleep for a while." His suggestion was frank, his invitation even more bald.

Summer nodded.

Again, he smiled that amazing smile. "What I meant to say was that some people—at least, some people in other parts of the world—would swear that you belong to me now. Not because of this, but because I saved your life."

Summer looked away. She couldn't seem to fall in with his evident joy.

"Hey." He nudged her chin with a finger.

She looked at him.

"Come on, Aphrodite. You have to know you rescued me today as much as I rescued you. Let's make a deal. Let's say we own each other. How about it?"

Mesmerized by the closeness of his eyes, of his face, of his happiness, Summer nodded. But as soon as she could, she turned away.

He seemed if not accepting of what little she could give then at least resigned for now, and he went off to shave.

Not wanting to think any more than that, Summer gave in to her fatigue. When he returned to the bed, she stirred. He smelled wonderfully of soap and after-shave, and she luxuriated in the scent of him and his warmth and comfort. Later, they made love again, then slept again.

When Summer awoke for the final time, light streamed in through the portholes like liquid gold. Reality finally ripped at her. The man sleeping beside her was a stranger.

Sick with remorse and embarrassment, she was afraid he'd awaken and pin her with that amazing green gaze and sudden startling grin. She crept away. Out in the main cabin, she donned her suit, and once down the ladder, she slipped into the water.

She'd wanted to disappear off the face of the earth, but had managed to disappear for only two and a half years. Worse, she was lying when she used her fears for Carrie as an excuse. She knew better than that. She'd avoided contact with Ryder Craig simply because she knew she'd been the one to throw herself at him.

Suddenly someone called her name. Looking up from where her knife had gone still on the cutting board in front of her, Summer saw Dee. Her friend's smile urged her back to the present.

"You've had it," said Dee. "You've been standing there for goodness knows how long, staring at the same chunk of kiwi like it's going to bite you. Come on, kiddo, it's time we're outta here."

"No, no."

"What do you mean, no? We're finished."

Summer glanced around. Dee had obviously washed up and put everything away without noticing her inertia until now. Summer hustled to cut the last of the kiwi with perfect strokes, then stuck the knife and board under the faucet. Dee slid the fruit into the industrial-size fridge.

"You're right—" Summer knew Dee watched her speculatively "—I've had it."

"But you're more than just tired, aren't you? You're worried."

"If you mean I'm worried about finding a house, yes. I rushed all over, looking at three more before I came here."

Obviously, Dee didn't believe that finding a house was Summer's only worry. But as usual, Dee accepted both what Summer had to say and didn't have to say.

"On my way tonight," Dee said, "I noticed a place nearby. It's for sale by the owner."

"Really? Not far from here?"

"It's nothing spectacular. Just your usual crackerbox. But it has a screened-in pool and looks like it's been kept up nicely. I wrote down the phone number and address," she added, handing Summer the paper.

"Thanks, Dee."

Dee plucked up her purse, then tugged on her lightweight jacket as they left the kitchen. "If it wasn't so late, I'd suggest we drive by it right now. But your grandfather is probably too tired for much more of this late-night baby-sitting."

They passed the final light switch, and stepping out onto the stoop at the side entrance of the church, Summer reached to flip it off. "He understands, but, yeah, I'm worried about him doing too much. And then Irma says she's working her last day tomorrow, and I dread her leaving."

"Irma What's-her-name? The one who's worked in the resort office forever since when?"

"Uh-huh." As they walked to their cars, Summer continued speaking. "I know this retirement has to be as hard for Irma as it is for Poppy."

Dee chuckled. "She's always seemed like a little owl to me. A polite little knitted-together owl," Dee amended. "She's really nice on the phone."

"I know what you're saying. Even for the twenty-odd years she's been around, I don't feel as if I know her. I mean, I know she has a group of close friends and her own house and a certain amount of financial security, but I've never really gotten to know her. Not until Poppy went into the hospital. And then, well, Irma was wonderful. A real support for us both."

"That's surprising. I thought the pair of them fought like cats and dogs."

Even Summer's laughter sounded sleepy. "They do fight like cats and dogs. But never in front of anyone. They think no one else knows." She sighed. "Still, Irma must be part saint for having stayed with Poppy all these years."

"Either she's a saint or she's in love with him."

Summer stopped short. "In love with him?"

"Stranger things have happened."

When Summer tried to absorb this, Dee nudged her with an elbow. "Come on, you. We'll never get home at this speed."

Snapping herself out of her latest lapse, Summer scanned the cozy nighttime scene. But then, she became aware of something odd. Dee even bumped into her as she stopped in midstep, this time to watch the shabby pickup that cruised slowly by.

"What is it?" Dee asked.

"I, uh..."

While the old rattletrap seemed familiar somehow, it left her view before she could place it. Then she pictured it again. She realized she had seen it before.

"Do you remember the other night?" she asked. "I mean, when I told you about that guy who followed me into the parking lot at the grocery store?"

Dee snorted. "The one the bag boys went out to do battle with? Along with *Arnold.*"

"Yeah, I think I just saw him—the guy who followed me."

"The same guy? Just now? Here?"

"Gosh, I must be losing it."

"Yeah." Dee frowned. "Come on, let's get some rest. How could the same creep find you here, and just at this precise time of night?"

Summer released a soft laugh. "Yeah, I'm losing it, all right."

THE NEARLY DIRECT drive west to east across the state of Florida from Sarasota to Palm Beach, was new to Ryder. Leaving on Sunday morning, he hoped to make it in time for lunch. Actually, he enjoyed driving, though he dreaded what waited for him on the other coast.

Ah, yes, Palm Beach. The town—so obviously in his mother's style—was the opposite of his own. More than anything he could name, it symbolized their differences.

Palm Beach was one of the richest addresses in the world. A tiny island with limited access, it was considered exclusive, extravagant and glamorous beyond anything except in the movies.

Its social season lasted from December through March. Beneath a tropical sun and an even more romantic moon, socialites gathered and gossiped, sunned and shifted for position, boozed and grew bored. In the Shiny Sheet, or rather the *Palm Beach Daily News,* they read about themselves seven days a week.

Like his father, Ryder's mother was also from an old New England family with even older money. And while his father had worked to the point of obsession, his mother had lived the life of the idle rich.

Vance and he had been sent off to boarding schools, and Evelyn Craig had tracked society's round from New York to the capitals of Europe to Newport to Palm Beach. Where society had been in season, Evelyn, with brief fly-in visits from her husband and children, had been there.

But Ryder didn't allow himself to look back. Only on his drive to Palm Beach did looking back become inevitable. And really, he didn't dislike his mother. Nor was he disdainful of her. He'd grown to see her for what she was—a woman who simply lived the way she'd been groomed to live.

And it wasn't that she was especially cruel, nor unintelligent. For a long while in his life, he would have given anything, anything, to have been the object of if not her love then of her approval.

But so many years later, he had reconciled himself to the kind of woman she was. Evelyn was perhaps incapable of loving anyone. Not without conditions. And her conditions were stringent.

To Evelyn, a man was supposed to be well polished, well dressed, attentive and entertaining. And rich. Above all, rich.

At about the age of ten, Ryder had put these truths together. And though he'd continued to love his mother, he'd also seen that he'd never measure up.

Already fiercely independent, even at ten, he'd rebelled. Rather than the manicured life she lived, he'd wanted freedom. He'd already liked boats, and she had disapproved of what she saw as his inexplicable behavior.

"He's so unlike us," he could remember her telling her friends. "I mean, like Vance or me or even Vanny. Where Ryder came from, I swear I can't say."

Oh, man, it had hurt.

Typically, hurt had led to anger and rebellion. But after many years of indulging his anger in rebellion, of using it as a protective shell, Ryder found he wasn't angry anymore. Years away from his family had dulled the anger, if not the pain.

And anyway, his pain was connected more to his father than to his mother.

His father, Vance, Sr., he'd truly loved. Ryder knew he'd never get over his father's death. After all, Ryder himself had been responsible for it, and his mother had told Ryder she'd never forgive him. To go to Palm Beach was to face those old truths in all their fury.

And yet, Ryder had to go to Palm Beach. He had to go for Carrie's sake. His family had to know about his daughter, and though he could be sure the family lawyer, with whom he'd been in contact over the past week, had prepared them, Ryder would be expected to give them the news himself.

Besides, his phone call to Vance had been surprisingly encouraging. Yes, Vance agreed that Ryder should come. And Vance had always been what his mother had wanted him to be, both as a son and as a man. Vance had met the prerequisites of their mother's conditional love, so Vance had been loved to the extent that Evelyn was able to give love.

Ryder smiled sardonically to himself in his rearview mirror. If Vance were to screw up, to really make a mess of something, Ryder wondered how far Evelyn's love would go.

Along with his anger, his envy of Vance had also disappeared. At least, Ryder didn't feel envious now. Nor had he sensed it bubbling up as it would have in the past when he'd talked to his older brother on the phone. He wondered how they'd react to each other when they met again.

He didn't have to wonder for long. Pulling into the curving driveway before the Mediterranean-style house that had been in his family for three generations, he cut his engine.

Slowly removing his sunglasses, he saw that nothing had changed. Although the large house wasn't presented like one of the jewels along Ocean Boulevard, it occupied an exclusive cul-de-sac close to the Atlantic. The tropical vegetation grew so thick few would guess there were other like houses nearby.

The red tile roof, the bright white walls, the sparkling windows—now open to the season—looked wonderful against the blue, blue sky, the green, green foliage. Color and light and a constant rustling breeze lent the place a holiday air—so appropriate to Evelyn's insistent, elegant, lifelong holiday.

Getting out of his car, Ryder was surprised to see Vance coming around the end of the house, walking in his direction across the flat stretch of Bermuda grass.

Ryder hadn't seen his brother since the trial almost five years earlier. Except for the night before last, they hadn't spoken, even on the phone, since the evening after their father had been buried in New York. Ryder had been on trial in Vermont. The proceedings had lasted two weeks, and the funeral had occurred in the middle of the second week.

Vance Craig, Sr., had died of a massive heart attack. Or so it was said. Actually, everyone knew that the shock of his son's being accused of murder and being brought to trial had been the true culprit. Aside from one exception, those facts wouldn't be stated more plainly than in this house. And that one exception was in Ryder's own heart.

"Ry," Vance said, smiling and extending his hand for Ryder to shake.

Ryder was surprised both by the use of the nickname the pair of Vances had used and by the genuineness of his brother's welcome.

Oh, it wasn't that they hadn't loved each other. It was more that they were so different. And then the ensuing years, the accruing differences, the subtle workings of their mother's tongue had driven them apart.

Ryder felt a nostalgic tug. Yes, Vance and he, and now Carrie, were alike. Their likeness shone especially in their smiles—in the sudden surprising Craig smile that was, except for Carrie's, hard-won and stingily given right up to the moment it broke.

"How are you?" Vance asked.

"Fine, and you?"

"Fine. You know, it's only Mother and I this weekend. B.J., uh, Brenda Jo, is still in New York, and the boys, well, like I told you the other night, they're in school."

"Yeah, I was glad to hear you took them out of the old alma mater."

Until the previous year, Vance's boys, like Vance and Ryder and their father and uncles, had attended a military boarding school up East. Family tradition. But Ryder was glad to hear that his nephews had been removed, and that B.J. had enrolled them in a school closer to their home in New York.

Oh, Vance still lived as he'd been reared to live. Conservatively. Work oriented. Class-conscious. He also continued to run the family business in exclusive real estate.

But Ryder wondered if his brother wasn't changing, too. Vance had intimated as much on the phone. Something was going on in them both, and Vance obviously sensed that, despite the slight awkwardness.

"Come on around," he said, indicating the direction from which he'd come. "Mother's at poolside, and lunch is nearly ready. I'm glad you made it on time."

Not expecting to, Ryder grinned. "I wouldn't dare be late for lunch. Not if I could help it."

Vance also smiled. He even relaxed with a slight shrug. He was admitting that their mother wasn't easy to live with. "Yes," he said, going so far as to voice Ryder's thoughts, "she's still the same."

Ryder stuffed his hands into his pockets. He hadn't meant to unearth the past. "How's she taking, uh, being on her own?"

Again Vance shrugged. "At first, after the funeral, she stayed in the apartment in New York for most of the time. But B.J. encouraged her to go out—perhaps before I would have. When B.J. explained that Mother's life had always revolved around socializing, we invited in a few close friends, and soon Mother was going out again. She hasn't skipped a beat since, and she hardly ever mentions Dad. B.J. thinks that's about the best Mother can do."

This reassessment of the mother Vance had worshiped as much as he had was new, and Ryder wondered if it wasn't Brenda Jo who had worked the changes.

Brenda Jo. He'd hardly known his sister-in-law. He only recalled that she, too, was one of their own. Vance had met her through their mother's circle, and Ryder remembered wondering if Vance hadn't just fallen in with family expectations by marrying her.

After they went through the lacy wrought-iron gates, Ryder and his brother walked across another stretch of green lawn with bright flower borders, overhanging banyan trees and high royal palms. The house was terraced in the rear, with precisely land-scaped gardens surrounding an azure pool reflecting azure skies.

Evelyn's world was dependably the same.

Ryder saw her then, sitting by the pool. The servants, and they had several here in Palm Beach, had erected an open white marquee, and she lounged beneath its glowing canopy, reading the Shiny Sheet.

Getting nearer, he saw that his mother remained unchanged. She was still slender and elegant, still perfectly made up and coiffed. She wore pool pajamas and dull silver sandals to match.

"Hello, Mother," he said, going beneath the canopy. Everything was picture perfect, pristine.

He tried to neither feel nor look like someone who had come, hat in hand, to make amends. After all, he hadn't. While he'd be willing to have a cordial, even friendly relationship with his mother, he'd never, never need her love again.

"How are you, Ryder?" she asked, removing her lightly tinted sunglasses and peering up at him from her chaise longue.

After she'd indicated chairs, both he and Vance sat down across from her. Tipping the end of her glasses to her lips, she observed them. One at a time. Openly comparing them. Always comparing them.

But this time, Ryder felt she had to be pleased in some ways. As men, he and Vance especially resembled Vance, Sr., and she'd invariably praised the looks of their dad. Primarily, she was impressed by the look of both things and people.

"You look," she said, proving his evaluation, "as if you're doing well. Every once in a while I hear from Calder Parks, and he claims you can do no wrong. But then," she added with a terse smile, "we, that is, you and Vance and I, know better, don't we? Unless you've changed," she stated, as if that couldn't be possible.

No, *she* hadn't changed. Why should others?

Much to his surprise, Ryder didn't take what his mother said as he would have in the past. He let her words, her insinuations, slide over him. After all, she had to get a little of her own back, and they hadn't seen each other since the trial in Vermont. Her pattern was to attack first, and once she got in her licks, she'd retreat to the cordiality of a semiclose friend.

By that time, there would be no more mention of anything "unhappy," as she used to call his doings. He'd begin to wonder if she'd forgotten whatever "antic" had caused her "displeasure." It was, in other words, the same old story.

In fact, Ryder felt so above the same old round that he nearly smiled. His newfound and unexpected dispassion where this person was concerned was amazingly freeing. If he had only achieved this detachment sooner, he would have saved them all a lot of grief.

Maybe those two years following the trial when he'd dropped out, stopped pursuing his career and spent all his time bumming around on his boat had been good for him, after all.

At the time he couldn't have said why he'd decided to drop out. All he'd known then was that he felt crushed by guilt and didn't feel he deserved anything better than the rootless life of a sea bum.

He hadn't killed the woman he'd been accused of murdering. He was sure of that. But on the other hand, if he hadn't been leading such a wild life, he never would have been accused of the crime in the first place. And then his father would never have suffered the heart attack that killed him.

But now, sitting by his mother's pool, recalling those years when he'd wandered the seas in a cloud of guilt and depression, Ryder realized he'd been punishing himself . . . doing a kind of penance.

At the time, maybe it had been the right thing to do. Not that any penance could ever really relieve him of his guilt or miraculously bring his father back to life. But at least those two years of time out had allowed him to see more clearly what was important and what wasn't. And his mother's slighting words were *not* important and no longer had the power to hurt him. But doing the right thing by Summer and Carrie was very important. And doing the right thing included telling his family about them—because Summer and Carrie now had to be considered family, too.

For once Ryder was glad lunch was served on time. Lunch diverted them. Ryder used the opportunity to prod Vance, to get his brother to talk about how he and the old family business were doing. As Ryder might have expected, Vance fared very well. In other words, the Craigs still made buckets and buckets of money, in this case, under Vance's supervision.

"I guess you know why I'm here," Ryder finally said, more for his mother's benefit than for Vance's.

As far as Ryder was concerned, Vance was out of it. Vance and he just might have something if they wanted to put in the effort. But for now, he had to zero in on his mother. When she acknowledged him with a negligent glance, he continued.

"I want you to know that I have a child. A little girl. She's nearly two, but I just found out about her within the past week. She's uh..." He hadn't expected to falter. But Carrie and Summer seemed more than miles away from his mother's judgmental stare.

"Well," he said, breaking into a grin, "she's wonderful and I'm very happy. I wanted you, and you, too, Vance," he added, turning to his brother, chuckling, "and Brenda Jo and the boys to know. To share my happiness, I hope."

Vance leaned forward to shake Ryder's hand. Hugs had always been out of the question.

"We are happy for you," Vance said.

That was enough for him, Ryder thought, releasing his brother's hand after a moment or two. Yes, he was content. Yes, there might be a possibility...

But no. Looking back at his mother's composed features, he felt the same old reaction from her.

She was an attractive woman, impeccably dressed and invariably in control. Her reply was as he could have anticipated—quick and aimed at the bone.

"How like you, Ryder. Another mess-up. This time, an illegitimate child even *you* didn't know about. And now, you come here and smile as if we should all be happy."

CHAPTER SEVEN

"HEY, Ry. My secretary says you're looking for me."

Ryder glanced up from the infernal, eternal paperwork on his desk to see Calder, standing in the doorway of his office, smiling at him. "Yeah, you've been scarce around here, and I want to talk to you."

"Great." Always enthusiastic, Calder settled on the chair across from Ryder, ready to listen.

Probably because Ryder seemed hesitant, Calder spoke first. "Yeah, I'm tired of the traveling. But then you know about the deal that made it worth my trouble."

At Ryder's smile, Calder continued. "I hear you've been busy, too. Working straight through Saturday."

Today was Monday, the Monday after Ryder's visit with his mother and brother in Palm Beach.

"So," Calder said, "I guess you got up to Palm Beach yesterday, didn't you?"

"Right."

"And what happened? What did they say? Vance was there, too, wasn't he?"

"Yes, Vance was there. And actually it went pretty well. Better than I'd expected after all these years."

"And your baby girl? What do they think?"

"They seem to accept her as a fact. Or rather, Mother does. In all fairness to Vance, he warmed to the idea."

"Well, that's good. I've had this on my mind, you know."

Yes, Calder would have had Ryder and his troubles on his mind, no matter how busy he'd been. It was their closeness that pushed Ryder on. Ryder owed it to Calder to be straight with him. Since the party at Calder's house, Ryder had worried about the feeling Calder had admitted to that night. Calder wanted Ryder as his heir apparent at Calder Parks Development. And as much as Ryder wanted to fall in with Calder's wishes, he just couldn't. Not yet.

Somehow he had to tell Calder about his extreme dissatisfaction with his career. About his desire to...to what?

If he were to leave Calder Parks Development, what would he do? Where would he go? Even in his years after college, he'd established himself in the same line of work, only then in New York. And also—purposely—in competition with his own father and brother.

Ryder had always been good at the business. He had the background for it. Had the connections. Had the merciless drive. And while he'd never done anything illegal or unethical, in those days he'd been glad to one-up his dad and his brother. And yes, Calder, too.

Ryder was ashamed of those days. The way he was of his trial and then of dropping out. He felt burdened by regret. He'd hurt too many people. If it hadn't been for Calder, he didn't know where he'd be. And looking at Calder, Ryder knew he had to explain.

Still sensing Ryder's flux of feelings, Calder made a stab at what was bothering him. "Your mother wasn't too hard on you, was she, Ry?"

"What? Oh, no. Not really. Anyway, I'm used to the way she thinks about me. That'll probably never change."

"And Vance? He doesn't hold on to that old stuff? I mean, from those days when you graduated from college and competed in the business against him and your dad. He doesn't hold any of that against you, does he?"

Ryder smiled cryptically. "You mean when I was out to cut them into ribbons?" Yes, he'd had times when he'd been an ass, and he hated thinking about that, too. Still, he answered Calder truthfully. "No, Vance doesn't seem to hold any of that against me. For him, it's water under the bridge."

"And it should be," Calder huffed, always in Ryder's corner. "Your dad was pretty good to you, Ry, but we both know he should have been there for you a helluva lot more. I mean, taking the occasional day off to play golf with you and me and Vance hardly made up for his hours at the office. And that's despite the great times we had. And as for your mother, well, I won't get into that again."

"No, let's not get into that."

"I'm just glad there might be some sort of reconciliation."

"Me too."

"It'll be good for that little girl of yours."

"Yeah, I..."

Again, Ryder's hesitation encouraged Calder's next stab at the problem. "You aren't worried about the responsibility of having a child, are you? Not that parents don't worry—"

"No. I mean, parenting's scary, but I also find the idea of it, well..." He felt his own smile. "She's so adorable that I don't think I could walk away unless I absolutely had to."

And that was scary, too, Ryder thought. If he couldn't stick it out here at Calder's ... If he couldn't force himself, and didn't know what else he could do... With a little girl depending on him, watching him, and him messing up again... It didn't get more frightening than that.

To be tempted to chuck it all again—

"So I guess that's what you wanted."

Ryder refocused on Calder's friendly expression. "What?"

"You wanted to tell me about what happened in Palm Beach."

"Oh, yeah. I mean, no." Even after a pause, Ryder still couldn't find the guts to say it. He simply couldn't tell Calder how hard it was to stay with him. "I wanted to, uh, tell you that I'm leaving early today. I'm driving out to see, uh, Summer and Carrie."

"Great, great. Hell, take as much time as you want. For over two years now, you've been working day and night, and you deserve some time away. Balance in our lives, Ry. That's what it's all about. As you know, no one enjoys working more than I do, but it's in the middle ground where we really live."

On a wink, Calder left.

Balance, Ryder thought. In the middle ground? What the hell did that mean? He was struggling just to keep going as he was.

He still despised big business, but he had nowhere else to go. And just as his recent past caught up with him in the form of a child he couldn't leave and a woman he couldn't forget, his distant past rushed at him with renewed force.

OVER THE WEEKEND, Irma had realized she'd painted herself into quite a corner. On Friday, she'd told Fred she'd worked her last day, and how could she go back on that?

If that was her last day at the resort, and admittedly there was nothing there for her to do, then that was the last she'd see of Fred. She'd have only flimsy excuses to visit him, and he sure as heck wouldn't think to come see her.

On Sunday, however, the light bulb in her head had blinked on, full force, right in the middle of church service.

The garage. Or rather, what they benevolently referred to as the garage.

Fred Miller had a few distinct qualities, and one was that he was a pack rat. In the twenty-two and a half years Irma had worked for him, she'd never seen Fred throw away so much as a soda straw. He'd been packratting anything one could imagine in the dingiest darkest building at the forties-style resort. But suddenly, during the sermon, no less, the garage came to her mind like a blessed vision.

Barely able to wait until Monday morning, Irma found herself at the resort. Across the parking lot from the office, she stopped her car in front of a long, low building that had been intended as a garage, but that had padlocks on its three large doors.

Luckily, Fred had no more imagination than to keep the key under the mat at the side door, and she pushed the smaller door open to the dank interior. Stepping in, for one could maneuver only so far, she scanned the stacks and stacks of boxes, the junk piled in bins.

"I don't know if this is inspiration or the bowels of hell," she muttered.

A broken ceiling fan, which had been removed from one of the bungalows and abandoned on an old chair, was now covered with cobwebs that gently wafted in the draft from the doorway. She remembered Summer saying that the dishes in the coffee bar had become badly chipped from hundreds of washings, and though Fred had grudgingly replaced them, sure enough, they sat in several boxes on the concrete floor. Car parts, more furniture in odds and ends...

"Golly Ned," she whispered.

Not unexpectedly, Fred came to the door, squinting in the dim interior. "What in hell?"

Irma braced herself. "You know, Fred, it would be nice if you'd say hello once in a while."

Since he didn't reply, she tried again. "I was thinking, uh, yesterday in church. Suddenly it hit me that this garage would have to be sorted through before the move. And heaven knows, Summer's got enough on her hands. I've decided to volunteer."

"Hell's bells, this is something I can do."

"Alone? There's an awful lot of stuff."

"Well." He put his hands in his back pockets. His eyes roamed where hers had gazed moments before. "I suppose there's more here than I recalled."

"I thought I'd hire Sophie Marshall's grandsons. You remember, the twins. Oh, I realize they're only sixteen, but the few times we've had them out here to help with this and that, they've done a really good job. We can take down every box and go through it. I'll keep a list, and you'll decide what's to be pitched and what's to be kept. I suppose you'll store some of it, huh?"

"Hell, I don't know. I haven't thought about it."

"What else can we do? We could get someone to haul it away as trash, I guess."

"What? There's some stuff in here that's worth a lot of money."

"Well then, what about hiring someone who knows?"

"Hiring? I'm not paying anybody to decide what to do with my stuff."

"Okay then, we'll have a yard sale."

"A what?"

"You know. We'll sort through it, then set it all out in the driveway and advertise. There's plenty of room for an open-air sale. I've been going to them for years, and I'm convinced people will buy almost anything."

Irma waited, holding her breath. Obviously Fred hated the idea. Still, the suggestion of the money to be made stuck like flypaper. Visions of people buying what he had stashed away since the dawn of time, well . . .

"I dunno," he said, eyeing her.

She eyed him right back, silently demanding another suggestion.

"I'll think about it," he finally said.

"Good." She pushed past him. "In the meantime, I'll go to the grocery store and get some boxes."

"Boxes? Why in hell boxes?"

"We'll have to repack everything. You start saving newspapers for packing, though my friends are sure to have stacks of newspaper."

Fred swiveled as she sailed out into the sunlit driveway.

"You bring down a webbed chair," she said, "and we'll put it right outside the door. We'll start this afternoon, and I promise I won't decide a thing. I'm just here to help."

"But what in hell?"

Irma got in her car and started it. She wasn't about to let him think about this. "While I'm at the store, I'll pick up some fish fillets, some fixings for a salad."

"What the . . . ?"

"I don't know about you, but I'll be ready for lunch soon, and I might as well grill some fish on that little grill just inside the door there. I'll bring charcoal, too, and that thingamabob you grill the fish in, and—"

"Now, wait a minute, wait a minute."

She slowed the car enough to listen to him through the open window. "Well, what? Doesn't fish sound good? I know you have to watch your diet, and—"

"Dammit, you know it ain't my diet. I told you I ain't gonna rush into this."

"You mean you prefer leaving it to Summer?"

Fred couldn't argue with that one. A bit of gravel spun off Irma's wheels as she departed. She was still hanging in there!

All through the grocery store, through rummaging in their stack of boxes, through getting everything in her car, her spirits grew. She was doing something meaningful.

Of course she didn't know a darned thing about cooking fish on a grill, and once she unloaded everything at Fred's—for he was nowhere in sight—and made her way to the contraption, she had to slow down.

Now what? The thing looked daunting. She was a career woman. She'd always cooked as little as possible. To grill the fish fillets, to use the basket thingy the butcher had recommended, well . . .

Well, she was determined. She could grill fish. She wasn't stupid.

By the time Fred returned from wherever he'd been, she had the fire going, and boy, was it going. The fish fillets didn't look like any fish fillets she'd ever seen, nicely presented on a plate at her favorite cafeteria.

"What in hell?"

Patience, patience. "Fred, I know the fish don't look exactly right, but I'm sure tired of hearing you talk like that."

"Don't look *exactly* right?" he responded.

Her gaze followed his to the smoldering fish. Pictures of the wimpy salad waiting in the fridge confounded her. Oh, nuts, she wasn't about to lose the battle that easily.

"Well," Fred said, glancing at her, "I'll fix us some scrambled eggs. Eggs and salads and English muffins are good."

"But surely you're not supposed to eat eggs."

"Hell, er, well, they aren't eggs. Eggs come in shells, and these darned things pour out of a milk carton. Summer bought 'em, but they ain't too bad. Come on, leave the fish. I'll clean up later."

Thinking she hadn't lost too badly, Irma went with Fred to his kitchen. Actually, he was downright nice about adding this and that to the salad, just to spice it up a bit. In fact, they had a very nice lunch. Even pleasant.

Oh, indeed, Irma knew why Fred was worth the winning.

AFTER PARKING his car in front of Summer's bungalow, Ryder walked past the empty swimming pool toward the beach. When he'd phoned Summer to tell her he was coming out, she'd said she was taking this perfect Monday afternoon to spend with Carrie.

As she'd told him, Carrie had been getting short shrifted since she and her business partner had accepted the wedding call he'd overheard—when had it been? That first time he'd seen Carrie, just over a week ago.

A week ago he hadn't known he had a child. Today, he felt as if he'd throw himself under a train for her.

Since his visit with Vance and his mother, his need to see Carrie and Summer had escalated. His emotions remained in such a turmoil that he couldn't describe how he felt, even to himself. He only knew he needed to be with Summer and Carrie, and he hoped to keep things on an even keel with Summer in order to do that.

Reaching the beach, he was struck by its emptiness, which was merely temporary. The nearby resorts were closed, waiting for the transformation that had changed so much of Florida's coastlines.

And then he caught sight of them. Carrie and Summer. His heart tripped. The air failed to reach his lungs. Gulls wheeled overhead, the sea pushed in like an old companion, but he saw only them. They were collecting shells, and the picture of them together was captivating.

Under a loose-fitting denim shirt, Summer wore a bikini. Carrie, too, was endearing in a bikini and eyelet cap. Summer bent down, then Carrie bobbed, scratching the sand like the nearby pipers did.

Looking up, Summer caught sight of him, waved and walked to meet him with Carrie at her side. Summer carried an ancient conch that was worn away to a handle, a center spindle and a nob on one end.

"See, Boop?" she asked. "You can use it as a telephone. Hello?" she asked into the shell. "Hello?"

Carrie giggled, then looked up at Ryder. When she grasped the old conch, Ryder put his fist to his ear.

"Hello, Carrie, hello."

Again she giggled, stomping the sand with bare feet in delight. "Hi, hi," she sang, grinning at him.

At Summer's next attempt, his heart turned over. "Hello, *Daddy,* hello."

Carrie's expression darkened. "No."

Summer must have read Ryder's suddenly drooping anticipation. She smoothed over Carrie's refusal to call him anything, much less Daddy. "Don't take it personally," Summer urged. "She's always reluctant to try a new word."

"I have to admit it," he said. "I can't wait for her to say it. Daddy, that is. Yesterday, I thought about it all day long."

Summer dusted her hands free of sand, closed a few of the buttons on her billowing shirt, scraped back a skein of red-gold hair.

Ryder absorbed every move.

"Well," she added, coaxing Carrie in the direction of the resort, "it won't be long. She's as sunny as she is stubborn."

Falling into stride with her and the child who toddled between them, then scampered ahead, Ryder kept his emotions from showing. If he didn't keep things between him and Summer on the up-and-up, she'd close him out. She'd told him so.

"Now comes the hard part," Summer said, sending him that tough little smile that tore at him.

"The hard part?"

Summer guided Carrie toward a shower head that extended from a nearby seawall. It was obviously used to get rid of the sand that, because of its fine grain, coated Carrie's skin like sugar.

Plucking up the child with a swift move, Summer turned on the spray and stripped off Carrie's suit. Sure enough, Carrie began to scream something fierce.

"She knows we're going in," Summer explained, washing the child and speaking over the racket. "As you can see, she hates going in."

As the complexity of raising children, of interpreting what they couldn't simply say out loud, sank in, Ryder experienced his first qualms about becoming involved with his child. It seemed so complicated. He felt so inept.

When Summer hefted Carrie to a hip, wrapped in a towel and screaming and kicking, Carrie got worse. Even so, Summer headed in the direction of the bungalow, and once again, Ryder matched his steps to hers, listening to her over the ongoing hullabaloo.

"Like I say, she loves the beach and hates to go in. And then, she's not very good at transitions."

"Transitions?"

"You know, from playing to having something to eat. That sort of thing. Going to bed at night can be really hard. Right now, she's tired from being outside, and she needs a nap, anyway."

Ryder's confusion was compounded. Kids came without instructions. Summer had learned a lot.

"Yes," she said, nodding at him when they entered the bungalow. "She's working herself into a full-blown tantrum. She can't handle it anymore."

"Tantrum?"

He wavered near the door.

Summer talked calmly to Carrie, but none of it helped. Summer even shot him a wry smile. "Haven't you heard the one that goes, 'There was a little girl who had a little curl right in the middle of her fore-head. And when she was good she was very very good, and when she was bad she was horrid'?"

Ryder shook his head, and Summer shared her verse with Carrie. But still, nothing worked.

When Summer moved with the child back into a small but cheery room full of baby furniture and toys—and also the large bear he'd brought—he couldn't help drifting after them, despite his shaky knees.

He remained by the door, watching. Summer un-wrapped Carrie from the towel, then fought her into a diaper, a T-shirt and some colorful overalls. All the while, Summer crooned to the child, talked to her, but the process looked torturous. If anything, Carrie grew worse. Summer finally had to put her down, and she lay on the floor and kicked her heels, screaming bloody murder.

"Okay, okay," Summer soothed, putting away the last of the mess and coaxing Ryder out of the room ahead of her. "You'll be fine. You'll be fine. Just calm down and when you're ready, we'll be waiting for you."

When Ryder would have shut the door, Summer pushed it ajar. "Don't ever close her in. She'll feel trapped."

He felt stricken. "Of course."

Summer relented with a little smile. "She's fine. It's just a tantrum. She reaches overload, and she gets so frustrated she doesn't know where to go with it."

Ryder followed Summer back into the small living room-kitchen area.

"Would you like something to drink?" she asked.

His throat was so tight he didn't think he could swallow. He shook his head, then nodded. "Maybe something to drink would help."

Again she sent him a tough knowing smile. The screaming hadn't abated, and he wondered if Summer's theories of childrearing weren't all wet. When she returned with a glass of iced tea, he grasped it and took a big drink.

"There," she said, indicating he should listen. "She's slowing down."

Slowing down, hell. He couldn't tell any difference.

He gulped more tea.

Although Summer seemed to enjoy his concern, she apparently felt sorry for him, too. "Usually," she explained, "children outgrow tantrums, and it takes a lot for her to get this bad. Part of it is that I've been so busy, and she's used to being with me."

"But isn't there something else that can be done?"

"Well, there're two theories about tantrums. At least, two I know of. One is to get them to a quiet place where they can settle down without any kind of judgment or discipline. Just a calm neutral place. She can't help how she's feeling. She just doesn't know how to handle frustration yet."

"And the other theory?"

"Well, there's a psychologist who says they're in stress, and that you should hold them and comfort them until they get it all out. But I find that the more I hold her and comfort her, the more the tantrum escalates. I think she needs to learn how to handle this, just like she has to learn how to handle falling asleep on her own.'' She shrugged. ''I don't know. It's never black or white, or wrong or right. I think it's more finding what's comfortable for you and your child.''

And me?

Ryder felt the ground move. He couldn't do it. Not in a million years.

When the phone rang, he almost jumped out of his skin.

''I'm sorry.'' Summer sent him an apologetic look. ''I've got to get this, and—''

He nodded, signaled with a hand. He took a long slow drink of his tea. In the other room, Carrie gradually grew quieter, and Ryder grew calmer, too. He even heard Summer's phone conversation.

''Right now?'' she asked. ''I don't know. I'm covered with sand, and Poppy and Irma are cleaning out the garage. He won't want to stop and shower and stay with Carrie, and she's in no mood for house-hunting.''

Ryder edged into the hallway. The small back bedroom seemed quiet. He would have taken a look, but he was afraid to start Carrie off again.

Then Summer caught his eye. ''Would you mind staying with Carrie? I mean, just for fifteen or twenty minutes?''

''Me?''

''Do you have time?''

''Well, uh, yes, but—''

She went back to the phone. ''It's all right, Dee. Ryder's here. I'll come as soon as I can.''

Ryder gulped down the last of his iced tea. He met Summer's eyes as levelly as he could. Oh, God.

"I hate to ask you to do this, but, Dee, my business partner, has told me about this house. You know, I've been looking at houses, and—"

He nodded.

"Dee just happened to catch the real estate agent at this house, and the guy says he'll wait and show it to me if I come right away. I know Poppy, er, my grandfather, will stay with Carrie, but he's been cleaning out a garage all afternoon and he'll want to shower first. It should only take him about twenty minutes. He's not by a phone, so I'll tell him to come down on my way out."

"It's okay." Ryder's own words surprised him. "I'll stay."

Her smile was almost worth it. Her smile made him want to give her the moon. But he wasn't ready for this—not this soon and not with Carrie's mood.

Still, Summer had switched into forward gear. "I'll change. It won't take a minute."

"Okay."

She disappeared down the now-quiet hallway, and once again, he was tempted to peek at Carrie. But no, he didn't dare. Maybe Summer could get away without their child catching on. Maybe Fred Miller would arrive and Carrie would never know the difference. Gingerly, Ryder sank onto the edge of the small couch and waited.

But of course the best-laid plans—well, Carrie peeked around the corner at him. Her nose shone pink. She hiccuped. She was so damned adorable that he had to do something.

"Come here," he whispered.

She tilted her head, considering it.

"Come on."

In the end, the little precaution she exercised amazed him. She toddled toward him confidently, obviously secure in the fact that no one had ever hurt her. Nearing him, she flung her small body at him, and he, even as off guard as he was, swept her up on his lap.

He was so befuddled, so aware of his growing sense of fatherhood, that he choked up again.

She was magic. Pure magic. She smelled uniquely of baby lotion and a little of Summer. He waited as her gaze glided over his face, measuring his features, his silence and surely reading his soul.

"Eye," she said, with a sudden strike of her pointed finger at his eye.

He ducked, chuckled. "Yes, eye." She dropped her gaze to his hand resting on his lap. "'And," she said. "Binger."

"Right. Hand. Finger."

No doubt about it, she was brilliant. A genius.

When she laid her hand on his, he stared at the two together. She was so small, so soft, so vibrant with life. She was like him. She was his flesh and blood. She belonged to him, and no matter what happened in the years to come, she always would. The idea boggled his mind. The emotions battered him.

Love.

Protectiveness.

He was rocked to the core. Surely, he was transformed.

"Well," Summer said, swinging into the room, "I'm ready. I promise this won't be more than twenty minutes or so. Poppy'll be right here."

Ryder cleared his throat. The look of Summer, even in a simple top, skirt and sandals added to his emotional load. "I, uh..."

"You'll do fine," she said, moving along.

He was vaguely disappointed, then, when she paused to pluck up an old bulky sweater and to shove her arms into it. Worse, she wrapped her soft vibrant hair around a hand before stuffing it beneath a baseball cap.

With Ryder still watching, she came to where he held Carrie on his lap. She bent to touch Carrie's cheek with her lips. "See you soon, sweetie."

But Summer's final words were directed at him as she put on a large pair of dark glasses. "And don't worry if she fusses a little when I go. She's beginning to deal with separation anxiety, and—"

"Separation anxiety?"

Summer chuckled. "Just talk to her. She loves to be talked to."

With that, Summer actually left him—left him alone with Carrie, who looked at him solemnly. He waited for her face to crumple, for the horrible screams.

Separation anxiety. It sounded significant.

"Eye," he said to her.

She grinned. "Eye."

Indeed, the old game worked. Ryder went on to name every feature Carrie knew, then some she didn't know but that she repeated. Still, she didn't cry. When he ran out of visible body parts, she slipped off his lap and trundled to her room and back.

She carried in a puzzle with enormous pieces, and proceeded to show him how very smart she was. His amazement had her hauling out everything she could, only for him to watch patiently as she quickly demonstrated this toy or that game.

She talked all the time, and occasionally he understood a phrase or two.

"Carrie," he said, coaxing her to look at him. When her big green eyes engaged his, he spoke softly, fixing her attention. "Say Daddy."

She studied him. He had no way of reading her thoughts, so he tried again. "Daddy, Carrie. Say Daddy."

She shook her head.

"Dada?"

"No," she stated flatly, picking up a bedraggled dolly.

But Ryder didn't have time to be disappointed. Barely knocking, Fred Miller came into the now-cluttered living room. Ryder got a hold on himself. As he expected, Fred Miller sized him up, too.

"How's she doin'?" Fred asked.

"She had a temper tantrum."

Fred lifted his brows. "Oh? Well, she'll be needin' a nap, then."

Ryder was again struck by how comfortably Summer, and now Fred, understood the tiny person who circled Fred's legs chanting, "Bopie, Bopie." But just that quickly she disappeared down the short hallway.

Left alone with Fred, Ryder wished he could say something to prove himself worthy. Here was the man who had stuck by Summer through all the times Ryder should have been there. Ryder both admired and envied him.

"So I hear you asked her to marry you."

Uh-oh, Ryder thought.

"'O' course she told me she said no. She's stubborn. I'm sure you couldn't convince her any more than anybody."

"No, I—"

"Heard about the money, too. Not that I don't think you shouldn't help support Carrie, but you've been damned generous, and I gotta admit it."

"Yes, er, like you say, I wouldn't feel right...I mean, even as it is, I don't feel right. I can only hope to do the best I can."

"Umm." Poppy went silent. Awkwardness prevailed. "You're doin' your best. But don't get me wrong," he added defensively, "she's doin' her best, too."

"Oh, I can see that. I couldn't ask for anything better for a child."

"Yeah, well."

The pair fell into the next uneasy silence, and it was again Fred who broke it. Digging in his back pocket, he produced two cigars, inexpensive and wrapped in cellophane sleeves. Handing one to Ryder, he unwrapped the other for himself.

"I just found these today. I gave them out when Carrie was born. Hell, I must have handed out a few dozen. So many friends then, you know. Here at the resort and along the beach.

Ryder sensed the old man's pain. "I'm sorry to see these little resorts being shut down. There're lots of people who'll never feel the same about visiting here again."

"Yeah, I've gotten all kinds of cards and notes. I've had clients come down every year the same two weeks of the season, and on the day they check in, they sign up for the same two weeks the next year. That's how you make the money, you know. Dependable repeat business. And then these people become friends. And that don't account for the friendships people renewed here, year after year, comin' down that way. People who never saw each other otherwise, people from all parts of the country spent weeks together, time after time, and no one can get closer than like that. Playing cards at night, sharing the beach during the day, only havin' each other for company.''

Even though the older man shrugged dismissively, Ryder saw that he hurt. But as Ryder considered a way of reaching out to him, Fred opened the door to the porch at the front of the bungalow.

''Can't light these up in here,'' he said of the cigars. ''Not good for Carrie.''

''Right.''

When Ryder joined Fred, Fred flourished a big old lighter that didn't work well, but he finally managed to get the cigars lit. ''Sorry,'' Fred mumbled. ''Found this contraption, too. Guess I shoulda thrown it out.''

Ryder suppressed the choking sensation in his throat. The cigar was two years old and tasted stale. Even so, he wasn't about to flunk another test with Fred Miller.

When Fred started to gasp, Ryder took the cigar from him.

''Damned things,'' Fred grumbled. ''Didn't keep at all.''

Ryder stubbed out the cigars in a nearby ashtray.

''S-sorry about that,'' Fred said, recovering his breath.

''I appreciate the thought. I've missed out on a lot.''

With that, they retreated into a mutual silent search for the next subject.

"Summer says you remember my name from the papers," Ryder stated, laying the main topic out in the open.

"Yep, I recall the tales in the paper," Fred replied. "You don't need to discuss the matter with me. I believe in this country and in what the courts decide. They found you innocent. That's all I need to know."

Ryder felt a tug of gratitude. Of course, he would've told Fred whatever he wanted to know, but Fred didn't say anything further. The best thing, Ryder thought, looking at the man again, was having faced the subject with him. He could tell Fred appreciated the opportunity to discuss it, even if he declined.

They each gave the other more than a wide berth. They grasped for something neither would want to define—something to make the situation better for everyone involved.

"So," Fred suggested, "I guess we'd better have a look, huh? It's awfully quiet in there."

Ryder nodded, then followed Fred back to the little bedroom at the rear of the house. He'd noticed earlier that the bear he'd brought for Carrie—the one that was three times her size and that had made her cry when she'd first seen it—now sat slumped in a corner of her room. The bear's friendly expression faced downward, but his red vest, his honey-colored fuzz, remained bright. Half seated on the bear's lap, Carrie dozed against its softness.

Fred and Ryder simply took a long look. "Told you," Fred finally said in a hoarse whisper, "that bear would be her buddy."

Ryder was almost brought to his knees by the sweet sight.

Even Fred's eyes glittered. "It's pictures like this that hold fast in your mind. They make all the hard times seem like nothin'."

Even for his inexperience, Ryder thought Fred had to be right. But other thoughts also assailed him. Carrie was so innocent, and a sense of unworthiness stirred restlessly in his soul.

CHAPTER EIGHT

"I HAVEN'T BEEN this tired since I don't know when," Summer said, deeply inhaling the cool night air.

Dee switched off the last light, and the pair left the church and headed for their car and van. "When you called me—what was it? Three weeks ago? When you told me we had a chance at that wedding, I should've said you were nuts. I still don't know how we did it."

"My feet can tell you," Summer responded. "But it was a real success, wasn't it? I bet we get at least three dates from this wedding. Everywhere I looked, I saw faces I've seen in the society sheets."

"Huh, I had two people come back to the kitchen, asking for our card, so that's two prospects alone. The second one, a woman by the name of Levy, commented on how wonderful you looked at the buffet. She said she simply has to have you in your white tux at her next party. I told her we'd be there, white tux and all."

Summer didn't tell Dee she was growing more comfortable with the little show they produced. They'd reached their vehicles—Summer's new van and Dee's equally new hatchback, both of which were marked with their logo for Dining In—and they were ready to go.

Dee paused to call out to Summer. "You sure you're not too tired to drive out to the key?"

"No, I'm fine. It's only a little after one."

Dee laughed. "Only a little after one, she says. Only a little after one."

With that they waved and got in their cars. Summer pulled off in one direction and Dee in the other. Tempted to drive by the house she'd decided to buy, the one Dee had seen originally, Summer realized how very tired she was. Still, visions of the lovely party they'd thrown, of the flowers and food and compliments, lingered.

Trying to order the next morning in her mind, Summer glanced into her rearview mirror, then into the one outside the door of the van. The guy behind her was following awfully close, and his lights—

His lights.

Summer's heart flip-flopped.

Don't lose it now, she told herself. *Don't let your imagination...*

But no. The driver behind her was tailgating. She couldn't see his car, but the angle of his headlights— the one slightly higher than the other—stuck in her memory.

Was she being followed?

"No," she said out loud, to hear her own voice. "That's crazy. First of all, *who*'d want to follow you? And second, *why* would they?"

Still, he stayed close to her. She was tempted to test her theory. By pulling off the main drag, she'd see if he did, too.

But she wasn't up to testing her theory. And besides, this guy was surely the one who'd trailed her that night into the lot at the grocery store. The one who, she could swear, she'd seen outside the church, no matter what she'd said to Dee.

Summer shivered. Counting herself lucky, she gripped her wheel. She'd reached the final lap. The bridge to Fiesta Key was just ahead and was—thankfully—lowered. No boat traffic would hold her up.

Briefly, she considered leading him away from where she lived. But then she realized he'd disappeared. Simply vanished. His lights didn't blaze in her mirror anymore, and the next set of lights behind her weren't lopsided.

Okay, so he'd left her with a spooky feeling. But she was nearly home. And he had definitely disappeared.

"Get a grip, Summer."

When she swung into the lot at the Flamingo Resort, she admitted the place had never looked so good.

"You're just tired," she said, catching sight of the light at Poppy's, then of the sporty red car parked outside her bungalow. "Oh, no," she groaned.

If there was anything she didn't need, it was Ryder Craig. Although she hadn't seen him in nearly two weeks, she wasn't ready to see him . . . preferably ever again.

Not that she didn't believe he avoided her as much as she did him. He came and went on the evenings she worked, always calling first and usually arranging his visits with Carrie through Poppy. She'd been left out of it. "Because," Poppy had explained offhandedly, "you're so busy."

But Summer knew better. The ground rules she'd established with Ryder Craig served them both. When she and he were together, they inevitably remembered the day they'd made love, and became embarrassed and awkward with each other.

"So what's he doing here this late?" she asked herself. "Lordy, Summer, you're losing it. Still talking to yourself, huh?"

Gathering herself, both against her fatigue and the sight of him, she opened the door to her small living room. Sure enough, he sat on the two-man couch, his long legs stretched to the desk chair. An album of Carrie's baby pictures covered his lap, and for some reason, the sight added to the turmoil she already felt from her experience on the road.

But she also recognized her reason for bristling. Guilt. For almost two years, she'd deprived him of Carrie.

"Hi," he said, looking a bit sleepy and dropping his stocking feet to the floor.

Oh, God, that was the worst. He appeared at his sexiest when he was vulnerable.

"Is everything all right?" she asked, keeping herself on track.

"Just fine. Carrie's asleep, and I told Fred, uh, your grandfather, to go on home."

"But he's okay?"

"Sure, sure, just sleepy."

"I know." She sighed and kicked off her high heels. "I've been asking a lot of him lately. I guess I'd better find someone to help with the sitting. But I'm glad—" she forced herself to say "—you've been coming out on nights when he's here. It's good of you."

"Good of me?" He sounded a bit offended at her formality, at her attempt to keep him outside. But he relented. "No, I want to be here. It gives me a chance to get to know Carrie, sort of supervised."

"Poppy says he's showed you how to diaper her, how to give her a bath and that no one coaxes her into eating her carrots like you do."

Ryder grinned. "Yeah." He smiled almost sheepishly. "It's great."

Oh, the guilt. Tugging herself out of her white tailcoat, Summer noticed the slow disappearance of Ryder's grin. He watched her every move, finally looking away.

"I hope you don't mind that Fred gave me this album of Carrie's pictures," he said.

"No." Summer placed the tux coat on the bar that separated the galley kitchen from the living room. "No, no, I don't mind."

"She's always been so..."

"Yes, wonderful, beautiful, charming, whatever you want to say."

His warm gaze played games with her resolve to keep him at arm's length.

Oh, Lord, she was so nervous. She wasn't up to this.

"You look beat. I mean, you look beautiful, but... Uh, sorry." He closed the album and, placing it on the table beside the couch, got up.

When his eyes met hers, she realized she was watching him, and it was her turn to avert her gaze. Taking off the tight men's vest and the white silk bow tie, she was left in tux pants, a frilled shirt and suspenders.

"Hey," he said softly, the sound, the single syllable, working magic in Summer's memory. "Are you all right?"

She nodded.

"No, you aren't. What's wrong? Didn't the party go well?"

"The party was fine. It's just that, on the way home..."

"What?"

"Oh, I don't know." Fiddling with the cuff links, the shirt studs, she sketched in her story about the jerk who'd followed her to the grocery store. "I must be crazy. I mean, to think I saw him at the church, and then tonight, following me. I couldn't even see his car—some creepy, rusted pickup. Only the head-lights."

"Did you get his license number?"

"I wasn't thinking about his license number. I was worried about how close he was, about who he was or what he was doing."

Anxiety crept into her voice. She sounded unrea-sonable. License-plate numbers were reasonable. Pulling off the road into a gas station or some inhab-ited place was reasonable. Calling the police was rea-sonable. But she hadn't thought of any of that.

She faced Ryder. She saw concern in his green eyes. She watched his jaw tighten.

"Look," she said, "it's nothing. I'm sure it's noth-ing. I'm tired, and we had that horrendous wedding to do."

"Yeah, Fred told me."

"Besides, I've had guys follow me before. Oh, maybe not like this. I mean, usually guys are more di-rect about what they want." She sighed, slid the sus-penders from her shoulders and untucked the large men's shirt. "The truth is, I don't want to think about it anymore. Not tonight."

He looked as if he wanted to argue with her, but he also relented. "Okay."

"Anyway, it's nice of you to play cards with Poppy. And every time I come home, I notice some new toy in Carrie's basket. You're very good to her, too."

"Well, uh, I've been getting too much like my boss, Calder Parks. Two years with my nose to the grindstone. Only he loves it and I have to force myself. Coming out here is relaxing."

Summer had to laugh. "Relaxing? Even I don't associate relaxation with Carrie."

He seemed to enjoy her laugh, and as she sobered, he spoke softly. "I've been wanting to thank you, too. You've been generous with me. I'm sure you had to wonder, at least at first, what I might want. This is a good time to tell you I'll never try any legal tricks to challenge you."

He picked up the book he'd left on the table beside the couch. "This is by Brazelton. But most of the books I've been reading on child rearing have agreed that the more involved both parents are with their child, the better the child does. That is, aside from unsafe situations and that sort of thing. Anyway, the point is—"

"Yes, I see, and I thank you for that. I must admit I've worried . . . well, more in the beginning, I worried you might take her."

His eyes looked so soft. "Oh, no, I could never do that. Not after seeing the two of you together. You're so right together it's a joy to watch."

Summer turned to place the studs and links from her tux shirt on the bar. She couldn't meet his eyes. She'd realized that he hadn't been taking her casual removal of the tux as casually as she had.

"I think I'll peek at Carrie," she murmured.

But when she turned back again, his hands slid onto the bar behind her. With his chest and arms, he caged her in. His gaze trapped hers.

"I haven't been involved with a woman since that day, and I don't want to be now. I especially don't want to remember. I don't want to look in your eyes and see the gulf, restless and blue on an August afternoon. I don't want to see your hair shining like the sun itself. I don't want to be here, but I can't seem to stay away."

Summer responded to the images he described. It was all so clear. The fantasy she nurtured, the one she used to fall asleep or when she was sad, was imprinted on his mind, too.

He moved closer to her and put his hands on her shoulders. "What are you wearing underneath the shirt?" he whispered.

Desire, as ready as the first time, flooded Summer. She wanted to resist, but she couldn't so much as think straight. "A man's undershirt. The starch of the tux shirt makes my skin—"

He interrupted her explanation. "And your stockings are white, transparent. And your underwear silken and—"

"No, just white cotton briefs."

His lips touched her throat just above the shirt collar.

Why didn't she stop him?

With his mouth against her skin, his words seemed to vibrate through her. "I don't want to dream anymore that I'm making love to you. I don't want to wake up in the middle of the night in a sweat. You're my worst nightmare, my sexiest dream." Then, abruptly, he dropped his hands and stepped back.

"And this is way out of line and I apologize. Like you've told me, we don't know each other, in spite of Carrie. Somehow I keep forgetting that."

He moved away from her.

She couldn't think of two words to put together.

"Besides," he added, turning back, "there's the obvious between us, and that can never be changed."

"The obvious?"

"My past?"

She wouldn't have thought of his trial, even if she'd had minutes to collect herself. As far as she was concerned, his trial, and whatever it involved, didn't matter that much.

"I can see my past hasn't troubled your mind too often," he said, sounding both sardonic and gentle.

"No, I'm more interested in who you are now."

His laugh turned short and sharp. "The past makes us who we are today."

"To a point."

"No. More than to a point."

"Well, I don't agree. I mean, that's not to say I wouldn't like to hear about what happened sometime, but—"

"Yes, sometime I'll lay it all out in front of you. I won't feel right otherwise."

Summer pushed back her hair. "Why don't you explain now?"

"You're too tired and it'll take time."

"I'm not too tired. In fact, I'm so wired that I doubt I'll sleep tonight. Why don't I fix us something to eat? Are you hungry? I realize I haven't eaten since lunch."

He shrugged. "I'd like to tell you, but . . ."

Rolling up the sleeves of her tux shirt, she headed for the galley kitchen. What she'd said was true. She wouldn't sleep for a while, if at all. And not because of this threat from the past. Ryder Craig in his present form was what scared her.

When he had nudged her up against the dining bar, she'd realized she could no more resist him now than she'd been able to that day. He'd been right in breaking off his embrace. They were a bad combination. Together they lost control. Only the fact that he knew that, too, and that he also kept a guard on what might tip the balance and throw them overboard into a sea of sensuality lent her any safety.

When he had pushed away from her, he'd demonstrated he could control what she could not. She trusted him, and she'd have to rely on him to keep his distance.

"So," she said, switching on the prepared coffeepot and opening the refrigerator, "what would you like?"

Lazing into the bar, he leaned on an elbow, and even that little move affected her. No matter how reasonably he spoke to her, the way he watched her made her feel wobbly.

But she had to stay in control. "If I'd have known about this two o'clock supper, I would've brought some of the leftovers from the wedding reception. Boy, we were really on tonight. Everything was sumptuous. But—" she peered into the fridge "—I only have, let's see, how about a Denver omelet and a blueberry muffin?"

"Sounds more like a morning-after than a midnight supper."

His voice, and especially what he suggested, added to her unsteadiness. "Still, it's that or nothing. Would you believe I haven't shopped for anything but my business since I can't remember when? Poor Carrie."

"Oh, yes, poor, poor, Carrie," he repeated dolefully. "But an omelet sounds good."

Easy was the best thing about Summer's menu. Within minutes, she and Ryder sat on bar stools, facing each other over the bar with coffee, orange juice—the whole breakfast bit.

"This is great," he said. "You can cook in my galley any day."

When her silence signaled that she was prepared to listen, he avoided her eyes. "Now that it comes down to it, I don't know where to start. I've never really explained my past to anyone from start to finish."

"Why don't you just start at the beginning?"

"Well," he drawled, "I was born thirty-three years ago in New York. Is that beginning enough for you?"

When he chuckled and she didn't, he read her seriousness. He turned serious, too.

"I was raised mostly in boarding schools, and, well, somewhere before the age of ten, I declared war on my family. Everything they were, I didn't want to be. Everything they wanted, I defied. I even lost a fairly loving relationship with my brother somewhere along the line. And with my dad, too."

He looked as if the ordeal might be too much, but when she remained quietly expectant, he went on.

"As I grew older, I got worse. I was the quintessential rebel in college, and then, once I graduated, I hit the money-making scene in New York at full speed. I'd been prepared for it, and I did pretty well. I took a power position with a real estate firm, one that was in competition with my father's, just to thumb my nose at him. By then my brother, Vance, had been with the family business for some time, and I included him in my competitive vendetta."

He shrugged. "Anyway, as I began to put matters in a saner light, I realized I'd fallen way short where my family was concerned. I mean, I hardly took the time to see them, much less to put any effort into settling my differences with them. So one Christmas, I decided to make a stab at fixing it and I showed up unannounced at my parents' apartment. Just to break the ice. To be sociable. Traditionally, they had an enormous party on Christmas Eve, and I thought that would be a good time to begin to change the situation.

"What I didn't take into account was my mother's strong sense of what's socially correct. She hustled me aside and read me a cool lecture on how impolite it was to simply show up uninvited and unannounced. When I told her I hadn't thought those rules applied to family, one thing led to another. By the time my father intervened, she was rigid and implacable, and I was in my usual controlled rage. Even Vance tried to get me to stay, but I was so angry I stormed out."

Summer saw that Ryder was trying, evidently not for the first time, to make sense of his past. She also saw that he blamed himself too much. That he was even ashamed.

"I had some friends who'd been bugging me about joining them for the following weekend in Vermont. They were old college friends, a wild bunch I'd been distancing myself from for some time. But they insisted, and I didn't have anywhere else to go. It was just for the weekend, and I'd been there often during our college years. Weekends skiing outside Killington were mostly a good excuse for boozing, and, well, for women.''

Although he cleared his throat and looked away, he went on. ''By that point, I was feeling I never did anything right where my family was concerned. I mean, I loved them, but Christmas Eve had been such a bust that I went into that next weekend more angry and more out on the edge than I had been in a long time. And the weekends at that cabin had been wild, and once I was there again, I saw nothing had changed.

''That week since Christmas had been especially cold, and for all the talk of making good use of the nearby slopes and the heavy snow cover, our three-couple party was just keeping up our old habits. We slept late. We scrounged around for something to eat. We skied a little. But mostly we stayed up late, played cards and drank. Drank a lot.

''By Saturday night, I saw I'd made a mistake not merely in coming, but in my choice of dates. Bunny Dale, a club dancer I'd hung out with in New York, didn't exactly fit in with the old crowd. After another evening of cards and particularly heavy indulgence, the host and his date went to bed.

''The second couple—another old buddy and, as it happened, my own ex-fiancée, Rochelle Waller—had done nothing except argue all afternoon. Because of that, my second friend also went to bed, and I was left alone with Rochelle and Bunny—an impossible combination to begin with.

''Bunny was, uh, pretty and, well, amiable and kinda shallow. She'd been taking Rochelle's digs at her fairly well. But frankly, as the three of us played cards at the table in the main room of the cabin, I considered driving back to New York, even in my inebriated state and with the mounting storm we could hear outside.

"Finally, I suggested that we all turn in. But Rochelle complained about being left with a great hand she wanted to play out. I could tell I was in bad shape. Worse than in years. I told Rochelle I was tired, and while I didn't want to aggravate her any more, I felt I was losing control. I threw down my cards and started weaving my way toward a bedroom, but somehow I ended up sprawled on the couch. I let my head drop back and . . . well, that was it." He flushed with embarrassment.

"I mean, for all my experience with alcohol, I passed out. I'd never passed out before.

"I..." He stumbled, then went on. "The next thing I knew, the police were swarming over the cabin and everyone was in the main room in various states of undress. Bunny Dale was dead in front of the fireplace, and Rochelle was claiming I'd gotten angry and shoved Bunny against the high stone hearth. Bunny had died on impact.

"God, it was like slogging through muck. I couldn't seem to connect with anything. I'm sure it was the shock, but the more I was questioned, the more frightened I became. It was a living nightmare. I kept telling everybody I'd passed out. And though I knew I was incapable of murdering anyone, my anger had always ridden me so hard...but I knew I couldn't have done such a thing. The worst was that I couldn't remember a moment beyond collapsing on that damned couch. The more I protested, the less people believed me. I saw doubt everywhere I looked. Everywhere but inside myself. Yeah, I'd been habitually angry, but, no, I couldn't have hurt anyone.

"That autumn, I went to trial in a county courthouse near the scene of what I now think of as the accident. My father's lawyer had found the best trial lawyers to defend me, and what had been nightmarish became nothing short of hell. I still couldn't recall what had occurred. In fact, I can't to this day, and I had no way of defending myself. I could have lied and said I remembered, but I guess I'm too damned stubborn to lie. Basically, it boiled down to my word against Rochelle's, and I had only my excuse of a drunken stupor.

"The trial lasted for two weeks. It attracted the media, mainly from New York and Palm Beach. My family's known in both places. My parents and Vance and his wife, Brenda Jo, came up to Vermont and attended the trial until the third day, when my dad collapsed in the courtroom. A massive heart attack. From then on, I remember events less clearly. Or rather, in confused order. Some things I recall as if it were yesterday. There was the trial during the day, of course, and in the evenings, even far into most nights, I sat with my dad at the hospital. Actually, for me, the trial became almost unimportant. My mother insisted on moving my dad back to New York so he could get the best treatment, but they couldn't stabilize him enough for the transfer. One afternoon he died while I was at the courthouse. I never got to talk to him. Not when he was fully conscious. Vance was there, but—"

The admission, the pain, had choked off his words.

Still, Summer's unblinking, nonjudgmental attention obviously coaxed him on.

"That was the worst. Not being with my dad, not asking him to forgive me for the pain I'd caused in his life. He was never around very much, but I loved him. And I think he loved me, despite the trouble I caused.

"In the end, I was found innocent. My lawyers took Rochelle's claims apart, and, essentially, I slipped by. After the trial, I tried going back to my old life in New York, to my career, but it didn't work. Or rather, I didn't fit in anymore. I hated the talk behind my back, the innuendo. Finally, I said the hell with it, and I bought *Spare a Dime* and followed the coast around from New York to Texas. I still drank a lot then, but on my sodden trip back, still along the coast, I stopped in to see Calder Parks here in Sarasota. He and I go a long way back, and though he offered me a job, I told him no. That was just a couple of days before you came along."

When Summer dropped her eyes, Ryder reached across the bar between them and took her hand in both of his. "I know it's embarrassing to think about that day. But it's also a beautiful memory for me. I'd never turn my back on it in a million years."

Summer shook her head, but he spoke before she could.

"I know. I know what you want to say. We shouldn't have. What we did was so irresponsible that few could approve. But that day was also very meaningful for me at that time in my life. When I woke up and found that you'd gone, I started asking myself questions. Questions about who the hell I was and what in hell I was doing. When I didn't like the answers to those questions, I decided I had to do something about my life. That's when I went to Calder, accepted his offer and got back to living in a responsible way."

Ryder stroked Summer's hand until she looked into his eyes. She saw that the warmth in his gaze equaled the warmth of his strong fingers.

"Aside from Carrie," he said, "I have a lot to thank you for. You got me going again. It was being with you that made me want to be, well...worthy. The truth is," he added softly, "I want you as much today as I did that day. Every time I see you, it's all I can do to keep from coming on to you, from wanting to be close to you again."

Summer tugged her hand from his, but he recaptured it.

"No, no, now, let me finish. What I'm saying is that's precisely why I'm glad you laid down the rules when I found you again. I need you to remind me that we don't know each other. Hell, we could count on one hand the times we've seen each other. And now, with Carrie, I don't ever want to do anything that would jeopardize my being with her. I've already caused enough pain in your life, and I'm already sorry enough about the past. I swear to God, I won't hurt Carrie. Even if that means keeping out of the life you've built here for her."

Finally, in forcing himself to go on, the shame spilled out, too.

"No, to hurt people so badly...to be so out of control as not to remember what I did or didn't do to another human being...to have everyone I know, and even those I don't know, look at me with doubt in their eyes...I mean, I'm grateful to have enough inner certainty of myself to know that I didn't kill. Not even in anger. But my mother, well, every time I looked in her eyes, I saw that she blamed me. On the phone the night of my dad's funeral in New York when I was still in Vermont, she said that she'd never forgive me, and she won't. And aside from her, there will always be others who'll wonder about, who'll downright disbelieve, my innocence."

"But can't you clear your name somehow? It seems to me that if you could get it all out in the open, in front of everyone, then you could finally put it to rest. You say you had only one accuser, Rochelle Waller, but that your lawyers took apart her testimony, if not exactly cleared you. Maybe if you went to her and got her to tell the truth..."

"Are you saying *you* think she lied?"

"What else? It's obvious. If you were engaged to her, and your engagement ended, uh..."

"Yes, as badly as it could have."

"But maybe the years have changed her, too. Maybe she'll reconsider what she said."

"Even if she stood on the rooftops and shouted that she set me up, it wouldn't make any difference. Rochelle Waller is only part of what happened. If I hadn't been so angry, so wild, if I hadn't been so careless as to get to the point of passing out...who knows? Maybe someone who'd mounted the witness stand could have painted a prettier picture of me. Maybe my dad would've lived longer."

"But people don't die of heart attacks because of how other people behave or don't behave. Your dad, if he loved you, wouldn't want you to think that. No, what you need is for Rochelle Waller—"

"No, what I need is for my dad to tell me he loved me, no matter how I screwed up. And he can't do that."

Ryder's words stopped Summer. She wanted to disagree again, but she didn't. This time, she took her hand away from his grasp. She left the stool at the bar and started clearing the dishes.

Ryder glanced at his watch. "Geez, it's after three. I better get going."

Summer didn't want him to go. But she knew he recognized the same impossibilities she did. They felt they knew each other, and yet, in actuality, they didn't. Yes, they wanted to make love again. But once again, it would be irresponsible. Just like the last time. A physical relationship without a foundation of knowing each other could end as quickly as it started. And this time, they had Carrie to think about. If they got to some point that they couldn't talk, Carrie would be the one to suffer.

Ryder went to the couch and slipped on his shoes. Slinging his jacket over his shoulder, suspending it there with his index finger, he met Summer at the door.

"Thanks," he began, and she only shook her head. They were too tired for anything more.

"Don't look for a sitter," he said. "Call me when things get tight and I'll come."

She couldn't help a wry smile. "You're going to retire from Calder Parks now, and be on call for baby-sitting?"

"No, but you'd be surprised how flexible I can make my hours."

She nodded.

They'd come a long way, reached their limit, and all that was left was for him to leave. Summer wanted him to get away before one of them did something to encourage him to stay.

CHAPTER NINE

DRIVING OUT to Fiesta Key after midnight had become second nature to Summer. Parties being what they were, she'd have odd hours and late nights for as long as she stayed in the catering business. And she didn't mind any of that. The big wedding they'd done over the weekend had turned out to be a boon. Ever since then, the phone had been ringing off the hook, and she and Dee weren't complaining about that.

Still, the job she was growing to love, in combination with the turmoil in the rest of her life, was admittedly too much. Worrying about Poppy and the move, thinking all the time about how to deal with Ryder Craig and the way he was affecting her life, feeling extra cautious in regard to Carrie and him preoccupied her.

But that wasn't all of it. And the quiet trip she made out to the key, usually late at night and always alone and after an exhausting day, habitually became the time during which she went over her concerns.

Ryder Craig. On Saturday night he'd opened up to her. He'd touched her deeply. Obviously he trusted her in the same basic way she had always trusted him. Even on that day.

But his telling his story had gone further than trust. It had showed how similar they were. How much they were struggling with those similarities. Having emerged from difficult childhoods, they'd both made a lot of mistakes because of their rebelliousness. In that regard, she could identify with him.

He, too, was working to establish a sense of equilibrium in his life. Neither of them wanted to be driven by the anger and insecurity they'd had built into them by their earlier experiences, and that drew them together as much as it pushed them apart.

Ryder was a man who'd been out of control since he was a child, and her heart went out to the little boy he'd been, despite the very competent male he'd become. Yes, they'd both made mistakes. But yes, they'd also taken control of their lives. Responsibility. Accountability. They wouldn't lose again what they'd worked so hard to establish.

She, better than anyone, respected him for that.

And yet she also had to admit to more than respect and trust and empathy. She had to recognize that the biggest threat to their hard-won ease with each other was their mutual and very physical attraction.

Suddenly an ill-matched set of headlights flashed in her rearview mirror. Right away, her heart began to pound. "Oh, no, not again," she said aloud.

This had to be the same guy. The one she'd encountered at the grocery store, and then on two occasions since. She felt half-angry and half-afraid. "Now what?" she asked herself.

He stayed right behind her. Even when she accelerated, he kept up. It was the same man, all right.

Since they were on a well-lit highway, she decided to change lanes. Maybe if she could pass the truck trailer just ahead of her, she could put it between this jerk and herself.

Stepping on the gas, she felt her van respond. After she'd passed the truck, she eased over in front of it. Forcing herself to loosen her grip on her steering wheel, she still couldn't help glancing into the rearview mirror. Now only the truck followed her.

Her next worry, of course, was that the creep would pull up in the lane beside her and try to get her attention. In that case, she still had the trucker behind her.

But then, oh, God, the truck flashed its lights, signaling for the next exit.

Should she turn off, too?

"No," she said to herself. "You're being ridiculous."

But then, when the truck did turn off and she felt somehow abandoned...the headlights fell into line behind her again.

She had to do something. Switching on her turn signal, she left the highway. She knew this area like the back of her hand, and just a few blocks down from the highway ramp there was a police station.

With a budding sense of triumph, she saw that the minute the creep noticed what she was up to and glimpsed the station, he veered off into the next side street. Once again, she was alone.

Pulling up for a stoplight at a corner, beyond which was the driveway for the police station, she wondered what to do. The light changed, and she pulled into the station lot. She was running on instinct, but she was mad, dammit!

Getting out of the car, she locked it and walked quickly toward the building. She was vaguely aware that there wasn't much activity as she went in the entrance.

She'd never been to a police station before, but she'd seen them in the movies and on television, and this one, with its rows of cluttered desks, had only a few officers on duty.

"Can I help you?"

Feeling a bit foolish, Summer focused on the man at the desk nearest the entrance. His white hair was like soft down, but his gaze was assessing.

"Is anything wrong, lady?"

She stepped up to the desk. "Well, no. I mean, yes."

"Is this an emergency?"

"No, but—"

He handed her some forms. "Take these and have a seat. Fill them out and a detective will be with you soon."

Summer choked out a little laugh. "No, you see . . . I don't need any forms. If I could just talk to you for a minute—"

"Sorry. Take the forms, fill them out and then we'll get someone to talk to you."

Feeling miffed at this officer and mad at the creep who had followed her, Summer went to the chairs that lined a wall and sank down on one. She didn't want to bother with formalities this late, especially when she still felt anxious, but she filled out the forms, anyway.

Then she waited. People came and went routinely. Gradually she calmed down. And although she wanted more than ever to go home and go to bed, she waited.

Finally someone named Detective Green approached her and introduced himself. He was a young, good-looking, African-American man who was all business.

"If you'll come with me, Ms. O'Malley," he said, "we'll see what we can do."

She was feeling that nothing could be done. Her story would sound flimsy.

Still, she followed him, and once they were seated at his desk, he focused on his computer terminal, where he entered even more information. "So tell me what happened," he finally said, looking at her.

"Well, I was driving out to the key, Fiesta Key—"

He nodded complacently.

"And I saw this pair of lights in my rearview mirror. I've had this same guy follow me before, so I recognized him right away."

"By his lights. You recognized him by his lights."

"Yes, the headlights. They're slightly out of alignment so—"

"Right."

"So anyway, I passed a truck so it would be between his pickup and my van, but then the truck turned off and I—"

"And you got off the highway and came here. When he saw what you were doing, he drove off."

"Well, yes."

Summer didn't know whether to be angry or not. Detective Green listened to her. But he didn't really seem to be taking her seriously. What did she expect? Compared to what he usually dealt with, she could have sounded simply overwrought.

Still, she was angry. She had her rights, too, and this creep was infringing on her freedom.

"And you've seen this guy before?" the detective asked.

"Yes. The first time, he was next to me at a stop-light a block or so before I turned off at the grocery store where I shop."

Green nodded, entering into the terminal the street names she gave him. "And did you see him again after that, before tonight?"

"Well, I thought I saw him outside of the church where my friend and I rent a kitchen for our business. It was late at night, but I was sure I saw him, cruising by when I was leaving to go home."

Again, he merely asked for precise information and entered it. "And were there any other occasions? I mean, before tonight?"

"Yes, and that's when I began to figure out what he was doing. I caught sight of his lights—the same lights—in my rearview mirror, just before I got home one night out on the key."

"So," he said, acting as if he'd finally tuned in, "he knows where you live."

To Summer this acknowledgment sounded ominous. She now saw the implications of having a strange man trace her to her home.

"And did you ever get a look at him?"

Detective Green's question slammed at her. "Oh, no. I purposely ignore these types. I never look at them. That only encourages them."

"And there's nothing concrete you can give me. Other than that he has lopsided lights."

Was this silly or wasn't it? "All I know," she said more stoutly than she felt, "is that someone has definitely followed me on three occasions. I see his lights, and..."

"And?"

"Well, when I looked at him the first time—I mean, when I glanced over at him at the stoplight that first time—I remember he seemed very large. He might have been wearing some kind of leather jacket."

"Anything else?"

Summer racked her brain. "No, nothing else."

"So," he said, "just for the record. You haven't ever seen this guy, and you have no description, no plate number. You're not even sure of the truck he drives, except that it's a clunker."

God, it all sounded sillier and sillier. Still, Summer figured she had this one chance, and remembering how she had felt, she stuck to her guns. "I know he's following me."

Detective Green looked at her again. "Even if there's some jerk out there who is following you, there's not much we can do."

"What?"

"I mean, following somebody is not against the law. Now, if he was calling you on the phone, we could arrest him for making harassing phone calls. If he was trespassing, like leaving notes on your door or even coming onto your property, that would also be illegal. If he had threatened bodily harm, or touched you somehow, we could get a restraining order. But this guy's just followed you a couple of times."

"But it's so intimidating. So scary. I don't know what he'll do next."

"He hasn't broken any laws."

Summer faced Detective Green over his desk. His gaze intimated they'd gone as far as they could and he couldn't do anything for her. Then he leaned toward her more confidentially.

"Look," he said, "there are lots of guys out there like this. We hear about them all the time. Except for a very, very small percentage, most of them never do anything but what this one is doing to you. He happened to see you at this stoplight. Then he followed you to the grocery store. From there, he followed you to the church where you spend a good deal of time. He's probably cruised by there dozens of times since, just to get a look at you. He probably lives in the area of the church and grocery store, so it's been easy for him to put together the general pattern of your everyday life. You say your van is clearly marked. But in all likelihood, he doesn't mean to harm you. Only to look."

"Likelihood? That's comforting."

"If you keep ignoring him, he'll probably give up."

"Probably? Likely?" Seeing that Detective Green was doing his best, she relented somewhat. "But *why* is he doing this?"

He shrugged. "Who knows? He probably doesn't have anything else going on in his life. He doesn't have other relationships, at least not meaningful ones with the opposite sex, and he's got all this time and energy to put into following you. From the little we're beginning to understand about this kind of behavior, he's probably feeling some sort of inexplicable connection to you. But take my word for it. We see this kind of thing all the time, and this kind of guy is almost always harmless."

Almost always harmless. Summer knew that Green was trying to make her feel better. "But isn't there anything I can do?"

He shook his head. "I have no official recommendation. Sometimes, however..."

"Sometimes?"

"Sometimes, if a woman feels she has the guts for it, if she confronts him, if she really tells him where to get off and why she won't stand for what he's doing, it's been our experience that the guy generally backs off."

Generally backs off.

"If, however," he said with emphasis, "you do confront this guy, remember that you can be prosecuted if you're the one to get physical. In the end, there's no right decision, no official policy."

Because Summer didn't reply, Green finished the conversation with formalities and a handshake. "My only other recommendation," he added, "is that you find a victims' rights organization. But honestly, Ms. O'Malley, I can almost guarantee that this guy won't do anything more than follow you for a while and then, if you ignore him, he'll give it up."

Almost guarantee.

It was the way Detective Green kept qualifying his reassurances that scared the daylights out of her.

"ARE YOU SURE you're warm enough, Fred?"

"Hell's bells, just a northern nip this morning. Been used to northern nips for years."

Fred shoved a large push broom across the filthy garage floor, so Irma went back to her own broom.

The stuff in the garage was now neatly stacked, and everything of any value was packed in well-marked cartons. Outside in the damp wind, a pile of discards waited for the trash removers. She and Fred had worked hard and their efforts paid off. The grime on her face proved it.

Glancing at Fred again, she saw him twitching uneasily in the salmon-colored sweater that she and a friend had assembled and blocked over the weekend. The darned thing still didn't look right, and she wondered if it didn't bind him through the shoulders somehow. And it looked so very salmon.

"Honestly, Fred," she said, stopping in the middle of the dust they raised, "you don't have to wear that sweater."

"Whaddaya mean?"

"I mean it looks uncomfortable."

"Chilly outside," he grumbled, back at his broom.

Finally Irma acknowledged what was really bugging her. They'd advertised the garage sale for next weekend. Starting on Thursday, actually. Four days, then. Four days to win Fred, and today she seemed further from her goal than when she'd started.

Oh, there'd been times when they'd gotten into discussing fairly serious matters and her hopes had soared. But times like this, times when he retreated into his shell of grumpiness, knocked her flat. His retreats, combined with the pressure of the weekend ahead—well, what excuse would she use for being at the resort after the sale?

Once again, failure threatened.

Once again, they paused, this time to observe the shiny new green car swinging into the resort lot.

"What the hell?"

As the car slowed, Fred went to the door, signaling to the driver to join them inside.

Ryder Craig.

Although over the past few weeks, Fred had talked of little except for his shared baby-sitting stints with

Ryder Craig, Irma hadn't met the young man yet. She waited to form her own judgment.

"Hell," Fred was saying to the newcomer who entered the spottily lit interior, "I didn't recognize you. Where'd you get the car?"

"I traded in my Mercedes for it. I couldn't imagine that a sports car would be good for chauffeuring children, so I bought this one and had a car seat installed."

Seeming pleased, Fred shifted his tall lanky frame and faced Irma. "I don't think you've met Irma, have you?"

Wiping her hands on her oldest pair of jeans, Irma stepped forward to shake hands with Ryder Craig.

"No, we haven't met," he said, "but I sure have heard about you, Ms. McGinty."

That sudden smile. It dazzled.

Well, here was something she couldn't wait to share with the girls. How often did any of them meet a man like this? She wished she could have taken a picture.

Indeed, Ryder Craig was what the girls would call a heartthrob. Occasionally one or the other of them would slip into the newer term *hunk,* but Ryder Craig could set any heart, young or not so young, racing.

But Fred remained Irma's concern, and after a short stay in the light of that transforming smile, she refocused on the older man. He'd gone on to show his visitor some of his most prized junk.

"What brings you out here on a Monday mornin'?" Fred finally asked, piquing Irma's own curiosity.

Ryder Craig glanced at his watch. "Summer called me at work. They burned the vol-au-vent at the church kitchen, and she needs to buy some stuff at the store."

"The vol . . . ?" Fred was lost.

"Patty shells."

Fred shrugged.

"Anyway, Summer said you were working in the garage, and she hated to pull you away to stay with Carrie. Normally, she said, she'd take her along, but she'll be in a rush, and you know how Carrie's having trouble with transitions."

"Transitions?"

"Yes, er—"

"Well, well," Fred interjected, brushing aside another explanation, "you'd better get going if Summer's waitin' on you."

"Yeah, but I'll come back with Carrie. I'm making a trip to the bank, and I thought this would be a good time to try the car seat."

Fred glanced at Irma. "We'll be finishing here soon, but if you need me, I'll be around."

"Thanks," Ryder's last smile for Irma was tinged with something tentative. "Nice meeting you, Ms. McGinty. Wish me luck. This is my first time solo."

Irma felt an emotional tug. Although Fred had told her about Ryder Craig's interest in Carrie, Irma easily read his doubts about his ability to handle the child. And Carrie could be a handful.

Still, there was something awfully sweet about this Ryder Craig. Something vulnerable. He was much deeper than a mere heartthrob. She couldn't wait to explore the possibilities with someone who'd appreciate all the ins and outs. With someone aside from Fred.

So THAT'S Irma McGinty, Ryder thought absently, maneuvering the new Volvo down to Summer's bungalow. Ms. McGinty was an odd little woman.

Still, she seemed more than merely the starchy spinster type, and Fred certainly mentioned her often enough. Ryder wondered what was going on between the pair. He thought that Fred himself would be hard-pressed to explain their situation.

After he'd reached her place and parked the car, Ryder knocked on Summer's door. She let him into an unusually messy living room. "Sorry about this," she said, comfortable enough with him now to let her harried state show.

"I told you I'd drop everything and come," he said.

She moved away from him, pushing a clip into her strawberry blond hair. She was so beautiful, but he had to remind himself that she was off limits.

"What are those?" she asked, indicating the three books he carried.

"Oh, I've been reading up on separation anxiety. I thought Carrie might be upset when you leave so I came prepared."

"She shouldn't give you any trouble with that."

"Yeah, but if she does cry, I'll know what to do. Most experts agree that you should sympathize with her. You know, tell her you understand how she feels."

"Sounds good to me." Carrie toddled from around the eating bar. She wore diapers and a T-shirt.

"I'm afraid she's only half dressed," Summer said, slipping on her own shoes. "But she's had her bath, so don't let the yuck around her mouth and on her hands deceive you."

Carrie stood beside him, smiling and extending the muck in her hand in his direction. Her smile captivated him, and he picked her up.

"Umm, looks good," he said, lying through his teeth. "What is it?"

Carrie grinned, pressing him to share whatever it was.

Summer sent him a wry smile. "Don't feel you can't refuse. Even I don't share her food."

"What is it?" he repeated.

"Cookie," Carrie said.

When he took the offering in his mouth, he knew it wasn't a cookie. Summer smiled. "Now that's above and beyond the call of duty," she said.

"Cookie," Carrie repeated, grinning.

Summer gathered her things—a jacket, her purse, more papers. "Actually, it was the remains of her toast."

Ryder swallowed. The toast was gone. And he'd learned another lesson. Never be cajoled, even by a smile, into sharing Carrie's food.

"Just wash her up and finish dressing her. You'll find her clothes on her changing table. She won't need anything to eat until lunch, and I should be back by then. The number at the church is on the list by the phone with the ones for her pediatrician and the poison center."

"The poison center?"

"Everything's baby-proof, but you know—safety first."

Summer dashed for her sunglasses and a baseball cap on the couch. "Just watch the bathroom."

Ryder's heart skipped a beat. "What?"

"Her latest game is unrolling the toilet paper."

Relief surged through him. No mystery waited in the bathroom. "Okay."

But his heart hammered when Summer, just about to leave, strode back in their direction. She stood close and kissed Carrie's cheek.

"See you soon, Boop," she whispered intimately. When her gaze caught Ryder's, he yearned in a way he never had.

But she'd become all business. "I shouldn't be too long," she said, finally closing the door.

Noticing the sudden quiet, Ryder looked at Carrie. He was afraid she'd cry, but she didn't. She studied his face. She was getting to know him. Her finger touched the cleft in his chin. She was so much like him that it was hard to believe.

"Say Daddy," he whispered to his child.

"Dada."

Ryder's heart lurched. He hadn't thought she'd say it, but the word had simply popped out. Still, her big green eyes regarded him intently.

Fatherhood humbled him. "Kiss me, Carrie, like you do Mommy."

"No." She shook her head vigorously.

Wondering if she was being contrary, if he dared upset the apple cart, Ryder passed his lips lightly across Carrie's plump cheek.

She smiled. But she also took his action for granted. She was accustomed to being kissed, to being loved. She smelled so good.

"I love you," he said for the first time. Tears stood in his eyes. "We've got a lot of years ahead of us, and I promise to prove I love you, Carrie."

Again, she studied him. Of course she didn't understand the words, but maybe she caught his mood.

Rather than worry her, than set her off, Ryder cleared his throat and smiled. "Well, if you won't kiss me, I guess we'll wash up. And then," he explained, carrying her toward the bathroom, "we'll get dressed. And then I'll put you in the new car seat. Everything's going to be just fine. I promise. But please, Carrie," he added, sneaking another quick peck at her cheek, "this is my first time, so be gentle."

Fortunately their round continued the way Ryder had promised. He felt so elated that when they hit the bank, when they slid into position in front of the drive-up teller's window, he felt jubilant.

The woman who waited on him, peering down at them from her glass cage, even commented on what a beautiful child he had. While waiting for her to complete the transaction, he turned on the windshield wipers because of the drifting drizzle, then patted Carrie in the car seat next to him.

"So far, so good," he said to her.

She grinned, fondling the fuzzy ears of her pink rabbit.

When the deposit slips came back, Carrie was suddenly fascinated by the envelope. Before he could figure out what the unusual lump in the envelope was, a red sucker in a cellophane wrapper tumbled onto the console between them.

She looked at it.

He looked at it.

She pointed.

At the hard honk from behind him, Ryder edged the car out of the lot. On his way to the stoplight, he swept up the cherry pop and stuffed it in his shirt pocket.

Carrie's concentrated stare, her impatient kick, told him he was in trouble. He fought down the rising panic.

"Okay, okay, we both know you saw that. But it's gone now, and—"

She kicked and said something as clear as it was unintelligible. She wanted the sucker, but he also knew Summer didn't give her candy.

"Geez," he muttered, focusing on driving, on reaching the haven of the bungalow.

But Carrie wasn't about to forget. She frowned at him, stretching a plump hand in his direction.

Ryder swept up the car phone and asked the operator for Fred's number. By the time he heard the welcome sound of the man's voice, Carrie was wailing.

"We just stopped at the bank and the teller put a lollipop in the return envelope. Carrie's seen it and—what?" In order to hear Fred, he plugged his ear. "Give it to her? But—"

"It's too late for anything but givin' it to her," he heard Fred say. "Should've hidden it if you didn't want her to have it."

"But I didn't know... Never mind. Thanks. We'll be there soon." Sure enough, when Ryder handed her the sucker, Carrie settled nicely into her seat.

Ryder was appalled. "Cute as a button," he muttered, "but as unscrupulous as a bandit." When she smiled, though, he thought even unscrupulous was all right. At least in her case. She was damned adorable.

"Well?" Fred said when Ryder answered the door back at the bungalow. "Sounds quiet now. Gave it to her, huh?"

"What else could I do?"

Ryder made room and Fred squeezed in. With bright red lips, Carrie sat on the living room floor in triumph.

"Dada," she said.

Ryder looked at Fred. He wondered how the older man would take this.

"Yeah," Fred said, sliding his hands into his back pockets and regarding the child levelly, "he's your daddy, all right. A sucker through and through."

Pleased at Fred's acceptance, Ryder found some words. "I, uh, remembered Summer saying no candy, and I . . ."

Fred appeared downright sheepish. "Hell, how do you think Boop recognized the damned pop? I've been sneaking 'em to her for as long as I've been taking her to the bank with me."

Ryder couldn't suppress his sudden chuckle. And then Fred laughed out loud. When Carrie joined in, acting silly, they laughed all the harder. They shared a secret—a secret rebellion against Summer's sweet despotism. If Fred had been one of his own generation, Ryder decided he could've expected a high five.

BY THE TIME Summer returned to the bungalow, lunchtime had come and gone. The day that had started out with a cold front, slumping in on gray clouds and stiff breezes, had settled into a steady downpour. She liked the rain—the occasional shift in the otherwise fairly predictable weather.

She felt guilty. She'd told Ryder she'd be back by lunchtime, but she was running late. She had disliked taking him up on his offer to sit, but he'd said he would, and Carrie and he had their rights to each other.

Still, she was cautious about what she'd find on returning to the bungalow, and she quietly opened the door. She'd expected some kind of fuss with Carrie, so she wasn't prepared for what she saw.

Because the bar was high, Ryder, who stood beyond it at the sink in the galley kitchen doing dishes, appeared naked—except for the dish towel across one shoulder. The long expanse of his back, brown and muscled and turned in her direction, was enough to startle her. When he swiveled to look at her, she felt herself flush. "I-is everything all right?"

"Great," he said in a whisper, obviously pleased. "She had lunch nice as pie and went down for a nap with a smile on her face. I tucked her in with no problem." He tugged the dish towel down to wipe his sudsy hands.

She tried not to stare. "I'm sorry I'm late."

She tossed her baseball cap and her other trappings onto the bar, and picked up a dish to dry. "It's all right," he said. "I squared everything with Calder. And, uh, about my shirt. Carrie tossed her carrots at me, so I hope you don't mind that I stuck it in the washer. It should be dry any minute."

"No, I don't mind."

She didn't mind that he wore only jeans or that his sexy presence dominated her house. Not much.

"I, uh, have a confession," he said.

"Oh?"

"When I went to the bank, well, Carrie had a cherry sucker."

Summer grinned wryly. "Join the club. While I haven't caught him yet, I suspect that Poppy's been letting her have suckers at the bank for months now."

When Ryder chuckled, then turned to hang up the towel, she tried to divert herself from watching him by putting the dishes away. But when he stood near her, with that gunmetal-gray light coming in through the windows and defining every perfect inch of his upper torso—

The dryer buzzed. Summer started. Ryder moved to pull out his shirt and then to pull it on. She walked away, into the living room, and he followed.

"I want to thank you for listening to me on Saturday night. To finally tell someone my story meant a lot to me. In fact, this morning I called my family's lawyer."

Summer sank onto the couch. Making no move to leave, Ryder stood in front of her, his shirt unbuttoned.

"Don't get me wrong," he said. "I still don't think I can clear my name, but I asked him to send for the transcripts of my trial. It's more that I can't recall much of what happened. I was so worried about my dad at the time that everything went by me. Anyway," he added on a sigh, "the lawyer told me the transcripts will run to about two thousand pages and I'm hoping I'll find something in them that will help me remember."

Summer searched for an encouraging word. "I'd like to read the transcripts, too," she surprised herself by saying.

He looked at her for a long moment. "All right." He also sat down on the couch and stared into her eyes. "I asked this lawyer about you, too."

"About me?"

"Well, about the guy who's following you. The more I think about the creep, the more it bothers me.

Of course, this lawyer isn't familiar with Florida law, but—"

"I, too, have a confession."

His gaze darkened. His mouth tightened. "That guy's following you again, isn't he?"

"Yes, last night—"

"Why didn't you tell me when I first got here? Why didn't you call me last night?"

"It was late. After we'd finished working. Anyway, I went by a police station—"

"I can't believe you didn't tell me."

Summer didn't know whether to be angry or not. Ryder Craig, looking as if he'd take the room apart, was hard to resist. Mainly because she didn't want to worry Poppy or Dee, she let down her guard with him. Telling him what had happened at the police station made her feel better.

Ryder felt worse. "Dammit, I could wring this guy's neck. What in the hell's the matter with him? Scaring you like this. And me, too, dammit!" Obviously thinking what she was thinking, that Carrie was asleep, he got a grip on himself. "And the police say essentially what my lawyer said. Except for that bit about confronting this jerk. My God," he added, "don't you even consider confronting him."

Although Summer hadn't made any decision about that, she didn't like Ryder telling her what to do. But before she could say that, he tugged a cylinder of Mace from a rear pocket and handed it to her. "Here. I was going to give you this, anyway. But not, and I repeat *not,* so you can confront this creep. You use it *only* if he comes at you."

Once again, Summer wasn't given a chance to reply.

"I looked into getting a gun—"

"A gun? My God, no. I won't even consider a gun. Guns disgust me. And besides, Detective Green—"

"The hell with Detective Green."

Summer saw that they both needed time to collect themselves and to think. She liked it that Ryder was concerned, could even appreciate it. But she'd make her own decisions about this in her own good time.

Taking the Mace couldn't hurt, though, and she said as much. "I only ask," she added, "that you don't tell my grandfather or Dee about this. In fact, don't tell anyone. I have a right to deal with this first."

Grudgingly, Ryder nodded. He also grew calmer. "Just promise to call *me,* will you? Tell *me* what's going on. I won't be left out of this. If you want me to drive you—"

"No, you're not going to drive me anywhere. This guy is not disrupting my life any more than he already has. Detective Green says he's probably harmless, and I'm going to assume he's right."

"The hell with Detective Green," Ryder muttered again, rubbing the back of his neck. "I feel so damned helpless...so frustrated. Just don't go confronting this nut. That's the stupidest advice I've ever heard."

"It wasn't advice. Detective Green—"

"If he can't protect you, then the hell with him."

"No," she said. "That's not fair to him."

"Not fair to *him?*"

"Yes. He did his best by me. You have to remember that officially he has no policy to go by, no law. He was as helpful as he could be under the circumstances." Since Ryder obviously didn't have a reply for this, she went on. "Anyway, I want to handle this on my own. Although I haven't thought it all the way through yet, I know I want to handle it. It's my decision."

"That's ridiculous. There's no reason for you to handle this on your own."

"No. You're wrong. There is a reason. More than a single reason, in fact."

Right away, Summer knew she'd gone too far.

He stood over her, his eyes drilling into hers, and she saw she'd have to tell him more than she wanted to. Whether or not she liked it, Ryder Craig had become embroiled in this aspect of her life, as well.

Not knowing where to start, not wanting to, she walked to a window. Outside it still rained in sheets, and her halting words were directed more to the gray day.

"I know what's happening," she admitted softly. "Where I couldn't see it before, I can now. This is all tied in to my feelings about how I look, about how I attract attention, uh, men, in ways and at times I don't want to. It's all locked in to my mother's expectations for me. She built those on my appearance alone. I still resent that, and I know I shouldn't. I mean, there are certainly worse problems for people to have than attracting attention. But it's such an intrusion."

Swinging away from the window, she faced Ryder.

"To be judged on your looks alone discounts the rest of what you are. I wanted my mother to see me, the real me, and all she did was preach about how to get ahead on my looks. I got so sick to death of it that at eighteen I married the high-school football captain, no less.

"I mean, just to show her, I went out and did the stupidest thing I could do. Sean, too, was interested *only* in my looks. Not that I blame him. We were both too young.

"Oh, that's not it, either. I'm over all that. It's just that I thought I was doing better. Wearing that damned tux, I thought I was really putting myself out there and developing a sense of balance, even a sense of humor, about how people react to me. But now this guy comes along and makes me feel all the insecurity I thought I was outgrowing. I don't know if I'm explaining myself right, if you can see—"

"I see." Ryder's voice was firm. "I understand."

Yes, Summer saw that he did. For the first time, she had someone who would listen to her without making her think she should just be glad she was beautiful. A sense of relief washed over her.

"If I could just handle this with confidence, I could finally make peace with my mom. Do you see?"

"More than you know."

At that instant, Summer longed for Ryder to enclose her in his arms and make love to her again. Physical intimacy would be as natural now as it had been on that first day. Because she'd gone over and over her memories of that day, she remembered him well. Now she longed to touch him.

Looking into his eyes, she saw his thoughts ran along a similar line. But he moved abruptly to step into his shoes, to do up the buttons on his shirt. As they had agreed over the weekend, they weren't going to act on impulse. They'd made mistakes, and they wouldn't make the same ones again. Ryder was hanging on to control. Hanging on for them both.

When he paused in the doorway, with the rain falling beyond the screen of the porch, he turned back. She was there, just behind him, she realized. She yearned for his kiss, and even as she thought he would briefly press his lips to hers, he didn't.

"Thanks," he finally whispered. "Thanks for listening ... for telling me."

Obviously afraid of more than that—as afraid as she was—he turned and left. Summer shut the door. Leaning against it, she let her knees give way. She slid down the door onto her haunches.

For the first time, she noticed there wasn't a toy on the floor or a thing out of order. Ryder had not only pitched in and watched over their daughter, he'd done what he could to be of assistance to her.

And the little can of Mace on the table by the couch—yes, he'd been thinking about her the way she thought about him. Constantly. With concern.

CHAPTER TEN

THURSDAY WAS the first day of the outdoor sale to dispose of some of Poppy's junk.

After the initial rush of early, even rude, buyers who regularly made the garage-sale rounds, other more familiar and more welcome people drifted by. Irma had recruited several of her friends to man the tables. They arrived with sunscreens and golf visors, with deck chairs and sun umbrellas, to sit and chat and assist as they could.

But Fred's friends, and Summer's friends, friends from the old days when they'd shared the resort life along Fiesta Key, came as well. Some came to help, some to buy, some just to hash over old times.

At first, Summer worried about her grandfather's reaction. As the afternoon wore on, however, Poppy loosened up to the point of acting as a host. When Summer saw him bargaining with a buyer, she knew he enjoyed the fray. All in all, it was a happy occasion made even more pleasant by the Florida sunshine and gulf breeze.

During a temporary lull at their table, Dee and Summer rearranged an odd collection of dishes and pots and pans from the resort's commercial kitchen, from Poppy's kitchen and even from Summer's bungalow galley.

"Uh-oh," Dee said, nudging Summer. "I think Jeffy has Carrie cornered over there."

Summer's gaze followed Dee's across the gravel lot to two ladies talking. Naturally, the women were oblivious to Carrie's plight—or rather, to Jeffy's.

"Frankly, Dee, Carrie's been asking for it all morning. She keeps sneaking off with his stuff, and he must be ready to strangle her."

"Yeah, well, it's the strangling I'm worried about."

When Dee would have acted, Summer restrained her with a hand on her forearm. "Wait a minute. Poppy sees them. Let him take care of it."

The pair observed as Fred sorted out the problem. Jeffy finally went off with his possessions, and Carrie was scooped up on Fred's arm. When he went back to the people he'd been talking to, Summer and Dee exchanged glances.

"He seems to be doing fine," Dee said.

"I'm glad. I've been concerned about him."

"I know—you're worried about his adjustment. What about the house? Does he like it?"

"He says he does. He'll have the one end with its bedroom and bath, and Carrie and I'll take the two bedrooms and bath at the other end. I know he's not interested in the pool, but his real problem is leaving the beach. We both love the beach. Living by an ocean becomes part of you."

Summer loved the gulf. The worst aspect of the move was leaving it. The rest she rather looked forward to. Especially to the space they'd gain at the house she was in the process of buying.

When Summer looked at Dee again, Dee grinned. "Isn't this fun?"

Summer smiled wryly. "Loads. As if we didn't have enough to do already. But really, Dee, it's great of you to help. And to take the party on Saturday night."

"Let's not start that. I mean, what about those two nights last week when Jeffy had the flu and you looked after him when I had to be out?"

"Okay, you're right. But still, I'm doing the grocery shopping tonight. I have Poppy set up for sitting, and I think Ryder's even driving out."

When someone wandered up to check out an old double boiler, Dee switched into high gear, loving the haggling Summer avoided. Summer thought she couldn't have found a better partner, a better friend.

When the transaction was over, both Dee and the customer considered themselves the winner. "Fun, huh?" Dee insisted.

But then Irma hustled over with a return from a not-so-satisfied buyer. She set the large pot Summer had sold earlier on the table.

"I'm sorry, Summer," Irma said, looking apologetic.

"I know. We gotta expect some returns."

"Not me," Dee declared with a grin. "Everyone who walks away from this table thinks they've made the deal of the century."

When Irma chuckled, Summer found her response unusual. Although the display of Irma's many friends on this day would deny it, Summer and Irma had just never connected. Probably because of the strict schedules they kept.

Anyway, Summer was grateful for the way Irma had hung in there for Poppy. Not for the first time, she wondered how Irma felt about her grandfather. Could the woman's attachment represent more than affection after years of loyalty?

"I understand the two of you have your hair done on Saturday mornings," Irma said.

"Yes," Dee replied. "I have a friend with a shop, and Summer and I have a standing appointment there."

"Well, I've always noticed how nice the both of you look, and . . . not that our ages don't make a big difference, but I thought I might try this person of yours."

Dee was delighted. "Sure, sure."

"I've always thought that to match my hair and glasses to my eyes—all gray, you see—was . . . well, I'm beginning to wonder if I haven't been settling for what's easy."

Dee loved nothing more than fixing people up, than making new friends, than involving herself in someone's business. "Oh, gosh, yes. I mean, there's nothing like a makeover, and my friend is wonderful with hair and suggestions. Why don't you come with Summer and me? We'd love to have you, and I'm sure my friend can squeeze you in."

"Even on a Saturday morning?"

"Oh, yeah, yeah."

As Dee talked about the shops along the mall where the hairdresser was located, Irma seemed absorbed. But Summer's attention was elsewhere.

Ryder had arrived.

She watched him walk across the drive toward Poppy, who stood with friends, keeping an eye on Carrie.

Carrie loved the excitement as much as Dee did. But it became obvious the child loved Ryder more. The instant she saw him, she bounced from one foot to the other, barely containing her joy. When she reached for him, and he caught her up and planted a kiss on her cheek, Summer was taken aback.

For better or for worse, Ryder Craig was in her life. He was good for Carrie, and that decided it. Although relinquishing even a few of her sweet responsibilities was hard, Summer now saw she had no choice. Carrie and Ryder had a right to the relationship that was clearly building between them, and with Poppy beside them as well, the three made a touching family group. Summer didn't know where she fitted in.

"Well," said Irma, forcing Summer back to her conversation with Dee, "thanks so much. I'm already looking forward to Saturday morning. See you then, too, Summer."

Summer smiled and nodded, and once the smaller woman was out of earshot, Dee whispered to her. "You don't think I pushed her too hard, do you? I mean, when she started talking about changing her hair color, softening it a bit, I itched to make other suggestions."

"No, I think she appreciated what you said. The two of you might even have fun on Saturday morning."

"Aren't you coming along?"

"Just to have my hair trimmed. I mean, I'm not working the party on Saturday night, but as soon as I can, I have to be here for the sale. We advertised for eleven, you know."

"Well, eleven should be plenty of time. Besides, I'll have prep work..."

Dee's words trailed off, and Summer knew why. She'd spied Ryder across the crowd. He still stood with Poppy, still propped Carrie on an arm, but he looked so good he would have been noticeable anywhere.

"Wow," Dee whispered under her breath.

Fortunately, they had another customer, and Summer was let off the hook. Ryder Craig was simply so attractive he drew even the attention of a faithfully married woman like Dee.

At last, he came toward Summer. With Carrie on his arm, he smiled that sudden, startling, absorbing smile. "Looks like a good day," he said.

Although Dee tallied her sale, Summer was conscious of her friend's desire for an introduction. Dee had seen Ryder, but now she was ready to accept him the way Poppy had, as a part of their lives. Carrie was a good reason to include him.

"This is so much fun," Dee remarked to Ryder, following Summer's introduction. "You really should jump in and enjoy it."

He chuckled. "Actually, I've had something crop up or I just might." He turned to Summer. "My brother called this morning. He says he and my sister-in-law would like to drive down to Sarasota tomorrow afternoon. They want to spend some time with me and, if possible, meet Carrie."

Summer had to admit she was stunned. Not only had she thought Ryder's brother would be unlikely to show up, particularly to meet Carrie, but she'd also assumed that Ryder and Vance had a strained relationship at best.

"Sure, sure." She forced herself to concentrate. "You can have her anytime this weekend. I'll be stuck here."

"Oh, but they'd like to meet you, too," he said, adding to her confusion.

"Me?"

He shifted uncomfortably.

"Well!" Dee grinned, oblivious to their unease. "This is working out wonderfully. Summer's taking off Saturday night, and things here should slow down on Sunday."

Summer sent Dee an icy glare. But Dee was undaunted. "This'll be great."

Ryder, of course, read Summer better than almost anyone. "Fred offered one of the bungalows. I mean, if I can't find anything else for them this late. I'd have them stay with me, but my cruiser sleeps only two."

Summer's flush rose to the roots of her hair. Who better than she knew about the sleeping accommodations in his cruiser?

"Well, this is better and better," Dee said. "Summer and I can set up one of the bungalows. We're selling as much of the furniture as we can, but I'm sure we'll find at least a bed and a card table."

Ryder smiled. "If it comes to that, I'll do what I can, too. But let's hope I locate a room for them someplace else."

"Yes, let's do," Summer heard herself say dryly.

At Dee's disapproving glance, Summer did her best to recover. "Sorry. Please bring them here. We'll scrounge up something."

Oh, God. She couldn't so much as picture entertaining Ryder's brother and sister-in-law. She knew the affluence they were used to, and though the Flamingo Resort was quaint, even charming in its own way, she couldn't imagine anything worse than welcoming Ryder's family, especially this weekend when everyone and his uncle was in and out.

Looking at Carrie, sitting happily with her arms around Ryder's neck, looking at Dee, whose glances said she should behave herself, Summer knew she had to put her own mixed feelings aside.

THE GARAGE SALE was more exhausting than Summer had imagined. It lasted until after sunset, and she wanted badly to go to her bungalow and collapse. Still, she'd told Dee that she'd do the grocery shopping for their weekend party. Poppy was ready to baby-sit, and then Ryder showed up to keep him company over cards.

When she was showered and on her way out the door, Ryder offered to drive her to the store. What he really meant was that their discussion about the man following her still bothered him. But he also knew better than to make a point of her refusal, so he watched silently as she got into her van.

Summer was hesitant to leave the resort. She'd been so busy setting up the sale that she hadn't gone out any evenings on her own. Now even the familiar drive and routine didn't help her escalating nervousness.

Tugging her baseball cap down, she wondered what good her little subterfuge would do. Nor could her worn slacks and old sandals, her chambray shirt and bulky cardigan mean much as a disguise. By now, the creep knew her van as well as he did her looks, and she kept scanning the traffic behind her in her rearview mirror.

She tried to divert herself with taped music, even with conjectures about the coming visit from Ryder's brother and sister-in-law. Tomorrow, Ryder had said.

But thoughts of Ryder also reminded her of the can of Mace in her purse, which rested on the other seat. He'd been worried, kind to get the Mace. But she couldn't imagine herself confronting the creep, much less spraying him in the face with it.

Glad to get to the grocery store, she did her shopping, still in her disguise, as she'd grown to consider her old clothes. Fortunately, people in Florida became so accustomed to sunglasses that she was sure hers remained inconspicuous, even late in the evening as she pushed her cart back into the lot and loaded her van.

Driving quickly to the church, she unloaded the groceries, then got sidetracked into a few chores that might help Dee. But eventually she had to face the idea of climbing back in her van and going home.

Outside the church, the streets remained quiet, and again she proceeded as quickly and calmly as she could. Really, she didn't know why the guy intimidated her the way he did. As Detective Green had pointed out, the creep merely followed her. What's more—Green had also said—she could expect that would be all he'd do until he got tired of his game and stopped.

But Detective Green's qualifying remarks stuck with her, too.

The creep's type was *almost always harmless,* she thought, maneuvering the van along the highway out to the key.

They *generally backed off* if confronted, she told herself, passing the exit for the police station.

Detective Green *almost guaranteed* the guy would only follow her.

Fortunately, she reached her last leg. The bridge for Fiesta Key would soon come into sight, and—

The lights were behind her.

Her heart began to pound. But yes, askew headlights were right there in her rearview mirror.

"Stay calm, stay calm. There's no other traffic, but stay on the road."

Gripping the wheel, she concentrated on controlling the van. The urge to floor the accelerator struck her as especially dangerous.

"Yes," she said, looking at the lopsided lights, "he's picked a good spot this time. But there's the bridge."

When she saw his lights dangerously close behind her, when she felt his truck nudge the bumper of her van, she feared panicking.

"You creep!"

Again he nudged her. And again it was all she could do to keep from swerving.

Frightened, shaking, she anticipated the bridge. The guardrails seemed to rush by, keeping her on the straight and narrow until she left the bridge and its lights and entered the dark and isolated area on the other side.

Now, she thought, now the stretch of old road to the Flamingo Resort. That's all she had to go. And yes, the creep still followed her.

Her thoughts ran on, as did her heartbeat. Leading him home had to be stupid.

But he already knew where she lived.

What she needed now was safety.

Anger took over. Yes, she was scared. Yes, she felt helpless. But, oh, she was furious! To use only the can of Mace in her purse didn't seem nearly the punishment he deserved.

Home. She was nearly there. But she had to keep her wits about her, too. She had to manage the turn into the softer gravel driveway without spinning out of control.

She did veer too quickly into the driveway and nearly ran into a pair of headlights that blazed into her eyes right in front of her.

Ryder. He maneuvered his car to speak through their open windows.

"Are you all right?"

"Yes, yes. But that guy followed me again."

He pulled off. "Stay right where you are! Don't move!"

Feeling her whole body begin to shake, Summer doubted she could do anything except what he'd ordered. She watched his rear lights as he gunned his engine. Gravel, spinning off his wheels, hit her van, then rained in a torrent as he squealed out of the resort driveway and onto the road.

Left in the sudden quiet, Summer tried to think. Where was the creep? Had he turned off? He couldn't have turned off. Not this far down the old resort road. He had to have . . . what? Turned around somehow?

Inhaling deeply, she released the wheel. With the panic draining away and leaving her limp, she considered Ryder's safety. Then lights came up in her mirror yet again—this time, Ryder's lights.

Glad he was back, she heard him stop and, abandoning his idling car, come up beside her window. Without words, he opened the door of her van and pulled her into his arms.

She could feel the tension in his body. But matching his grasp on her, she also felt his warmth. Oh, God, he felt so good. So strong. So capable.

Oh, God, she needed him.

Taking off her baseball hat, he tossed it on the seat of the van. In the stark light of his headlights he searched her eyes. "Are you all right?"

She nodded. "I'm fine. He just scared me. And you? I guess you didn't . . . ?"

"No. I saw the last of him just as the bridge closed down and he got away."

"No description, then. No plate number."

"No," he repeated softly, grimly.

When Summer trembled, Ryder loosened their embrace and took her hand. "Come on, you can't go back to the bungalow like this."

"Poppy?"

"He fell asleep on the couch, so I left. Carrie's fine, too."

Keeping her hand tightly in his, he tugged her to his idling car. There, he reached through the front window to switch off the lights and engine. The night enclosed them almost cozily.

Still tugging her along with a warm grasp on her hand, Ryder opened the rear door of his car and urged her inside. She sank onto the seat with a sigh. After closing the door, Ryder sat back, still holding her hand and obviously letting the quiet settle him, too.

When he spoke, however, his words were at odds with the calm of his voice. "If that creep were here, I think I'd kill him."

Summer chuckled.

"No, really I would."

"I know what you're saying. I was really afraid out there on the road. I panicked."

He squeezed her hand.

"What I can't figure out," she said, "is what motivates him. *Why* is he doing this?"

Again Ryder squeezed her hand. She felt him looking at her in the darkness. "You gotta face it, Summer," Ryder said softly. "Despite your little disguises, and don't try to deny them, you're a walking, talking turn-on for most guys. It's just that some guys handle turn-ons better than others. Hell, not that I didn't handle it the worst of anybody."

Summer knew he was referring to that day when they'd met and made love. They were both on track now. They had their lives in control. At least until this creep business. Yes, she'd been reduced to hiding herself, and she wasn't proud of that.

"I guess there's no point in calling Detective Green," Ryder said, heaving a sigh.

"No, he can't do anything. He said so. Besides, I've embarrassed myself enough over this. The first time I saw this guy, I actually turned to a security guard at the grocery store."

"I still think I should drive you where you need to go in the evenings."

"No, no, I won't do that. I've retreated enough because of this jerk. Besides, Poppy would wonder what was going on."

Summer absorbed the quiet for a minute. "No," she said. "More and more, I realize this is something I have to face on my own."

"If you're going to talk about confronting this creep, I won't stand for that."

"No, I don't necessarily mean confronting him. It's more like learning to stay calm when he starts doing his thing. He's really predictable, you know. Detective Green says that if I ignore him, he'll probably get bored and stop."

"No," he added more firmly, "the only answer is for me to drive you back and forth to work. Like you say, he'll give up, and then—"

"No, you're not driving me. I'm not giving up any more of my independence." Summer saw that she and Ryder could have gone on arguing, but she didn't want to argue. She'd decided what she'd do next, and she thought Ryder could tell that, too.

This time she'd told him she wouldn't be dissuaded. But she also wanted to convey her gratitude to him. He really cared. As in the past, she felt close to him. Especially in the dark and with her hand enclosed in the warmth of his.

"Like I was trying to tell you the other day," she said, forcing herself, "what I'm feeling has a lot more to do with my past than with this guy. I don't know exactly how to explain it, but my mother made such a big deal out of my looks that I almost hated her for it. And for not even trying to look at the real me. Yes, I do tend to play down my looks. As you said, to disguise myself. And I don't feel good about that, either. But I just can't get around feeling that people should accept me for who I am, for what I've been doing with my life, rather than just for my appearance."

Because Ryder's silence encouraged her, she made herself say what she'd never told another human soul.

"From what my mother used to tell me, I began to think that the *only* thing I had going for me was my looks. Still, inside myself, I thought surely there should be more. I certainly felt more than merely beautiful. But gradually, those truths of hers became a constant fear for me. I mean, I'd ask myself, 'What's important about me?' Or, 'Doesn't what I do or feel or think count for anything?' Later, when I started dating, I really questioned myself. My value, in particular. Yes, I've had guys who took me out only to show me off to their buddies as their latest conquest. I've dated businessmen who wanted only an armpiece. Guys that might have interested me wouldn't approach me because they thought I probably wouldn't be attracted to anyone who was less than my own physical match. At the age of fourteen, I had an older man come on to me when I 'started to bloom,' as he said, and he scared me to death.

"And then there are the people who use your looks against you. Their attitude is to keep you from getting by on good looks alone. As if I want to. Those people love it when you goof up or lose. And the Blond Bimbo Syndrome. There's a winner. As far as some people are concerned, being blond is a guarantee that you're either brainless or sexually loose.

"Other women can be especially cruel. After all, women are taught by our society to compete with one another. Especially in the looks department. Some women won't even give me a chance. I had high-school friends who turned on me just because they got jealous and petty about some juvenile behavior on the part of a boyfriend, for pete's sake. Often older women, supposedly grown women, don't want to hear you complain about your problems. They can't imagine you even have problems because you seem to have so much else. In those cases, I'm always tempted to put myself down just to make the woman feel comfortable.''

Summer sighed in the darkness. "In that way, Dee's been really good for me. She accepts me for who I am, and I love her so much. She's my first real friend.''

Having finally opened up, and sensing that Ryder sympathized, Summer confided the last.

"That day, I mean, when I was swimming and I thought about suicide...''

Ryder's stillness coaxed her on.

"It had been over a week since my mother's funeral, and at her funeral, an older man, a married supposed friend of the family, took me aside and said he'd see to it that I was taken care of...that he'd even set aside some money for Poppy if I'd move into this apartment he had, and, as he put it, make myself available to him. That day, when you rescued me, I was thinking my mother was right. And I hated her for being right. I hated that old family friend, and I hated myself most of all. But you—you never once said I was beautiful.''

Ryder stirred as if to take her in his arms.

"No," she said, still hanging on to his hand, still grateful for the darkness. "You've told me you've never regretted that day, and I don't, either. It changed my life. It changed me for the better. It gave me Carrie. But you're right, you know. I can't risk the stability I've established, both for Carrie and myself, without being really sure this time. And the truth is, I—''

"Yes," he said for her. "You know as well as I do that I'm not sure of myself. You met me as a dropout, and you think...hell, *I* think I could drop out again.''

Ryder's soft admission left them with nowhere to go. And they both knew it.

Still, he seemed reluctant to call it a night. Summer knew she was reluctant. She grew extra quiet, luxuriating in the feel of her hand in his, of his thumb rubbing the inside of her palm.

"You know," he finally said, "I admire you. I think you've shown a lot of courage. And not just tonight."

She groaned, shaking her head even when he couldn't see it.

But he sensed it. Felt it.

"Hey," he said as a soft rasp. With his free hand, he reached across them to move his fingers along her neck and into her hair. He coaxed her chin so that she peered into his face in the dimness.

"Hey," he repeated. "You *are* beautiful. To think that you feel something you shouldn't feel when you hear that hurts me. The way you look is only one part of everything else that's beautiful about you. Beauty, both inside and out, is rare, in fact. And as far as I'm concerned, it's the rest of the world that's screwed up. Not you."

Summer didn't want to hear any more. She shook her head against his gently restraining fingers. She felt him leaning toward her. She knew he was going to kiss her and she wanted him to. Comfort. Kisses. And then...

Yes, she wanted it, all of it, to happen again. She wanted Ryder.

But his kiss was merely soothing. Tenderly, he touched her lips with his. Then her forehead, her eyes, her cheeks. He was ministering to her with masculine sweetness and generous kisses. "Yes," he whispered, "you're beautiful. So very beautiful."

For the first time, Summer reveled in her beauty. For him, she wanted to be beautiful. She wanted to share her gift with him. Only him. The taste of him drove her wild.

"We can't do this," he whispered, his mouth back at her lips. "This's what happened the last time, you know."

Summer didn't reply.

She invited his kisses.

And he obliged. "I want to give to you," he said more urgently. "I want to be close to you again."

"Yes."

"Just one more time," he said. "Just for you. Just so I can remember."

She nodded into the curve of his throat.

Ryder's hands slipped into her clothing, and he gently and quickly opened her shirt and bra. His hand, then his lips and tongue claimed her nipples.

"Just this one more time," he insisted. The front zipper on her old slacks gave way to his fingertips. "Just for you"

Summer yearned for him. She had for so long. Acute now, the yearning became an ache. She ached for him to stroke her, and when his hand slid into the opening of her slacks, down into her briefs, she heard the slight pleading sound that escaped on her breath. He began to rhythmically caress her as he kissed her throat, then her navel.

Summer groped for the buttons on his shirt. She wanted to feel the warmth of his chest, the texture of his dark hair.

"No," he said, bringing her closer to the edge. "Don't undress me. Don't touch me. This is just for you. Oh, God, Summer moan for me again."

She couldn't help it. The little sounds kept erupting as he stroked her.

"Come on, my beautiful, beautiful Summer. Just for me."

At last, she gasped. She arched her back and, spreading her knees, pressed her hands to keep his hand, still and strong, against her.

"My sweet, summertime Summer," he said, the heel of his palm firm against her, exactly as she wanted.

Summer felt drained. When she snuggled into Ryder, he kissed her slowly. Vaguely she wondered how he was dealing with his own wants and needs. His words had seemed true—he'd wanted the pleasure for her.

"Come on," he whispered. "You've had enough for one day."

At the bungalow, after a few more of Ryder's lingering kisses, Summer went inside and urged Poppy on his way.

When she fell into bed, she slept as she hadn't slept in ages—so deeply that she didn't have to think anymore. Not about the creep. Not about how much she had to do. Not about meeting Ryder's brother. Not about how much she loved Ryder Craig.

"YES, sirree, folks, you don't want to be in New York today. Read it and weep, New Yorkers. Minus—yes, I said, minus ten degrees windchill. And down here, folks, well, what is it out there on this lovely Friday afternoon in Sarasota? Warm along the beach and

*even warmer inland. Yeah, snowbirds, if you don't
have to fly back to New York yet, don't!"*

Switching off the radio in the galley kitchen aboard
Spare a Dime, Ryder looked at his brother. Having
just sat down on the banquette at the table, Vance
smiled at him. "Sounds like we missed it, B.J. and I."

"Yeah," Ryder replied. "Windchills like that sound
bad, even for New York. Especially this late in winter."

After flying into Palm Beach and then driving down
to Sarasota, Ryder's brother and sister-in-law had arrived at his old cruiser. Ryder hadn't seen his brother
since that day when he'd told Vance and his mother
about Carrie. In fact, this was the first private contact he and Vance had had in years.

Ryder felt the awkwardness keenly, but there was
also a feeling of hope based on the old ties.

"Are you sure B.J.'s all right?" Ryder asked. "I
mean, the marina's a great place for walking and
chatting with people, but you just got here and—"

"She'll appreciate stretching her legs. And she's
giving us some time on our own."

Again the awkwardness pressed at Ryder. "I never
gave B.J. a chance to know me, and I see now how nice
she is."

"Yeah, I know what you're saying. And you're
right, she's great. She's been good for me. She be-
lieves in family, and for years she's been urging me to
get in touch with you."

Ryder smiled. "Not that I've been easy to get in
touch with. Nor that I would've appreciated her efforts. At least, not until lately."

"Yeah, well, I haven't always been so great, either.
And I'm sorry about that, Ry. What with B.J. and the

boys, with my life running along smoothly, I'm realizing that things in our family weren't so good or so black and white, as I was led to believe.''

Ryder thought that maybe they were moving too fast with this—what was it? Reconciliation?

Oh, he wanted to reconcile. But to talk about their original family so openly and so abruptly—well, he wouldn't chance any more disagreements with Vance.

Then again, Ryder understood his brother's effort. He'd obviously been encouraged by B.J., and Ryder remained more than willing, if not exactly able, to face the past and improve the present.

"As I get older," Vance said, looking at the beer that had begun to sweat on the table, ''I see that I've allowed mother in particular to influence the way I think about things. Not that I didn't fall in with what she, and especially Dad, wanted from us. I mean, I've liked taking over for him, both with the business and family obligations. But Mother always claimed you were different. And in a very negative way. She said you weren't like Dad and her and me, and I guess I grew to believe that, too. But lately I can see that you simply wanted different things. That you hated the life I accepted without question. Mother shouldn't have set us against each other. Right from the start, both she and Dad should have seen your differences and appreciated them. I've learned that with my own two sons. With my own stumbling attempts at parenting. We have to allow our children to be who they are. Not just mold them to fit some tradition.''

Vance's words stunned Ryder. For his brother to come around to seeing things as he himself did amazed Ryder.

And though part of Ryder had always admired the brother who was five years older than he, part, the rebellious part, had resented Vance for having a personality that dovetailed with those of their parents. And then, Vance had also taken their side when Ryder had acted out because the younger brother hadn't fitted in.

Ryder began to allow himself to admire and even to love his brother again.

Still, there was more. Much more, particularly involving their father. Ryder knew the complexities couldn't be addressed in a single afternoon.

"I haven't spoken to Mother since driving over to Palm Beach and telling her about Carrie."

"No, she hasn't mentioned either you or Carrie since. Sorry, Ry, but I don't think you can expect Mother to change."

"Oh, I know that. I just don't want her taking out her feelings for me on my daughter, or on the woman who gave me my daughter."

"We'll simply have to work around Mother. That's what B.J. and I have decided. But we want you and yours to be in our lives, Ry, and we're willing to stand up to Mother so that can happen."

Again, Ryder was stunned. Stunned enough to admit the truth. "I doubt there'll be much standing up to Mother. She's always tolerated me to a point. It's more that I don't kid myself, Vance. Mother will never feel any differently about me. She'll never forgive me for Dad's death. Nor would I want you to put yourself on the line for me. She needs you."

Vance nodded.

Once again, Ryder sensed the unaccustomed optimism in himself. Maybe he could live the conventional life he'd been raised to live. That life he'd fought so long. That life he was now reestablishing at Calder's.

Maybe he could make himself worthy again. Maybe he could do it for Carrie. For Summer.

Oh, God, Summer. He loved her so much. Last night when he'd held her in his arms...

But if he was going to stay on the straight and narrow, he had to get himself together before he involved Summer. He couldn't drag either Summer's feelings or Carrie's emotional security into his life until he knew he wouldn't drop out again. First, he had to prove his own stability to himself.

"I hope," Vance continued, "that I haven't come on too strong with all this getting-back-together routine."

"Oh, no."

"You look tired."

"Just didn't sleep last night."

"And Summer? Are you sure she doesn't mind us staying at the resort?"

"Well, actually, I didn't talk to her when I called there this morning. They're into their second day with the yard sale, you know, and it sounds busy out there. But I did talk to Fred, uh, her grandfather, and he said they'd be glad to have you."

"It's not my doing, you know." Vance seemed a little sheepish for one usually so confident. "It's more that B.J. wants to meet Carrie and to get to know Summer. She's interested in Summer you see. I've warned her not to take this family bit too far, but still—"

"No, you don't have to worry about Summer. She's really great."

"Yeah, she's gotta be one helluva woman to have you settling down." As he studied Ryder's obviously preoccupied expression, Vance was aware that they all needed more time.

CHAPTER ELEVEN

NERVOUSLY, Summer glanced beyond the open front door of bungalow number four. Sure enough, they arrived in two cars. Ryder's barely familiar green Volvo stopped in the circle of bungalows ahead of a spiffy yellow convertible.

Since Ryder had called Poppy, evidently saying that he hadn't been able to find a room for his brother and sister-in-law, she had thrown herself into getting one of the bungalows in shape.

It was after nine in the evening. Carrie was in bed, and the hubbub of the sale in the upper lot had died down for the night. Poppy and Irma had retired early, and even Dee's energy had dwindled to the point that she'd gone home.

Tired herself, Summer couldn't believe she still had to deal with Vance and B.J. Craig. She worried that Ryder's family would find the resort inadequate. Even in its heyday it would hardly have suited the sophisticated New York-Palm Beach couple who climbed out of the yellow convertible.

As she stood smiling in the doorway, the porch light revealed the two men lifting the few pieces of luggage from the trunk, while the woman, who had to be B.J., watched with her dressing case in hand. Finally, the trio turned toward Summer, their soft voices growing louder as they entered the porch.

Summer smiled more broadly. "Hi," she said.

Briefly Ryder introduced them. Though she couldn't help thinking about what had happened the night before in the back seat of Ryder's car, she forced herself to focus on the newcomers.

Vance reminded her so much of Ryder, and even of Carrie, that Summer was thrown into a whole new quagmire. These people were *related* to her daughter.

B.J. was one of the few women Summer had ever met who was tall enough to look her straight in the eye. She had ash blond hair, cut in a neat sweep. And while her clothes—casual expensive resort wear—were the best money could buy, her sunburned cheeks, her steady stare didn't jibe with what Summer had pictured. Vance was openly standoffish, if also very polite, but B.J. captured Summer's interest.

"It's so nice of you to do this for us, Summer," the woman said, smiling and holding Summer's hand in a tight grasp. Not that the grasp was hard or insistent, just sincere, like B.J.'s clear gray gaze. "Ryder explained your situation here, and I feel bad about putting you to this additional trouble."

"No trouble at all." Summer glanced at Ryder.

B.J., however, went on. "We had such a nice drive down from Palm Beach. Vance and I almost feel like honeymooners. It's been a long time since we've been on our own, without business calls, the boys and all that."

"Well, I'm sure Ryder's glad you're here. And I'm happy you'll meet Carrie."

"Yes, yes, Carrie. I can't wait. Ryder says she's already asleep. And then, I'm a mom, so I know how it is once you get them down for the night. There's no way short of a fire that you'll wake them up."

Everyone chuckled, and Summer indicated sheets across her arm, which she was about to put on their bed.

"Oh, here," B.J. said, "let me help you. Vance, you can bring in the luggage, and then you and Ryder can be excused for a while."

Yes, Summer thought. B.J. ran the show, but with a benevolent hand.

When Summer entered the bedroom, B.J. and Vance came in after her. Setting down the luggage, Vance left with a smile.

"Well, this is charming," B.J. said. "Just charming. I hate to see it gobbled up. And so does Ryder. He talked so much over dinner that I feel I already know you and Carrie and your grandfather."

Checking B.J.'s gray eyes, Summer read the woman's genuine concern. She had the style Summer had expected, but she was pleasant and open.

Summer moved to put the sheets on the bare mattress.

"Here," B.J. offered, "I'll take the other side."

While Summer would have sworn B.J. didn't put on her own sheets, she pitched in.

"We didn't bring much," she said. "Unfortunately, we have to go back to Palm Beach on Sunday morning, and then catch a plane for New York in the evening. It's hard to leave the boys, but, as I said, I've enjoyed the break."

Summer noticed that B.J. didn't mention Ryder's mother, whom they had to have seen in Palm Beach. Summer was curious about that woman, too. But Evelyn Craig wasn't discussed offhandedly, and that said a great deal.

"I've never been to Sarasota before," her guest continued. "I've heard about the museums and theater, and I wish we could stay longer. But, well, we just can't take the time away except in short weekends. Oh, my," she added, catching her reflection in the mirror over the dresser. "I *do* have a sunburn. Vance kept warning me, but after New York, the sun felt so good that I insisted on the convertible when I saw it."

"Does your face feel hot?"

"Yes, and I'm afraid I didn't bring anything except the usual."

"You might try yogurt."

"Yogurt? For sunburn?"

"We use it all the time. I have some if you'd like to try it."

"Yes, I would. Thank you. I want us to be friends, and now I hope you do, too."

Summer felt confused. She hadn't anticipated anything but a mutual interest in Carrie. At best.

"You know," the surprising visitor said, "Vance and I want very much to be in Ryder's life again, and I can see that includes you. Since I've never had a sister and there are few other relatives, either in my or in Vance's family, I honestly think we might make a go of it, you and I."

Summer was astounded by B.J.'s frankness. Still, looking at her direct gaze, Summer couldn't doubt she meant every word she said.

"Tell me," B.J. continued, plucking up her case and heading for the bathroom, "would you, just by chance, know someone who can help with my hair? I know it's last minute, but with the car and all, it's a mess."

Summer watched B.J. peer at herself in the bathroom mirror and tried to figure out the woman. She finally put her finger on it. While Summer felt that she and Vance were more alike in their reticence, in their standoffishness, B.J. was one of those good old girls. Summer thought she'd returned to a dorm room.

B.J. was the full-blown team supporter, the resident athlete, the one girl every other girl could depend on, no matter what. Amazingly, Vance Craig had married the opposite of himself.

"As a matter of fact," Summer heard herself say, "I have someone who does my hair. My friend and I have a standing appointment with him on Saturday, and if you'd like to join us in the morning, I'm sure he wouldn't mind."

"Love it."

From just that much, Summer knew that B.J. and Dee would also hit it off. And they did. The next morning, they not only had a grand time at the hairdresser—making over Irma—but afterward they went to the mall, continuing to decide what should be done about the older woman they had by the elbows. Fortunately Irma seemed somewhat flabbergasted but willing to try anything.

Summer, of course, had to go back for the open-air sale, but when B.J. and Dee and Irma also returned to the resort, Summer was in for more surprises.

Irma looked ten years younger. Her hair was softened by a rinse, and the pink sweats that Dee and B.J. had insisted she buy and wear for that afternoon made her appear more feminine than Summer had ever seen her.

But the biggest surprise was the way B.J. insinuated herself into their lives. While Ryder and Vance took Carrie to the beach, then out for hamburgers and back to Ryder's boat for a nap, B.J. insisted on staying on at the sale. If anyone proved she could outwork Summer and outhaggle Dee, it was B.J. She was as unpretentious, as confident as anyone Summer ever hoped to meet.

IRMA'S MIND SPUN round and round. Really, she'd seldom had such an amazing day. Summer, who had always been nice to her, had been downright kind that morning. And Summer's friend, Dee, and then Ryder's sister-in-law, B.J., had positively swept her off her feet. The younger women had been so determined to redo her hair, and then to suggest a new wardrobe, that she was sure she could take them into her confidence.

She'd decided days ago to approach Summer and Dee for their advice. But she'd never in a thousand years expected their response. She felt like the changed woman she'd always longed to become. Even her friends had been amazed.

And now, she felt pleasantly exhausted and exhilarated at the same time. The final flow of customers had left the parking lot, and she, Summer, B.J. and Fred covered, with a collection of canvas and newspaper and cardboard, the last of the remaining goods.

Naturally, Irma's gaze sought out Fred. He was on his last legs, and she yearned to tuck him up and hover over him. Still, she knew better. She doubted Fred had ever been tucked up. And while he often played the mother hen with Carrie, Irma couldn't imagine him accepting her clucking.

She still believed Fred was worth the winning. But once again, she felt further from a victory than when the opportunity of the garage sale had flashed into her head. She'd offered to help with the last of the packing for the move, when the time came for it, but she knew that once again her chances were limited.

Even now, she had no excuse to stay. It was only eight o'clock, but Fred both went to bed and got up early. She wondered what he thought of her new appearance.

"I guess that's a wrap," Summer said. "We've done better than I thought we would. Tomorrow will probably be slower."

When Summer actually smiled at Irma, even pulled her into a quick hug, Irma was speechless.

"Thanks so much for your help."

Irma was afraid that behind her new glasses, tears might spring into her eyes.

B.J., who looked on, smiled broadly, tilting her head to observe them with her level gaze. Really, this B.J. was the nicest person.

"Well," Irma managed to say, "you're welcome. I enjoyed it, and I know my friends did, too. Now remember, I'll be here on Monday. The people from the charity will have the final choices before the trash men come on Tuesday."

"Yeah," said Fred. "I get a tax deduction for anything the charity takes, so you gotta be sure, Irma, that they give us an estimate of what our donated stuff is worth."

Irma nodded, oh, so reluctant to go.

Beyond the lights of the resort, the gulf water rippled. In the evenings, the air grew cooler, the breeze stiffer, but the nights were as pleasant as the days.

"So," Summer said, looking at Irma, then at her grandfather, "I guess you owe Irma a cup of tea, Poppy."

"Huh?"

"The least you can do is offer her a cup of tea before she drives home."

Summer winked at Irma, and again Irma was nothing short of floored. Could Summer be encouraging something?

"Yeah, yeah," Fred said. "Come on, I'll fire up the kettle. Not too late yet. And you," he added, turning to B.J., "you were a big help. It's too bad you came all the way from New York just to work your tail off."

"No, no," replied B.J. "I was happy to do it. A nice change of pace. I kinda hate to go back."

"Yeah, well," Fred bragged, "everybody feels that way once they get here. No snowbird likes to fly back to the snow."

B.J. laughed. "This snowbird certainly doesn't. Still, I guess I'd better, and that means I'd better say goodbye until next time. Vance and I leave after breakfast tomorrow."

With final words and a mutual exchange of good wishes for a safe flight home and profitable end of the sale, Summer and B.J. walked through the old resort toward Summer's bungalow.

"They look nice together, don't they?" Irma said to Fred, who remained next to her, watching.

"She's just as tall as Summer, but she ain't as pretty."

"Well, there aren't many girls who are as pretty as Summer. B.J.'s just as nice, though. And just as trim. I think they like each other."

"Umm." Fred headed for his rooms behind the resort office, which were as familiar to Irma as her own little house inland. Once inside, he turned in to the kitchen, urging her into the TV room with its couch.

"Don't know what's on," he said, "but it'll be good to sit down for a minute."

"You can take off that sweater, you know," Irma called after him.

The darned thing still looked uncomfortable, no matter how much he wore it. And so salmon!

Finally, he came in with two mugs of tea laced with honey the way they liked it. He set the mugs on the coffee table and picked up the remote for the television. When he leaned back beside her, Irma wished for days and days just like this.

"It's nice of you to make tea for me, Fred."

He looked at her then. Really looked at her. "You look damned pretty, Irma."

She blushed. Actually blushed.

Leaning toward her, Fred pressed a kiss on her lips. "I want to thank you for all you've done, Irma."

She beamed into his face and passed a gentle hand along his stark jawline. "Oh, Fred, don't you know I'd do anything in the world for you?"

"Yeah, well," he said, his face still close, his eyes glinting, "you stay outta the kitchen and we'll do just fine."

WHEN SUMMER TURNED from Poppy and Irma to head for the circle of bungalows, B.J. fell in with her. Their silence was companionable. Way out, the gulf rolled like silver under a starlit sky.

"I hope you don't mind," B.J. said, "that I didn't spend more time with Carrie on this trip. But I thought that Ry and Vance needed some time together. You know, brother to brother. They haven't seen each other in years, and lately, that's bothered Vance a lot. Besides," she added with a sideways glance at Summer, "I wanted to get to know you."

Summer smiled wryly. "Nothing like working at a garage sale to get to know someone."

B.J. laughed openly. Summer thought she could really like this woman.

True, they were from different worlds, but B.J. seemed oblivious to that. Not that she made an effort to hide her affluence, either. She was a natural—comfortable in any circumstances. As Summer was not. Perhaps, Summer thought, that's why she admired B.J.

Approaching Summer's bungalow, they saw Ryder and Vance waiting on the screened porch. A pile of blankets indicated their desire to leave Carrie, who had to be asleep, and to go down to the beach for a while.

"I don't know," Summer hedged when Ryder said as much.

"I'll come back and check on her," he offered. "She'll be okay."

Summer knew that she could hear Carrie if the child got loud enough. "Yes, I know she'll be fine. It's just that..."

She couldn't suggest she'd be uncomfortable with Ryder and his family, especially in the light of their own shaky situation.

And indeed, the beach at night on such a starry night was spectacular. Sitting down on towels, each of the couples wrapped up in the blankets the men had brought. With their backs to the warmth of a seawall, they felt very relaxed. For a while, the four simply absorbed the peaceful atmosphere.

But Summer also fought down her thoughts about the last time she and Ryder had been so close, two nights ago in the back seat of his car...after the creep had followed her home.

She didn't want to think about any of that. Besides, she couldn't remember when she'd been as tired as she was lately.

"The sand's still warm," B.J. commented. "If somebody doesn't talk, I'll fall asleep."

"I'm afraid," Vance replied, "that the only thoughts you'd hear from me on an occasion like this would be bittersweet. This kind of night gets to me."

"Hey, yeah," B.J. said, springing to life. "My dear hubby doesn't get nostalgic often. Let's hear it, honey—something bittersweet."

Although everyone chuckled, Vance sounded willing to expose his feelings, perhaps because he knew they'd be received gently.

Summer found his stumbling start touching.

"Well, uh, I associate Florida with the vacations we spent in Palm Beach. I guess those were my favorite old times because the four of us were together. Remember, Ry? That's when we had the most access to Dad."

"Yeah," Ryder said, also recollecting. "I remember those vacations as being the best, too. Real time with Dad."

"And real time catching hell from Mother. She hated it when the three of us went out fishing together. I think that's when she started getting hard on you, Ry. Because you liked those trips so well, and she despised anything to do with boats."

"Anything to do with ignoring her social round, you mean."

"Yeah, I guess that's right, too. And then Dad always took your side about the boating. That really frosted her."

After lapsing into a brief silence, Vance resumed speaking, obviously reaching for something positive. "Later, though, as we got older, we played a lot of golf with Calder Parks. Remember? You and me and Dad and Calder. Those were good times, too."

"Really good," Ryder murmured, still holding Summer close beneath the blanket. "But," he added more firmly, "I can also see now that I used boats, or rather getting away on boats, as a means for getting back at Mother."

"Not that you didn't need the distance sometimes, Ry."

Summer could see that the brothers were trying hard to sort through their shared past. Again, she felt the poignancy of their attempt.

B.J. could say whatever she wanted. "Speaking of Evelyn, we really want you to drive over to Palm Beach the next time we fly down, Ry, in three weeks. Of course the boys won't be able to come even then. Not until spring break. But couldn't you meet us there? We'd love it. We'll have fun."

"Oh, I don't know about that."

"No matter what Evelyn thinks," B.J. insisted, "the rest of us have a right to be together. And Carrie should get to know us, too. We want to know our niece. Besides," she added, "Carrie can win over even Evelyn with just a smile"

Ryder snorted. "Oh, really?"

Summer thought that was as far as Ryder and his brother and B.J. could go for now, but she felt good for them. She felt cozy nestled into Ryder's side, and the exchange between him and his brother warmed her heart. At peace for the moment, she drifted off.

"I think they're both asleep," Ryder whispered to Vance. "They've had one helluva a day."

"I'm glad to see them making friends so quickly."

Ryder liked B.J. already. He wanted to visit with her and Vance again in Palm Beach. But going to Palm Beach meant dealing with his mother.

The night was too nice for contemplating that. And he was too tired. The simple pleasure of Summer's weight and warmth on his chest would be enough— enough, if he didn't think about wanting her.

"She's the most beautiful woman I've ever seen," Vance said, breaking in to Ryder's train of thought.

"Yeah, every time I look at her, she stuns me. But best of all, she's caring and intelligent. A genuinely good person. I'm in love with her," Ryder blurted out. "I've been in love with her since the day we made Carrie together."

"Then why aren't you with her?"

Ryder shrugged. "It's complicated, but I'd be willing to court her. For two and a half years, I've been faithful to what I've been feeling, so you know I'm a goner. It's just..."

"The past?"

"No, more like the future."

"I don't get it."

"Well, think about what we've been discussing. The bit about changing, about getting on the straight and narrow because you have kids. Have you ever seen anything more innocent than the faces of your children? How will I ever look into Carrie's face and tell her, 'Yeah, sweetheart, if you keep your nose clean and try hard, everything will turn out fine.' I mean, I'm hardly in a position to preach about trying hard and keeping my nose clean. And what about the day when I have to explain the trial?''

Ryder felt so ashamed that he was glad his brother couldn't see his face clearly. "What about when I have to tell Carrie about Bunny Dale's death? About the fact that I was so drunk that I still can't remember what happened? How will I tell her about Dad?''

"You'll have time to tell her, Ry. In bits and pieces. By the time she's old enough to understand, she'll love you. We all know you didn't do what Rochelle claimed you did, and Carrie will, too."

"I wish I could believe that."

"And if you can't? What do you do then?"

"In the short run, I'm getting to know Carrie and Summer."

"And in the long run?"

"Yeah, that's the big one. And I can't answer it yet. Can I be what Carrie needs? At this point, I'm feeling I'll be involved in Carrie's life as much as I can be, but more from the sidelines. I'll let Summer handle the everyday stuff. Summer's a wonderful mother and I trust her. The only thing I'm sure about is that I have to decide something soon. I want to do the right thing for them. As soon as possible I have to be honest with Summer about how much she can count on me."

"Well, it looks to me as if you could have it all."

"Yeah, but I also need to know I can live the conventional routine. And, man, I'm having a helluva time sticking it out at Calder's."

Their next pause did little to comfort him, and Ryder allowed himself to focus on Summer, on the way her lush curves fitted into his body, on how much he wanted her.

"You know," Vance said, "I've heard Rochelle is in New York."

Ryder was clearly startled by this news. "I've been thinking about asking you if you knew where she was. I've been reading the transcripts from the trial and wondering if she'd talk to me. Do you think she would?"

"That's hard to say. She's engaged again, to a guy who's a friend of a friend of mine. From what I've heard, she's turning her life around. Why would you see her?"

"For my own information more than anything. If I could remember what occurred... Even the transcripts haven't jogged my memory. I doubt I'll ever recall, and that's the worst. That's also the aspect I dread explaining to Carrie. How can I say I was so out of control that I can't remember a night like that?"

Ryder sighed. His shame over his past was always the final wall he couldn't get around, and he wanted to awaken Summer and call it a night. When he said as much to Vance, his brother surprised him.

"No," he said. "There's one more subject."

Although Ryder didn't know if he could take any more, Vance seemed insistent. "When Dad died I was with him. Just me, you know."

"Yeah, I remember."

"He wasn't conscious, not really conscious, except for one time toward the end. He woke up and smiled at me, his mind as clear as crystal."

Ryder yearned to cut Vance off. But his brother was obviously recalling something painful for himself, too.

"He said he loved me," Vance admitted. "And then," he added softly, "he told me he wished you were there so he could tell you the same."

"I knew he loved me," Ryder choked out.

"Yes, but he also said he wanted to ask your forgiveness."

"*My* forgiveness?"

"Yes. He said your behavior had been as much his fault as yours. He said if he'd been around more, if he'd taken your part more against Mother, that you wouldn't have had it so hard. That you wouldn't have reacted the way you did. He said that was the single regret he had in dying. That he couldn't finally stand up for you."

Ryder let his head drop back.

His dad's forgiveness.

Tears of relief threatened. He would have given anything to allow the wrenching emotions. Instead he concentrated on Vance's words.

"I'm sorry, Ry. Sorry that I didn't tell you sooner. I wanted to. Especially since the boys. And well, B.J.'s nearly driven me nuts with saying I should call you. I should have—"

"Don't apologize. I've been a hardheaded ass, and the way I see it, we're even. But," he whispered, hoping he could finish, "I'm glad you told me. I'm glad to know, now, how he went and what he thought of me when he died."

Ryder reached out his free hand to his brother. Sitting there, the pair grasped hands for a moment.

Finally, Ryder dropped Vance's hold. By silent agreement they turned to the women beside them. Ryder gently kissed Summer awake.

"Hey, sleepyhead," he said quietly.

"Where...?"

"On the beach, remember?"

She sat up, breaking the spell. "Oh, yeah."

Ryder stood, reaching a hand to tug her to her feet. He glanced at Vance, who whispered his response.

"I think we'll stay for a while. B.J. says we're sort of on a honeymoon..."

Ryder smiled, and dropping his blanket next to his brother, said, "See you in the morning."

"In the morning," Vance replied. "And you, too, Summer. For breakfast, I hope. Before we leave."

"In the morning," she repeated, still sounding somewhat disoriented.

Taking Summer's elbow, Ryder guided her toward her bungalow.

"You didn't hear Carrie, did you?" she asked.

"No, just the waves and the night critters."

"It's pretty spectacular."

"I can understand how you'll miss it. I've got salt-water in my veins, too. You will go to breakfast with us in the morning, won't you? Before Vance and B.J. leave?"

"I'd like to, but—"

"I know, the last of the sale. And I'm sorry, but I won't be able to take Carrie for the day like we planned."

"Oh?"

Ryder entered the screened porch behind Summer. And while she didn't switch on the overhead light, she did turn to him in the doorway.

"Sounds quiet," she said.

Ryder remembered the conversations on the beach. He used them to keep his focus on the beautiful, vulnerable woman who was so near to him, and yet so far.

"I talked to Vance," he said. "While you and B.J. were asleep. And I'll ask Calder for time off to go to New York to confront Rochelle. Tomorrow, I'll see if I can fly back with Vance. If not, I'll leave on Monday."

Summer's eyes met his, obviously searching his face.

"I'm okay," he said, realizing she had to be both curious and concerned. "I'd better go," he added.

But he just couldn't resist her. He leaned forward and pressed his lips to her soft ones. Everything about her was lush and inviting. He kissed her again. The ache he suppressed slipped out as a groan. She was so sweet, so sleepy. He grew crazy with desire.

She was also responsive. He saw that she'd let him touch her... maybe.

He pulled abruptly away, grasping for coherence. "You're half-asleep. Tomorrow, we'll both be sorry if I don't go now."

"Tomorrow," she said, with that defensive tilt to her chin, "you're going to New York. Good luck."

She stepped inside, leaving him on the porch.

He couldn't believe how close they'd come again— both of them and so easily. What in the hell could he do when neither of them could say no and mean it?

WINTER WIND CUT through the streets of New York City, far from Sarasota's summerlike warmth. Pushing his fists into the pockets of his trench coat, Ryder increased his pace. Although his head was down against the cold, a display window caught his eye.

Evermore Antiques.

Almost colliding with another pedestrian, he stopped and consulted his watch. Just enough time to step inside and have a look at the hand-painted miniature that had attracted him.

He had to meet Vance for lunch, and he dreaded telling Vance that Rochelle Waller had just shot him dead in the water.

"May I help you, sir?" The salesman greeted him as he entered the shop.

Ryder took in the natty gentleman in English tweeds. "I saw the miniature in the window. The one with the blue satin ribbons."

"Yes, yes, a delight," the fellow announced. "I knew we wouldn't keep it for long. Not that it's anything of real value. You do understand that, don't you?"

Going to the window, the gentleman opened the small door and stretched inside. Even as he handed Ryder the miniature, Ryder knew he'd buy it, no matter what.

"It's a fairly good likeness of Botticelli's Venus, don't you think? I mean, you do know the picture, do you not? His *Birth of Venus?*"

Like almost everyone, Ryder had seen photographs of the Renaissance painting.

"The miniature was done by an amateur, of course—some young chap on his grand tour in the early part of the century. But it's good."

Delicate filigree framed the oval that fitted into Ryder's palm. The mythological Venus, as Ryder recalled, represented love, grace and beauty. Honey hair flowed around her body, hiding her nakedness. Standing modestly on a cockleshell, she averted her eyes.

She seemed shy about her beauty. He had to have it.

"I'll take it," he said.

"Very good, sir. If you'll step this way..."

"It needs to be packed well."

"Yes, I have a nice jeweler's box and some bubble wrap. I'll only be a moment."

Left alone in the shop, separated from the Venus, Ryder glanced at the collection of antique furniture and began to muse about the morning he'd had.

Rochelle Waller. Showing up on her doorstep just after breakfast, he'd caught her off guard. As he'd expected, she lived in a fashionable high-rise apartment overlooking Central Park.

"Ry?" Getting a look at him through the barely open door, she gasped. "How did you...?"

"I lied to security."

She bristled, peering at him through the slot. "Just like you."

"Would you have seen me if I'd called first?"

"No."

He shrugged.

"What's more, I won't see you now," she said, shoving the door, but not quickly enough.

He wedged his foot against it.

"What do you want?"

"You know what I want. I want to know what happened in Vermont."

"Well, you won't get that here."

"This is the only place I can go, remember?"

She stared at him. Then, much to his surprise, she moved to let him enter.

Ahead of Ryder, Rochelle tugged at the ties of her slate gray silk robe. He followed her across an opulent living room to a long curving couch. While she sat on the couch, he remained standing.

She was still pretty, he thought. Lively, strong-willed, small, dark haired. Still the same Rochelle.

He wondered, now, how they'd ever become engaged. He didn't recall anything more than being drunk, both when they'd decided and then decided not to get married. Even drunk, they'd had enough sense to know they'd never make it together.

God, no matter how much time went by, his past continued to torment him. He was desperate to clear his name. He'd been toying with the hopeless idea since he'd found Summer again. Now, with Carrie in his life, he'd become dead-serious.

"Really, Ry," Rochelle said, forcing a small hand through short dark curls. "I don't want to do this."

"Well, I do."

"Too much time has gone by."

"For you, maybe, but not for me. There'll never be enough time to put Vermont behind me."

"Look, I'm engaged now. To a really nice, stable guy. I don't want to remember."

"At least you have the luxury of remembering."

There, that had struck home. She glanced away from him.

He stood waiting.

"I can't do anything for you," she said stiffly but no longer hostile.

"That's funny. Since you were my only accuser, you're the only one who can help."

She shot up from the couch. Fiddling with her sash, she went to a window.

Ryder didn't know exactly what he expected of her. But even without remembering what had happened in the cabin in Vermont, he knew he hadn't done what she'd claimed he'd done.

"I can't help you," she insisted so softly that he barely heard.

"Listen, if you lied on that stand—and I know you did—if you want a new life—and I certainly understand that, too—you owe me."

"Owe you what?" She swung on him. "Even *if* I lied," she said, "who's it going to help now if I say I did? Let it go, Ry. We're doing fine now. I've heard as much about the new life you're making with Calder Parks as you've evidently heard about mine. Let it go, for God's sake. No, for my sake, let it go."

So she did hint at having perjured herself. If she'd lied on the stand, that was a crime.

"I won't take any legal action on what you might have to tell me," he said, a little shocked by his own statement. "I swear that. I just want to know. I want you to tell me what I can't remember."

"No, Ry. You say you know in your heart that you didn't murder Bunny Dale. That'll have to be enough. No matter how much we reform, we'll always pay for parts of that life. Your payment is to live with it as it stands. Considering how you treated people, how you treated me in particular, I think you should count yourself damned lucky."

Ryder ached with the knowledge that he still didn't deserve to be with Summer. Or with Carrie. He hadn't begun to clear his name, and now he never would.

CHAPTER TWELVE

SUMMER SAW HIM right away, of course. Ryder. Even in the client's steamy, crowded kitchen, she would have been aware of him.

The last time she'd seen Ryder, he'd told her he was leaving for New York. He'd told her that they couldn't make love. That they'd regret it.

But Summer had sensed that regret had been only an excuse. Oh, regret was reasonable enough. And they would certainly be taking a chance in falling into a physical relationship. But she was precisely at that point. Yes, she loved him. And yes, she was willing to chance emotional disaster for herself.

She could tell that Ryder cared about her.

She also knew he was unsure in a major way.

But still, she was willing to bet that whatever was holding him back could be worked out.

She loved him that much.

He leaned into the wall, arms akimbo, just inside the kitchen door. He watched her. Waited.

She adjusted the tailcoat of her white tux.

Although she hadn't expected to see him, she wouldn't let him know that, either.

Get it together, Summer, she warned herself. *You're finishing up here, and he wants to talk.*

Finally, he made his move. He joined her at a countertop where she hefted a final box into her arms.

"Can I help you with that?"

"It's more awkward than heavy."

He took the box, anyway.

She had to be sure that everyone had left, and then to carefully close the back door behind them. "The client says it'll lock when I pull it," she explained, tugging the kitchen door and hearing it shut. "She and the last of her guests are settling in for cards, so I don't want to bother her more than I have to."

Scanning the wide driveway at the rear of the house, Summer saw that her helpers had gone. Already on her way out, Dee waved and tooted her horn. Waving back, Summer unlocked the rear of her van. "Just put it in here," she said.

Ryder slipped the box inside, and sure enough, they were alone behind the house.

"I was worried that the creep would be out again."

"No, no, I haven't seen him since the last time."

She looked at him in the patchy light. He was a wonderful sight, even in casual slacks and a pullover.

"How was your trip to New York?" she managed to say.

"Fine, but I'd like to talk."

"There's a coffee bar not far from here."

"You don't mind? In the tux?"

"Well," she lied, "no." She did mind the flashy tux, but she wanted to hear what he had to say.

Even more curious, Summer had Ryder follow her to the church where they unloaded the van. They then drove to a nearby greasy spoon. She and Dee occasionally went there to take a break.

It was an old-fashioned, round-the-clock place with high stools and a counter. Summer slid onto a bench in a booth. Soon they had cups of coffee in front of them.

His trip to New York intrigued her, and having found a private spot, she waited for him to look at her.

"I've only been gone four days," he said, "but it seems like forever." He told her quickly, haltingly, about his confrontation with Rochelle Waller. Summer felt disappointed for him. More than disappointed. Ryder was obviously miserable.

"I admit it," he said in despair. "I'd begun to hope that I might clear my name, that in some burst of reformed fervor, Rochelle would confess that she lied. That she might even go over what happened that night in Vermont. I mean, I really need an explanation for Carrie. I just can't picture myself sitting down with her someday and telling her all that garbage, especially if I can't remember it myself. Now I don't have even what Rochelle could have given me."

Summer didn't know what to say. While she hoped that he had reached a turning point, and that he could begin to let it all go, somehow she doubted he'd reached that point.

Rather than watching him struggling like an animal in a trap, Summer searched for another subject. "Are you still thinking about going to Palm Beach to see your family?"

He shrugged. "I suppose I should. No matter what my mother does, I can't react to her slights by turning my back on her anymore. Other people are involved now. Vance, Carrie..."

Summer had noticed that Ryder seldom spoke of his mother, and when he did, he didn't talk against the woman. While Summer sensed that his relationship with his mother had never been good, she admired

Ryder's restraint in discussing what had happened between them.

"If I do go," he said softly, his gaze roaming over her face, "I'd like you to come along."

"Me?"

"B.J. will have my head if you don't. And I'm still unsteady about taking Carrie on my own for the whole weekend. And I could, quite frankly, use the support."

Summer didn't know how to reply. She sipped her coffee. "Well, I have some good news," she said to bring his gaze back to her face. He could use some good news. "Poppy and Irma are getting married."

A look of surprise appeared on his ruggedly handsome face.

She chuckled. "I could hardly believe it myself. I mean, those two have been at each other since I was a kid. Still," she said on a soft sigh, "something's happened. They've decided Poppy will move in with Irma. She has a house inland, with a park across the street. Her neighborhood is into cards and socializing and the programs they offer in their community. Frankly, I think Poppy's not just accepting the inevitable, but he's contemplating a revamped life. At least, Irma and I hope so."

"And how will that affect your own move?"

"I'm not sure. I mean, we need to vacate soon now, and the papers for the house are being processed. Carrie and I have to live somewhere, and since Poppy insists on making the down payment while I handle the monthly mortgage, I still think it's the best deal I can hope for. I'll take the bigger bedroom at the one end, and . . ." Again, she sighed. "Actually," she added, ensuring that Ryder knew her feelings, "I couldn't be happier for them."

"Nor could I."

"So," she said, "I guess if that's all, I'd better be on my way."

"Just to be on the safe side, I'll follow you out. But first..."

Ryder groped through his pockets.

"What are you looking for? Money? I've got money."

"No, no, I bought something for you in New York, and, damn, if I haven't left it at home." He sat helplessly back on the bench seat. "Where's my brain?"

"I'm sure whatever it is can wait."

"No, it can't. It's so perfect—damn!"

She hated to see him disappointed. "Why don't I follow you to the marina? You can give me this perfect gift, and then—"

"Then I'll follow you out to the key. I'd like a peek at Carrie. Even asleep, she gives me a boost."

"Yeah, that's her best boost." Summer felt her own crooked grin. "When she's asleep. But I'm afraid she isn't at the bungalow."

"Oh?"

"Poppy and Irma have her at Irma's house for the night. Since they actually enjoy keeping her there, I generously gave them a turn."

Again her smile was dry, and Ryder glanced away. "I don't know, then," he said, sobering. "It may not be a good idea."

Naturally, Summer took his point. No matter what else they might discuss, their irresistible attraction to each other was always there.

If he could hold his ground, so could she. She wasn't afraid to be aboard *Spare a Dime* again. At least, not for a few minutes.

"So," she said decisively. "Let's go. I need to get home."

The night was warm and balmy—an exquisite night where exquisite nights were typical. Summer followed Ryder to Pelican Point, to his marina, tucked under a bridge along the Intercoastal Waterway.

The Ryder Craig who came to assist her out of her van was a far cry from the sea bum of her fantasies. This Ryder Craig was in control.

Taking her elbow, he guided her along wooden docks where a variety of boats bobbed in their slips. An old dog, a homely mix of breeds, came up to them, barked, then accepted Ryder's pat on the head.

"His name is Cuss," Ryder said, "and it's appropriate."

Satisfied, the dog trotted off, his long toenails clicking against the dry planking.

And then, there it was. *Spare a Dime.* Only it couldn't be *Spare a Dime,* Summer thought.

Ryder smiled at her, reading her mind. "Yeah, you could say I've been busy. I stripped her down to bare wood, then caulked and painted her. I overhauled her motor, refinished the decking, polished the brass and laid on lacquer to keep it shiny."

Ryder helped Summer on board. "Steady as she goes," he urged, conscious of her heels and flicking on the running lights.

When Summer wobbled at the first wash from a slowly motoring sailboat seeking its slip, he grabbed her elbow. "I guess you'd better take off the heels."

For all his good show, he was still as reluctant as hell to have her there. "The present's below," Ryder said, averting his face and bounding down the short steps to the cabin.

Summer followed him. When he turned on a small lamp, she glanced around the immaculate main cabin. Beyond, a refinished louvered door stood open to the darkened sleeping quarters.

She recalled everything as if it were yesterday.

Ignoring the flood of memories—the way Ryder was obviously trying to do—she accepted a small box from him.

Since he waited for her to open the box—rather impatiently, as he wanted to get going—she unwrapped the small package. Evermore Antiques was embossed on a gold seal. "Even the wrapping's pretty," she murmured.

She removed the tissue to reveal a miniature of Botticelli's lovely, naked Venus on a cockleshell, looking shyly away. It was so incredibly elegant.

Clearing his throat, Ryder said, "When I saw it in that window in New York, I thought of you. You know, beautiful Venus emerging from the sea."

Summer chuckled. "You obviously know more about mythology than I do."

Looking into his eyes, seeing his concern about something happening between them again, she longed to reassure him.

"Like you say," she murmured, "this is perfect. And obviously you feel about that day as I do. It was wonderful, and it brought us Carrie. But you don't need to worry. That's not going to happen again. That day I needed you. I needed your understanding and your warmth…and your body. But I'm not needy like that anymore. I'm doing very well. The truth is, I know that what happened was my fault. I came on to you. Because of that, I was reluctant to find you afterward. I can admit that now, too. My pregnancy was my own fault, and I didn't feel I could show up on your doorstep."

He choked out a bitter sound. "Don't be ridiculous. I wanted it, too. I knew what I was doing."

"I realize that. It was a special day, and this gift says you see it the same way. I'm grateful for that. I know we have a lot of time ahead of us. We'll be sharing Carrie. And while I'm happy for you and her, when you visit with her, you shouldn't think that I need more from you. As far as I'm concerned, that day was a fantasy and it won't be repeated."

He stared at her, desire evident in his eyes. "I don't want to hear you say that. I don't want to see you in that tux, and I don't want to see you out of it. I don't want to take you home, and I don't want you here."

She started to tell him that she felt entirely levelheaded. But she was within arm's reach.

He stood over her too quickly.

She lost ground too fast.

His jade green eyes were shadowed by the soft light of the cruiser. She felt the boat sway gently. Or was that her knees? He bent forward, and she watched his lips part. Hers responded likewise. He made a possessive search of her mouth with his tongue.

"I don't want to do this," he whispered, "but you're not just Everyman's fantasy, you're mine, too."

He kissed her lingeringly. His hands slid inside her tailcoat, slipping it off her shoulders. His kisses went on and on, and she melted as, one by one, her vest, her tie, her suspenders, the cuff links, the studs and then her shirt fell away.

The tux pants dropped to the floor, leaving her in the transparent white, lace-edged thigh-high hose, cotton-knit bikini briefs, and a men's white cotton undershirt.

He pulled her undershirt over her head, revealing her luscious breasts. Stripping out of his own knit shirt, he bound them, naked chest to naked chest, in a grip that forced the air from their lungs.

He locked his lips to hers in the same frantic way. Vaguely, she tasted her power over him, she luxuriated in it. Slowly, she rubbed her breasts against his solid, warm chest.

When he set her away, she nearly lost her balance. His intense gaze caused her to cross her arms over her throbbing nipples.

He pushed a hand through his short black hair. "You'd better call Irma to let her know where you are. Give her my number."

Pausing for only a moment, she picked up the phone. His reluctance was really getting to her.

When Summer hung up the phone, she looked back at Ryder. He was catching his breath, rubbing her kisses away on the bulge of his upper arm. He peered at her over a thick shoulder.

She grabbed her shirt. "I told you I'm in control," she said tartly. "I'm going home."

"The hell you are." His voice was a rasp. "Just give me a minute. Somehow, I gotta... I gotta slow down and think."

They were in control, all right. Just like that first day.

She couldn't even figure how to get the studs back through the holes in the tux shirt.

"What are you doing?" he asked, still frowning.

What she was doing was obvious. She just couldn't seem to get the shirt fastened.

"I'm going home," she said flatly.

Unexpectedly, his warm hands gripped her upper arms. Since she refused to look at him, his voice gentled her. "I don't want to regret anymore, Summer. I want to do the right thing. The best thing for all of us."

"Do you think I don't?"

"The way I see it, I gotta get my life together and clear up my past. If I come to you and Carrie, I want to do it with clean hands."

God, why did this man get to her the way he did? Her eyes flooded with tears. Finally, with a finger to her chin, he lifted her face to his.

"I don't want to look in your eyes like this," he whispered. "I don't want to remember the way I do every day of the year. I don't want to sit with a client, so bored out of my skull that I go over that day just for escape. I don't want to think again that I can't live another day without your touch. Without seeing you. In the days to come, I don't want to dream about the way you look tonight. I just can't afford it."

Summer was so mesmerized by his soft litany, by the depth of his sincerity, that she hadn't noticed his fingers nudging at her shirt. He had the studs back out of their holes, and stretching around her, he placed them on the built-in table. He parted the shirt and let his gaze roam over her breasts.

"I don't want to look at you like this. I don't want to want you."

She didn't want to want, either.

He stepped back to balance himself against the table, to slide out of his shoes and socks. His slacks joined her scattered clothes, and then his briefs.

He edged close again, stroked a thumb down her cheek. "I don't want to think about the way you look and feel. I don't want to kiss you," he whispered, kissing her, "because we'll make love, and then it'll start all over again. It'll go beyond my control."

Ryder kissed her, stroked her, nudged her toward the darkness beneath the bow. There, in what little light penetrated the portholes from the quiet harbor outside, the sheets remained a pool of pale blue welcome.

Lingeringly, he smoothed down her stockings. Her bikini briefs.

"Only with you," he said, worshipping her with his eyes, "do I ever feel such a complete and utter love. You amaze me."

He crawled into the bed next to her, his hands touching where his eyes had marked out the way. "I want to stop myself, but I swear I can't."

"No one knows what you're saying better than I do. I don't want to make any more mistakes, either."

He silenced her with a deep kiss, opening her mouth with his. At that point, he seemed to surrender.

And, oh, she wanted him to.

Getting up from the bed, he went to the small bathroom and returned with a condom. Without hesitation, he put it on and turned back to her, knowing that she'd watched.

He'd switched gears. The way he looked at her showed her he no longer felt anything but desire.

His fingers, his eyes, gauged the changes their child had made in her body. "I don't believe it's possible, but you're even more beautiful now than you were that day. Your beauty is deeper, more lush. Your nipples are big and dark," he said, fingering her.

"I wish I could have been with you. I wish I could've helped. Don't you see? It seems that all I do is act, then pay in remorse."

Summer ached to comfort him, to wash away the sorrow, to tell him they wouldn't waste any more energy on it. But Ryder took every thought and yearning and set it afire with a present urgency. She couldn't both regret and be on fire. Nor could he. In the moment, all that mattered was the drive to belong to each other.

"I can't hurt you somehow, can I?" he asked, positioned above her, swamped in their need.

She smiled at him. "You can only hurt me by not loving me enough."

"Then I'll never hurt you." He plunged into her, and every aspect of her—mind and heart, soul and body—welcomed him.

PALE ROSEATE LIGHT filtered in through the portholes, further illuminating the soft look in Ryder's eyes. He leaned on an elbow, just above Summer, as close as he could get.

He'd wakened her with another round of urgent loving, then threw aside the sheets, intent on a long, slow exploration of her with his eyes and fingertips. And questions. A thousand questions.

His fingers left a trail of pleasure on her stomach. She tried to ignore it and, unlike him, also tried to keep her eyes to herself. She just couldn't be that bold yet.

"Did you have morning sickness?" he asked.

"Some, but actually I had an easy pregnancy."

"And what was the birth like? Easy, too, I hope. I wish I'd been there."

"There wasn't much you could have done."

"Yeah, but I could have talked to you, you know, been there."

Summer permitted herself to study him. He had very large feet. Brown and callused from going barefoot, they were also well kept.

Despite his rugged features, he could be defined as a beautiful man. Especially in the nude. He was like a sculpture, but with the deep shadow of a beard. He reminded her more of the sea bum than of the polished power player. The veneer had vanished and he was revealed to her.

His thumb lightly circled her nipple. "Did you nurse her?"

"For a few months."

He bent and kissed her, his tongue playing a tender game with hers. "We make great children together."

She touched his cheek.

"I want to hear all the baby stories, you know."

"And you will."

He reclined against the pillows, as comfortable with his nudity as she was not with hers.

The hard masculine strength of his body seemed at odds with his vulnerable core. He had long tapering legs with well-muscled thighs and calves. Most of him was nut brown. Pale creases fanned from the corners of his eyes as he often squinted at the sun and sea. But the shadings from his waist—a toasty brown at his belly, then light tan to the creamy white of his most private area—fascinated her.

When he spoke, she averted her eyes. "You know, don't you, that I don't see this as a fantasy anymore?"

"Me neither."

"This is real."

"About as real as you can get." She tugged the sheet across herself, but not across him. While he welcomed her as she snuggled into his chest, she continued her covert study of him.

"Actually, we have a lot in common. We've both had a lot to overcome. What with my absent father and yours abandoning you, we've had rocky starts. We've both worked hard since."

"That's true."

"I think we might be able to..."

Summer thrilled at the hint of hope in his voice. Yes, they might be able to...

"You've got to remember, though," he said, turning to her suddenly, almost desperately renewing his embrace. "I'm really different now. I mean, if I had seen you, say when I was in college...God, I would've gone nuts at the sight of you. I would have been so intent on having you that I would've watched your every move. I would have badgered you, tracked you. Yeah, I had a real attitude. And even if I had convinced you somehow, I wouldn't have recognized what I'd won. I wouldn't have appreciated you. You do understand all that, don't you? I was that different."

"You don't need to confess to me," Summer replied. "I understand. And anyway, you've put all that behind you."

She could tell he wasn't nearly as sure as she was. And there was something else, something he wasn't telling her.

She wondered if he didn't yearn for something other than what he did for a living. Just as he told her enough about his mother without exposing the specifics, he also hinted at a deep unhappiness with his work at Calder Parks Development.

Above all, Summer knew he hadn't entirely surrendered to her, and especially not to the future. No, even though he kissed her with real need, deep inside, he was still holding back.

CHAPTER THIRTEEN

CARRIE SCAMPERED along the deserted beach, bobbing for shells, challenging the gentle surf with her chunky feet. Ryder and Fred followed her in a more direct line. Often, Fred joined Ryder for his Saturday-afternoon stint of baby-sitting, and when the day was perfect, the three sauntered down the beach, then back to the Flamingo Resort.

The west coast of Florida was a fisherman's paradise. Fishing and boating outdistanced golf and tennis as favorites and always had. Naturally, Fred's conversations ran to the old days. But Ryder's tales of the battles he'd fought with big-game fish had also become a staple—marlin off the southernmost keys, tarpin and kingfish right off Sarasota, then sail- and swordfish farther out.

"Now, this was off the shallows of Biscayne Bay, you know."

Fred trudged beside Ryder, his hands in the back pockets of his baggy slacks. "Yeah, yeah. Off Miami."

"In three-foot seas. I tell you, my fishing buddies had everything they could do to keep down their lunch. But when I pulled that red snapper out of that green warm water, it was like pulling out the sun itself. It was a perfect fish. All golds and reds...myriad shades, shining like the sun. A perfect day. A perfect fish.''

And then, Fred was never outdone by Ryder's fish stories. ''It was just about here,'' he said a little later, stopping to survey the gentle swell of the ever-changing beach. ''I told you about that, didn't I? The day I met up with that blue heron? He stood as confident as you please, not too much shorter than me, looking me straight in the face. I said hello, and walked on by. Of course, the fish are doin' better than the birds. Used to be terns nesting here in their season, and the herons like that were common. Fewer and fewer birds now. Even less and less in the future. Yeah, yeah,'' he said, picking up their pace, ''it's just as well I get out now.''

Ryder's eyes traced Carrie's erratic path. She clapped her hands at the laughing gulls swarming overhead. Ryder thought she was as native along the beach as the wildlife. He wondered how much of her time here she'd remember. He wished they could all live by the gulf—he and Carrie and Summer and maybe...

Since that first night on his boat, Summer and he had made love regularly and always with contraception. And while he dreamed along the lines of family and permanency, dreams didn't equate to reality. Not to the reality he lived.

Somehow, for all his dreams, they couldn't outweigh his nagging caution, his constant need to prove himself—to say, see, I can make the kind of money my family has always made. I can do it as well as anybody. Worse, his struggle clouded these happy days with Summer and Carrie.

If he could only release the struggle, let go of the past.

"You know," Fred said, eyeing him as if he understood more of Ryder than anyone, of that most private aspect of Ryder—his dream, "I've been talkin' with that friend of mine who lives up in Bradenton. The one who owns Crane's Full-Service Boat Rentals."

Ryder's ears perked up and Fred knew it.

"He's real anxious to sell out and retire. Now, it's a really big operation, you know. All kinds of boats for rent. Deep-sea and offshore charters and guides. The whole bit."

Ryder rubbed the back of his neck and squinted against the bright white sand. "It sounds ideal. But I don't know."

"You don't know what, precisely?"

As in former conversations about this, Ryder hedged. "It would take the juggling of the century to pull off the finances. A combination of my money and loans from my family money and a bank, and, hell, it's complicated."

"Yeah, but it's something you're used to figurin'."

"Oh, yeah, I know *how* to do it. But it would be risky. At least for the next several years."

"New businesses are always risky. Damn, nowadays old businesses are, too."

Ryder simply didn't have an answer. His biggest dream of having Carrie and Summer and a family was followed by this close second. To not only have a business of his own, but to have one that dealt, daily, in fishing and in what he liked most, messing around in boats... It was all too good to be true, and he'd never lived too-good-to-be-true. Not until lately had he even approached it.

If he could just do it.

If he could just feel he deserved to do it.

"You know," Fred said, measuring him out of the corner of his eye. "I've got a little money from the sale of the resort. Not much," he qualified, "but I'd be glad to help you out."

Ryder shook his head, bowing it and keeping his gaze to the sand. To hear Fred make that kind of offer, when Fred had invented penny-pinching and caution, cut Ryder to the core.

"Thanks," Ryder finally managed to say, still avoiding the old man's stolen glances. "That means a lot to me, Fred, but it's more than the money."

"Yeah, yeah, I know." Fred Miller understood a man's pride. A man's need to prove himself through his own efforts. A man's push to make up for the past and to ensure the future of those he loved. In those needs, Fred was of the old school.

Despite the warm day, despite even the growing relationship with Fred that meant so much to him, Ryder felt bleak.

WELL, OF COURSE, Summer thought. All of her questions concerning her and Ryder were tied in with how much he planned to be with her and Carrie. And that point led to the house she was buying. If he was going to be with them as much as he had been, the move into a bigger space would be a relief. That meant he should like the place they silently inspected.

The next question she had to ask herself was whether they were coming together as a family? Could he do that? There were times when she knew he could, when he seemed to know he could, too. Since they'd first made love again on his cruiser, she'd tasted what it could be like with them—with the three of them.

But then, moments like this cropped up. Moments when he distanced himself. The house was musty and especially dank on this damp day. The power had been turned off weeks ago, and the air hung so heavily that Carrie seemed to feel it, too. As they walked through the empty rooms, ending up in the one that would be Summer's bedroom, Carrie leaned limply into Summer's shoulder.

"Here, let me take her," Ryder said, reaching for the child.

Carrie went to him readily, then hung on him in the same way.

"She's just cranky," Summer said. "It's nearly suppertime, and all day, while Dee and I worked in the kitchen, she fussed."

Ryder hadn't seen the house before. Yet when she'd asked him to meet her here, he'd easily agreed. Summer didn't really know why she'd wanted him to come so badly. With or without his approval, she'd buy the house. With or without an outright push on his part, she'd move in, too.

"Where will you put the bed?" he asked, bringing her eyes back to his.

They tended to share her double at the bungalow, and she'd told him about the queen she had ordered for this room. Still, the subject of the bed reemphasized their problem. Yes, they slept together. They shared Carrie and their everyday lives. And yes, most of the time they were happy.

But...

Summer pushed back a damp curl. She looked at Ryder.

Carrie's head nodded close to his, her two fingers in her mouth indicating her fussiness. With their faces so close, the comparison was inevitable. Green eyes. Dimples. The same smile. At times like this, Summer realized how much they had at stake.

Oh, God, she loved to look at them like this. Ryder and Carrie were so good together. So natural.

She focused on his earlier question. The bed. "I thought I'd put it over against that wall."

Nodding, Ryder snuggled Carrie's droopy head to his shoulder and looked at Summer squarely. "I like the house. Really, I do. We'll have a lot more room here, and I'll do whatever I can to help. With the move. With the money. It's just that..."

"It's just what?"

"Rochelle Waller called Vance."

In her mind, Summer tallied the facts. This was Friday, and tomorrow she and Carrie and Ryder were supposed to drive to Palm Beach. Actually, they'd been looking forward to it. They were eager to be with Vance and B.J. again, and Vance had been encouraging about Ryder's mother. Evidently, Evelyn, too, approved of the visit.

So now what? Summer asked herself, trying to contain the irritation that bubbled inside.

"Vance says that Rochelle was interested in getting in touch with me, and when she found out I'd be in Palm Beach over the weekend, she asked if she and her fiancé could fly down for Saturday afternoon. She wants to talk to me again. Frankly, I don't know what good any more conversation will do. I mean, not if she can't tell the truth. Which she obviously can't do without trusting me. And my family, too. Still, she's coming, and with Mother there, I have to admit I'm worried.''

Once again, Summer admired Ryder for not cutting up his mother when he had the chance. Mother. Mother. They always pussyfooted around the subject of Evelyn Craig. Remembering her situation with her own mother, Summer fidgeted with her car keys.

"Dada," Carrie said softly.

Summer felt doubly stunned. First, to hear Carrie say Dada, and then to see Ryder break into one of his totally unanticipated grins brought her up short.

Still, his words, applied with a kiss to the top of Carrie's curly head, were for Carrie. "Just one more minute, honeybunch. We'll go soon."

Stepping up to Summer, he enfolded her with the arm that didn't support their wilted daughter. "I know you have to go back to the church for a while."

"What with taking off the weekend, I can hardly leave Dee in the lurch."

Ryder nodded. "I'll take Carrie home, and you come when you're ready."

Damn, he was always so understanding. He was also potent. He wove a quick spell on Summer's mouth.

"The bed," he whispered, letting her go, "will be fine against that wall."

Well, Summer thought, watching Ryder walk away with Carrie and voicing the word, at least, to herself. *I have that much commitment.* But no, that wasn't it, either. She knew she and Carrie had Ryder's commitment. And he told them often enough that he loved them. It was just...just so damned confusing, she told herself.

By the time Summer left Dee, her inner turmoil had subtly escalated rather than abated. She tugged her baseball cap close to her sunglasses.

On the highway out to the key, she noticed that the heavy grayness had begun to dissipate at the horizon. Maybe tomorrow would be better, if not with the situation in Palm Beach, then with the weather.

Because it was dusk, Summer reached forward to switch on her headlights, and just as hers went on, so did the lights in her rearview mirror.

"Come on now, come on now," she said to herself, her gaze going back and back again to the odd slant of the lights. "Don't panic. You're out here on the highway, but the next exit is yours, and then . . ."

She gripped the wheel. She thought about the Mace in her purse. "And then what? Are you gonna cave in to this? Run away?"

The emotions that had only simmered lately now reached full boil. What right did this creep have to—

"To what?" she asked herself. "What's he doing? Aside from intimidating you? What in the hell are you afraid of? You've never even seen the jerk's face!"

Turning off at the exit with steely determination, Summer watched the lopsided headlights follow. The driver even adjusted the distance between them, keeping close.

"Okay, okay. Come on, buddy. Just come on."

She recognized her anger. But she also felt as cool as a cucumber. Once over the final bridge out to Fiesta Key, there was that straight stretch, deserted now, of course. Then, the Flamingo Resort. But it was the straight stretch she concentrated on.

Good, good, she thought with one glance in her mirrors. The cockeyed lights kept up in her rearview mirror through the last light of day.

Surprising herself with a neatly executed maneuver, Summer all but swerved across the road and slammed on her brakes. The van shuddered to a stop.

Behind her, the pickup screeched, its wheels locking in a blue haze as it also jerked to a halt.

Out here, they were alone, would probably continue to be. But dammit! She'd had it!

It had finally boiled down to the two of them.

Poppy couldn't know.

Detective Green had said the police couldn't help.

Ryder, who waited for her at the resort, would be so furious.

This guy could be one of that small percentage who wouldn't back down, but...

Reaching into her purse and grabbing the Mace, Summer jumped out of her van. Aside from that, she was beyond considering right or wrong, crazy or caution. She stalked back to the chugging pickup.

Obviously trying to get the old rattletrap to react, the driver inside finally went still at her approach. She saw him only as a dark hulk, but she barely registered that, either.

"Okay," she muttered.

Retaining enough sense to stand somewhat back, she stopped level with his closed window. She licked her lips, tightened her grasp on the cool cylinder at her side.

But then she saw the black-booted foot meeting the pavement, and heard the pickup's door protesting as it was shoved wide-open. A giant pulled himself out of the ominous pile of junk—a great hulk of a guy in black leather and with a dawning smirk on his lips.

"Whooee, baby. Ain't you a beauty. And all riled up, too. Gave me a little surprise there," he admitted, nodding at the pickup that sat dead in its tracks.

Fear drained from Summer. Rage filled in. "What the hell is the matter with you?"

"Why, nothing—" he hesitated "—nothing's wrong with me, honey. Nothing at all."

"You don't think that following a woman around and scaring her half to death doesn't make you sound like you have a screw loose?"

His smile slipped. "Why, honey, I've been paying you a compliment. Don't you know that?"

"Paying me a compliment?"

"Why, sure. I was just getting to know you. Kinda watching you and thinking that we might, uh…"

His suggestive grin sent her into a rage that she hadn't known she was capable of.

Still, she kept a lid on it. This guy wasn't worth her fear. He was merely a creep. He was one of that large percentage who did no more than get some kind of warped kick out of following women.

He disgusted her. "Let me tell you something, buddy. I've got your license number now. And your description. I've been in contact with the police, and it wouldn't take much for me to invade your life the way you have mine."

That got his attention. His smile died.

"If I ever see your lights in my rearview mirror again, if I ever catch so much as a glimpse of you, I'm going to find out where you live and work. I'm going to raise such a stink that you won't know how to get away from it. Have you got that?"

Although the man's demeanor became less cocky, he made a macho attempt to retaliate. "What in hell's the matter with you, lady? I said I was paying you a compliment."

"And I'm telling you that there isn't a woman alive who thinks that being scared is a compliment. If you want someone in your life, buddy, then get a therapist."

"The hell! It's you that's crazy, lady, not me! You're just too damned stuck-up! Think you're too damned good for me!"

As he climbed in his pickup, he flung his final remark at her over his shoulder. "Who needs you, bitch? You won't see me again! I wouldn't give you the satisfaction!"

Summer listened to the door on his truck slam shut. Standing her ground, she watched the creep grow even more flustered inside the cab as he worked to get his heap restarted.

And while it took what seemed like forever, Summer didn't budge.

And he knew she watched him.

But finally, the pile of junk came to life, and after maneuvering along the narrow old road, the creep gunned his engine and laid down a trail of rubber and pale blue exhaust as he peeled off.

She was rid of him. She'd also gotten lucky. He hadn't been one of that small percentage who could have done her real harm, and she was grateful for that.

She let down her shoulders and, feeling the can of Mace slip from her nerveless fingers, went to her van.

CALM BUT oddly determined, Summer parked in front of her bungalow. The last daylight revealed a broken bank of clouds on the horizon and turned the gulf to a worn bronze sea. Plucking up her baseball cap, she headed for the bungalow, feeling the changes both deep in herself and in the weather.

Indeed, inside, short crisp curtains fluttered, welcoming the soft breeze. She could hear Ryder, back in her bedroom, crooning an old rock song obviously adapted for their daughter.

"Carrie, Carrie, Carrie, do you love me?" was more a deep murmur than a melody. "Carrie, Carrie, Carrie, do you care?"

Standing silently in the door of her small, crowded bedroom, Summer saw Ryder sprawled across the mattress. He wore only jeans, and one large bare foot tapped out the rhythm of his song against the floor.

Carrie was perched on his bare chest, giggling. All bathed and ready for bed, she wore Minnie Mouse pj's and a hat Ryder had formed from a paper bag.

"Carrie, Carrie, Carrie, do you care?" he repeated, getting lost in the exact lyrics. "Come on, Carrie. Give me a kiss. Plant one right here. On my cheek. You got a hat. I get a kiss."

He pointed at his cheek, and bursting into a renewed string of giggles, their child shook her head. "No."

"You kiss Mommy."

"No."

"You kiss Poppy."

"No."

"Yes, you do," he insisted softly.

But Carrie had glimpsed Summer. "Mamamama," she called.

Summer forced herself forward. Emotions pounded at her. Somehow she smiled and dropped a peck on

Carrie's fragrant round cheek. "Hello, honey-chunk."

Mostly, Summer felt Ryder's eyes on her. His study became so serious that he got up from the bed, still with Carrie in his grasp. "Say night-night to Mommy," he urged. "She's ready. Really sleepy, in fact," he said to Summer.

After more kisses and more good-nights, he disappeared with Carrie, only to return in record time. By then, Summer was pulling down a stack of baseball caps she had stashed on the shelf of her closet. She dumped them in a wastebasket.

"What's going on?" he asked, frowning.

"I just met up with the creep."

"What?"

"Oh, don't look like that. The jerk is no more than a king-size bag of wind. Large, harmless... brainless."

"What in hell are you talking about?"

As Summer described her brief encounter, she kept pushing the baseball hats into the trash can.

Ryder thrust a hand through his hair. "I don't know whether to find him and cut out his heart, to turn you over my knee and spank your butt or to shake your hand."

"If I have a choice—" an unbidden smile tilted her mouth "—I'll take the handshake."

She opened her drawers and started pulling out bulky sweaters, formless slacks—the whole ugly wardrobe she had collected over the years.

Her disguises.

"Actually," she said calmly, "now that I'm more clear, I'm not so sure that I'd recommend a confrontation like that to anyone else, with the same problem. In fact, I wouldn't. I only know I'm glad it's over."

Ryder's gaze followed her every move.

"Look," she said, dumping the accumulation of clothing from her arm onto the floor. "All I know is that I'm not hiding behind sunglasses and baseball caps and big clothes anymore. I'm not going to be afraid anymore. This is the way I look. How other people react to me, how they perceive me, is their problem. I'm not knocking myself out anymore, anticipating what others will do or think. The truth is, I'm me, however I look. And frankly, looking the way I do isn't half-bad."

Finally Ryder smiled. "Lady, it ain't half-bad at all."

Swiftly he caught her up against him, lifted her off the floor. What with the few boxes she'd packed, and now the mess she'd made with her clothes, he nearly tripped. But he caught his balance. He was strong and vital and sweet. His rare laughter warmed Summer.

His face was close. "I'm so glad you've made peace with your dragon. I've always felt I couldn't push it, but you're so beautiful, so beautiful, so beautiful. You're my summer sun. You dazzle me." He fell with her onto the bed. "I love you so much."

Yes, Summer thought, looking into his face, fingering his hair, his barely bearded jawline. Here again was her sea bum. He was so good for her. So good to her. The miniature he'd given her, which rested on the bedside table, meant so much.

The copper light slashing into the room in a last blaze, the precious sight and sounds of Ryder with Carrie that she'd witnessed on coming home—

She felt as if everything was within her grasp. And she knew Ryder remained unsure of himself. But surely it wouldn't slip through their fingers. Perhaps it was just getting through tomorrow. Through their trip to Palm Beach. They'd come this far; they could make it through Palm Beach.

In Ryder's escalating kisses, Summer felt his urgent need for her and felt the need herself. When he pulled back, studying her face, she peered at him questioningly.

The wind in the window puffed out the white curtains, stirred his dark hair. The sensual assault was pure pleasure. She waited, wanted, looked into his green eyes as they examined her.

In this precious moment, at least, he wasn't holding back.

CHAPTER FOURTEEN

SUMMER FELT THAT beyond the cloistered atmosphere of the Mediterranean-style home of the Craigs, Palm Beach represented the fast track. She'd been impressed by that idea at lunch. And lunch was obviously an important ritual for Evelyn Craig. Everyone had been on time. Everyone had let her dominate the conversation. Everyone had listened to her chatter about the Palm Beach social round.

Now, as Summer changed and put Carrie down for a nap, she felt as if she'd landed from the moon. She'd never fit in at Palm Beach. Nor would she want to. Society and wealth and the games they demanded were beyond Summer's comprehension and interest.

Of course, following lunch, things had gotten somewhat better. Evelyn had retired behind her newspaper on her wicker lounge. The rest of them—B.J. and Vance, Summer, Ryder and Carrie—had swum in the perfect pool in its perfect setting.

With Carrie there, they'd fallen easily into a sense of family. And if they could take steps toward becoming a family, that would make the trip worthwhile.

Vance's welcome had been surprisingly genuine. In Sarasota, Summer had wondered if she could like him. Now, she knew she'd have to. He had warmed to her, and because he looked so much like Ryder, Summer found it hard to dislike him.

But of course, B.J. really lifted Summer's hopes. When she and B.J. had spoken of her boys, Summer had seen how much she missed them.

But now, as she stood in her assigned bedroom, Summer's easiness vanished. She wondered if her palazzo pants of raw white silk could stand Evelyn Craig's scrutiny.

Looking at her clothes strewn across her bed and the Italian double dresser, she thought of how her background and family differed from Ryder's. Not that that seemed to matter to Ryder. Ryder, the sea bum. Ryder, who chafed against the work he did no matter how well he did it.

A soft knock interrupted her musings, and Summer went to the door. B.J., in a flowing beach caftan, stood on the other side, her short ash blond hair perfectly arranged.

"Is she still asleep?"

"Sure." Summer opened the door. "You can come in. Once she's down, she sleeps for hours."

B.J.'s gaze traveled from the unpacked clothing to the crib where Carrie slept, then back to Summer. "I see you're ready."

"Do you think this is all right?"

"You could wear a gunnysack and it would be all right."

"Yes, but you know what I mean."

"Unfortunately I do. Evelyn always holds court at lunch like that. You'll probably get used to her sooner or later. It's either that or having nothing to do with her at all. Evelyn doesn't unbend for anyone."

Summer's discomfort with talking about Ryder's mother must have showed in her face, because B.J. went on in her frankest fashion. "Look, I don't like talking about her, and I don't want to sound two-faced. The truth is, Evelyn and I get along. But the reason we get along is that I want us to. I've always wanted a family, and since there wasn't any possibility of that on my side, I've done what I could to make it easy for Vance and the boys. And Evelyn, too. But don't get me wrong. I know what she's like. If she'd treated Vance the way she treated Ryder, I'm sure I'd feel differently. Only Ryder has ever gone against Evelyn's wishes. And then only because he needed more from her. Even Vance, Sr., let her rule the roost." Sighing, B.J. plunged ahead. "But what's most important now is that you and I are up front with each other. Honestly, what Vance and I build with you and Ryder means a lot to us."

Having said all that, B.J. lapsed into easiness. With a big smile, she admitted as much. "I'm glad I got that out. What's more, you don't need to watch what you say about her, either. As far as I'm concerned, people like Evelyn leave themselves open to the opinions of others simply because they're so judgmental themselves."

Summer felt better. But before she could comment, B.J. went on, her voice low for Carrie's sake, but her movements and expressions animated.

"I mean, just look at this. Making you share a room with Carrie, and ignoring your right to decide whether you sleep with Ryder."

"I can respect her wishes under her own roof."

"Yes, but she's such a hypocrite. I mean, in *Palm Beach*. Palm Beach is the height of sleeping where you want and with whom you want, just as long as you respect the money. Well, anyway," she said, shrugging and going on, "when we came down before we were married, Evelyn turned a blind eye to Vance and me sleeping together. She's just making one of her queenly statements.''

''You mean she doesn't approve of Carrie's illegitimacy?''

''No, that's not it, either. Besides, that's no one's business but yours and Ryder's. No, what she's doing is making a show of disapproving in case any of her friends drop by. Which, let's hope, doesn't happen. We have only tonight, and then you leave in the morning. And while I know this thing with Rochelle Waller can't be helped, I must admit I'm disappointed we can't simply go out to a movie and have a hamburger. I mean, you and I and Vance and Ry.''

Once again, Summer would have agreed, but B.J. was on a roll. ''And I also want you to know that when Vance helped you out of the car and hugged you, he meant it. He likes it that you're with Ryder. He wants what I want for all of us. It's just that sometimes he's more slow to accept people.''

Summer raised a hand. ''I understand what you're saying. I'm afraid he's like me in that regard. And yes, I've decided I'm ready for a family, too.''

''Great, great. Now this bit with Rochelle just has to work out. Then we'll all have the fresh start we need.''

''I must say I'm nervous about Rochelle Waller.''

B.J., who had ended up by the French doors that opened on to a little balcony overlooking the pool below, parted the draperies and peered down. ''They aren't here yet. Vance says Rochelle's fiancé is really nice. Vance thinks he's the real mover behind this meeting. Who knows what Rochelle is up to. She can be a hell-raiser if she wants to be.''

''You know her, then?''

"Oh, only what I've heard down through the years. Ours is kind of a closed circle."

"Yeah, well, that makes me feel left out."

B.J. came to give Summer a quick hug. "I know," she said. "Palm Beach is enough to strike fear into any heart. But don't worry. Vance and I don't do that scene, either. Only Evelyn. And she won't insist. Because you're so beautiful, she might occasionally want to show you off at lunch, but only if you marry Ryder. We'll worry about that bridge when we come to it. For now, there's just us chickens."

"Yes, us chickens. Us chickens in this humble chicken coop."

B.J. laughed. Then, with a cautionary peek at Carrie who remained asleep, she coaxed Summer to the door with an arm around her shoulders. Because their heights were the same, B.J.'s gray eyes looked directly into Summer's blue ones.

"Just a few rules will get you by. No matter how unnice she is, be nice to Evelyn. Be attractive. She *loooves* attractive. And no matter what she says, she's actually more shallow than she's cruel. In fact, it's only with Ryder that she's cruel, and that's because she knows he expects more from her and always has. Vance says that Ryder has pretty much given up caring what Evelyn thinks. Frankly, that's the best any of us can do. In her heart of hearts, Evelyn doesn't care, so why should we give her more than she can accept? It sounds cynical, I know, but just give her what she wants and she'll be happy."

Yes, Summer thought. Behind that easygoing nature, B.J. was no dummy. What's more, B.J. had a heart of gold. She was obviously the one behind their coming together.

RYDER WAITED with Vance by the pool. Rochelle would arrive soon. And while he was anxious, he'd learned to disguise his feelings. Except with Vance, now. He wondered if, with his calm gaze, Vance didn't read him right.

"Are you okay, Ry?"

Ryder smiled. "Piece of cake."

Vance didn't smile.

The afternoon shadows lengthened into early evening. Although lunch with his mother had been typical, the few hours in the pool had been fun. Being the center of attention had delighted Carrie. He reminded himself that he was doing this for Carrie. For Carrie and their future together.

Ryder peered down into his glass of mint-garnished tomato juice. Vance nursed a Bloody Mary, and Ryder longed for a little numbing, too. But it had been years since he'd had alcohol.

"You say," he stated, "Rochelle's fiancé, this, uh..."

"Patrick Fleming."

"Yeah, Patrick Fleming. That he didn't explain what she wants."

"My impression is that Rochelle wants to run the show. But like I say, Patrick Fleming is such a laid-back guy that he wasn't too clear. He just said she wants the whole family here."

Ryder squinted. The sun made a glittering path across the water's surface.

His best childhood memories were, like Vance's, tied in with their vacations from school. Here, in Palm Beach. And while the place was familiar, it wasn't home to him.

Home was now represented by Summer and Carrie and by that little bungalow at the Flamingo Resort. No matter what happened today—and he had to admit he was afraid of what might happen—the tender ties that now bound him would never be broken. Not in his heart.

Finding that thought as unnerving as what lay ahead, he got a grip on himself. He had to stay sharp. He had to face whatever Rochelle Waller would have to say without letting it get to him.

Just as in the past, he would also have to swallow his mother's certain judgments. And while he had no more answers for her now than he'd had then, the old resistance to her disapproval burned in him.

He couldn't believe it, but he felt like some damned kid again. It staggered him. As a kid, he'd been so angry and he'd never known why.

"Are you sure you're okay, Ry?"

Ryder looked into his brother's steady gaze. "Yeah, yeah. I just have to concentrate on finding out what happened in Vermont. On discovering the truth, if I can. I'd like to clear my name. I'd like to reclaim a sense of belonging. I need to keep my life on an even keel," Ryder shrugged. "Who knows? Maybe Rochelle will help."

Vance appeared as doubtful as Ryder felt. Rochelle Waller had a reputation for being anything but helpful.

Ryder's smiles remained slightly sour. "As if all of this isn't enough, I'm thinking about leaving Calder."

Amazed, Vance halted their leisurely pace. "Leaving Calder?"

"Yeah, I know it sounds like I'm just dropping out again, but . . . Well, you know Summer's grandfather, Fred Miller."

"Right."

"He and I have been talking a lot. It seems that as I'm getting older, I'm gaining some generous mentors in my life. I mean, Calder's always talking about second chances and finding the middle ground. At first, I didn't know what he meant, but, uh..."

Ryder looked at his brother. He wanted to see if Vance understood what he was talking about. In the past, Vance would have drawn a blank, but maybe not now.

"No, no," Vance said. "I think that's good. I mean, about finding a middle ground. Especially with how we were raised. Like Dad had been raised. To inherit money and then to make more money than our family ever had. It's a lot of pressure, but I just happened to take to that programming better than you did. Not that you don't make one hell of a competitor. Nobody knows that better than I do. I should be glad you're leaving the business."

Ryder thought it was good to kid around with Vance. Better yet to confide in him and have him understand.

"On the other hand," Vance continued, "you have to be fair to Calder, too."

"No one knows that better than I do. He treats me like a son, he wants me to take over his business, and I owe it to him to be straight with him. But it's more that I haven't made up my own mind. I have to be sure I don't screw up again."

"I know. I know," Vance murmured.

"And what do you think Dad would say now?"

"I think he'd want you to be happy. He might not understand that point of Calder's about finding the middle ground, but I know Dad would want you to be happy, Ry."

The pair began to pace beside the pool again, still more uneasy than relaxed.

"And if you leave Calder?" Vance asked. "What will you do?"

"Fred's been telling me about this charter-boat fishing company that's coming up for sale soon. The guy's retiring."

Again Ryder glanced at his brother to see how this idea hit him.

"I think it sounds good for you," Vance said.

"It's not what the family—"

"No, but it sounds good for you, Ry. That's what you gotta think about now. I'm learning that we're not all the same, and that we each need to do what's good for us."

Hearing the door that opened on to the patio close, Ryder and Vance turned to see their mother coming out.

In flowing green silk trousers and emeralds and diamonds, she was dressed for the evening. She surveyed the pool area for the least imperfection.

Ryder took a drink of his tomato juice. "And Mother?" he asked Vance. "What do you think she'll say if I start—as she used to put it—shunning the responsibilities of life again and messing around in boats?"

Vance gazed at Ryder, then, suddenly, surprisingly, grinned. "I think she'll say what she's always said, Ry. Over and over and over. She's not going to like it one bit."

"Well," Evelyn said, coming toward them and interrupting their shared chuckle, "at least you're here. I hope the girls won't be late. Rochelle and Patrick should be here any minute, and I hate it when anyone's late. It's so impolite."

Evelyn peered at the drink in Ryder's hand. "I hope that's nonalcoholic, Ryder. Your behavior gets even worse when you drink, and with Rochelle, we'll certainly need our wits about us."

"It's just tomato juice," he said very calmly, he thought.

But inside...

To feel a renewing sense of the same old rage and guilt these years later was as ridiculous to Ryder as it was true. In the past he'd invariably lost the most control after an encounter with his mother. Like the first time he'd tried to reconcile with his family on Christmas Eve and she'd seen his advances as impertinence, as a social blunder. That occasion had set him up emotionally for the ski weekend in Vermont.

And yet, Ryder also knew he was too old to blame his mother for anything anymore. He was a grown man, and he saw her now for what she was and always had been.

Then why in the hell was she getting to him? And especially today? Today when he didn't need it. It was the shame, of course. That old cloak he'd worn and tried to discard by keeping his nose to the grindstone. He was ashamed to face the past, but even more so to face it in front of Summer.

He thought he'd never put it all behind him, and the old impulse to run pounded at him equally hard. That was the scariest part, of course. Going off the deep end again. Returning to *Spare a Dime* and the life of a bum.

But then he had to think straight. Across the pool, Summer and B.J. joined Evelyn in a circle of white wicker chairs. He barely had time to fortify himself with just looking at Summer when Rochelle Waller stepped onto the patio, closely followed by a pleasant-looking guy who had to be her fiancé, Patrick Fleming.

SUMMER DID what she could to keep her eyes from Ryder. She was afraid for him, and he had to be worried enough. He and Vance walked toward them in the circle of chairs. And while the polish that Ryder strove for was native to Vance, both men had something about them that attracted attention. With similar smiles, they accepted the round of greetings and introductions and sat down.

Naturally, the discussion started innocuously enough. The weather and the trip down were topics that had to be aired. Summer thought Rochelle Waller was as uncomfortable as the rest of them. Aside from Evelyn. Evelyn was in her element. As for Patrick Fleming, he simply observed with a pleasant smile accenting his pleasant features.

Summer hardly had the patience for the next subject—gossip about mutual friends, both in Palm Beach and New York. Another round of drinks was served, and while she and B.J., Vance and Ryder and Patrick Fleming grew more quiet—and even Rochelle only murmured responses—Evelyn wouldn't shut up.

Rochelle appeared more uncomfortable by the moment, Summer thought. And though Summer knew the woman had to be confident, even outgoing, Rochelle looked anything but. She was small, dark and pretty and dressed expensively, like Evelyn.

Why didn't they put Ryder out of his misery?

But then, Summer only surmised that Ryder was miserable. When she looked at him, he appeared contained, even indulgent toward his mother. Still, knowing him as she did now, Summer also knew differently. He had to be in pain. With his mother, he suffered pain.

Finally, Rochelle was talking in terms that grabbed everyone's attention.

"I know," she was saying, "that I'm taking a chance coming here today. Still, I'm pretty certain it isn't too much of a chance." Looking at her fiancé, she smiled slightly. "Patrick has encouraged me to come. And while this is hard for me, he and I have discussed some sort of meeting like this often enough for us to think it's the right thing to do. And that," she said, facing Ryder, "is really why I'm here, Ry. I know you're trying to make a fresh start just like I am."

Any other conversation was out of the question. Everyone sat, absorbed by Rochelle, by what she endeavored to bring to the surface.

"Not too long ago, Ry, when you came to New York, you asked me to help you with the things you can't remember. I saw then that you have a right to know what I both know and recall. In fact, I think I can't go on until I get it all out. So please forgive me if I take my time—if I'm not sure how to do this. Anyway—" she cleared her throat "—I see now that I was the one who had maneuvered Ryder into our college engagement. It was more my doing than yours," she said, actually looking at Ryder, "and now I see that. But then, well, I really did love you, Ry. Much more than you ever loved me. I knew you were capable of loving someone, but that someone wasn't me. I could never be the one for you, and there would be only one. I think every girl who knew you recognized that. That's why you seemed so dangerous, so alluring. I wanted to be the one, but I couldn't be, and that made me angry enough to..."

Taking another encouraging cue from Patrick, Rochelle went on. "Your rejection hurt me deeply. But in my heart, I also knew you were being honest in breaking it off. Years later then, at the cabin in Vermont, well, that night, we'd all had too much to drink. That's not an excuse but a fact. I'm sure you, Ry, remember playing cards with me and Bunny Dale. Or at least you said you did at the trial."

Ryder nodded.

"I was so mad at you, Ry. I realize that you'd broken our engagement long before that, but I was still very, very angry. When you walked over to the couch and passed out, I felt as if I'd been deprived of my first chance to vent my anger, and . . . well, I must admit I was tough on Bunny. Not that I did anything to her physically. It was more that she tried to get you to bed, and when she stepped back from the couch, she . . . well, I guess she tripped over the hearthstones somehow. She'd had a lot to drink herself."

The story was embarrassing to recount. Everyone felt the embarrassment. Even Evelyn, Summer thought.

However, with another look at Patrick, Rochelle forged ahead. "After Bunny fell, I went to her. I could tell something was really wrong with her. I got panicky, and I also tried to wake you up, Ry."

Because her eyes were locked on Ryder's, there was no question about the focus of Rochelle's thoughts. She remembered now. Vividly. She remembered the whole scene, and the center of that scene had been Ryder.

"God, I beat on your chest, I shook you. I was so frightened. I was so damned mad at you. You'd always been so heedless, so above it all—"

She broke off, still holding Ryder's gaze.

He nodded. "Yes, you're right," he admitted. "I'm sorry about that now, Rochelle."

"No, no, you were only careless, Ry. I was the one who was wrong. I was, in fact, angry enough to want revenge and then to take my opportunity when the police came. Really, I hadn't planned it. It just spilled out. I was so frantic, so angry that you still didn't seem to care, that I started lying without considering the cost. I told the police that you and Bunny had argued, and that you'd pushed her into the fireplace and she'd . . . Of course you hadn't pushed her, she'd simply fallen somehow . . ."

Rochelle's eyes pleaded with Ryder. "Later, I couldn't go back on what I'd told the police. I just couldn't. I was afraid to. Even these past years since, I still thought you deserved what I'd done to you. That was, until Patrick. It's been Patrick who's set me straight, Ry. And that's why . . ."

When Rochelle's dark gaze zeroed in on Summer, Summer felt the impact of everyone's eyes.

"That's why," Rochelle said softly, "I can understand your need for a clean sweep. Like me, Ry, you've found the one, and neither of us can be happy without setting the past straight. I know I can't be happy until I apologize to you and your family for all the pain I caused, and I do that now."

Summer felt the silence. No one moved. Not until Ryder nodded again.

"Thanks, Rochelle," he said, remaining remote. "Thanks for coming."

"Yes, well," Evelyn said, resettling on her poolside chair. "That's all very nice of you, Rochelle. However, it doesn't change anything. You see, Ryder's always been good at getting himself into bad situations that turn even worse. If he hadn't been drunk to begin with, none of the rest would have occurred.''

Surprisingly, it was Vance who moved to the edge of his chair. ''Mother—''

But Ryder laid a hand on his brother's arm. ''Mother's right,'' he said, curbing Vance.

Silence spun out for only a moment more. Then Evelyn went on. ''So now that that's over with, why don't we have another drink before going to Taboo. Reservations are for eight.''

LYING IN BED that night, after dinner on Worth Avenue and drinks at Lulu's, Summer tried to absorb what had happened. She supposed she felt more numb than anything.

Even without talking to him, she knew Ryder hadn't survived Rochelle's shameful tale by the pool early that evening. Even with his relative conviviality during his mother's evening out, she knew Ryder had suffered. Only the fact that Vance and B.J. seemed to understand that, too, gave Summer any comfort.

And, oh, God, it had been awful. Not that she didn't know people made mistakes. She'd made some herself. What mattered was what you did with the mistakes. What they did to you. And Ryder, well, until this, he'd been doing okay. She'd sensed his shakiness all along, his holding back. But this . . . this . . .

Behind his remote facade, she'd recognized his shame. And his pain. She wanted nothing more than to comfort him. But after they'd gotten home and his mother had gone to bed, he'd made it evident that he needed his space. She wouldn't see him tonight.

Her only hope was tomorrow. In the car, on their drive back to Sarasota, surely everything would look better. Surely Carrie would have her usual softening effect on him. Surely she herself would be able to reach him, talk to him, convince him that he didn't need to be ashamed. Everyone made mistakes, and he'd done everything he could since that first day on his boat to regenerate himself.

She knew he still didn't remember anything Rochelle had told him. He'd said so at dinner. But with her and Carrie, he'd find the strength to go on. Although he remained shaky from the encounter, it could serve as a turning point from which they'd move onward and upward.

Tears of doubt and hope and commiseration blurred Summer's gaze. The pale-gold-and-white bedroom was slick and cool and silent. Only the floating sheers at the two sets of French doors lured her thoughts elsewhere.

Carrie. She was having such a good time that it wore her out. Carrie loved the attention that Vance and B.J. showered on her. If she wasn't smiling happily, she was falling asleep.

Evelyn, too, had been nice to Carrie. But nice defined Evelyn's limits, and Summer preferred shallow niceness to solid rejection.

And the woman was so capable of rejection. Even toward her own son. More and more, Summer respected Ryder for never speaking badly of Evelyn. Like tonight. He'd gone through hell with Rochelle, and then he'd also taken his mother's summation with polite acceptance. He hadn't even allowed Vance to defend him.

As if that hadn't been enough, Ryder had finally joined his mother's party for an evening out in Palm Beach and had acted as if he'd enjoyed it. Worse, his mother had acted as if everything he did for her was her due.

Really, Summer could have spit nails. She tossed on the large bed. She tried to think of something else. She watched the rhythmic dance of the curtains in the French windows.

She couldn't wait to get home. Palm Beach was so different from Sarasota. Although they were in the same state, there were distinct differences between them.

She dreamed of lacy foam-edged fans, overlapping in silvered slices on the white beaches of Sarasota. She dreamed . . . well, she thought she dreamed of Ryder entering her room. At first, he was an intruder in slow motion, outlined by the dim light from the hallway. He wore only a towel, and closing her bedroom door, he glided across the carpet to peer down at Carrie in her crib.

Summer wondered if she dozed, or—

He moved toward her, through the soundless shadows. Passing the French doors, he was outlined briefly and fully. He'd left his towel draped on the railing of Carrie's crib to serve as a barrier. He came to Summer with that quick, masculine grace that always sent her senses reeling.

He knelt at her bedside. His breath, his light kisses, were warm against her cheek. She reached to smooth her fingers down his jaw. Capturing her hand, he pressed devouring lips into her palm.

He whispered in her ear.

Summer stirred enough to caress the back of his neck. Quickly Ryder picked her up from the bed. Ducking his head and shoulders against the gossamer curtains, he took her out onto the balcony. There, Summer saw more than gentleness and grace and strength in him. Again she saw desperation.

The warm breeze heightened her awareness, and she saw that when he moved, when he pushed her against the stone balustrade, his back was reflected, pale and shadowy, in the glass of the French doors behind them.

She watched his muscled torso, the hardening of his tight buttocks, as he bent over her. He plundered her mouth with his tongue and pulled her nightshirt over her head.

She wanted him, too. Urgently, just as he wanted her.

The way his mouth teased her breasts soothed her aching need for him. She was as driven as he. She urged him to fill her.

Still watching in the mirroring surfaces—the smooth flow of muscle in his back and shoulders—she adjusted herself to him, too.

He spread her legs and stepped between her thighs. She opened eagerly.

He plunged into her, demanding and hot, holding her tight against him.

Making love on the small balcony felt so free. The balmy night air whipped her hair into his face and into hers. It released the intoxicating scent of him, combining it with the perfumes from the garden below.

She arched her back, lifting her arms to the starry night sky. Ryder gasped, and she could feel him luxuriating in her pleasure.

She trusted him completely. Let go completely. She reveled in his mounting surrender, in his own wild abandon. He arched, too, away from her, gripping her but straining in the opposite direction. The sight of his arms reaching out to her, of the span of his naked chest, of his throat laid bare to her, made her want to laugh and cry at the same time.

For one precious moment, he lent himself to her, to the night, to a vulnerability that accentuated the sweet experience of his release into her.

At that instant, nothing, nothing in sea or sky or space could separate them. In the silent shining night, they belonged to each other, at that precise point of physical and mental and emotional coupling, forever.

As if to prolong the moment, Ryder held Summer still, remaining still himself. But finally, he slipped from her, then embraced her again.

"Rochelle was right, you know." His husky voice betrayed his emotion. "You're the only one for me. You always have been and you always will be, no matter what happens."

Obviously no longer able to trust himself, he helped her to the floor of the balcony. Their physical communication had been so total that Summer was speechless.

From the balcony sill, she watched him go inside her room. Grabbing his towel from Carrie's crib, he dropped a kiss on their child's cheek. Then, as silently, as smoothly as he'd come, he was gone.

Summer shuddered with a lingering presentiment. Without words, he was saying goodbye.

CHAPTER FIFTEEN

SUMMER SAW that in Palm Beach the mornings were spectacular. Whereas the sun set on the gulf, it rose on the Atlantic, painting everything with soft peaches and golds. Even the pantries and kitchen at the home of Evelyn Craig.

Because she and Ryder had planned an early start returning to Sarasota, and because the housekeeper had been given the morning off for having kept Carrie the night before, Summer and her companions had scrounged around for breakfast on their own. Throughout their scramble for this pan or that piece of toast, a companionable if also bittersweet mood had pervaded their activities.

Since the housekeeper hadn't come down, neither had Evelyn. While Ryder joked with them, smiled with them, the trio shared an unspoken sense of his pulling away. Like Summer, B.J. and Vance had to wonder if Ryder could overcome this latest exposure to his past.

After cleanup, when Ryder got their bags from their rooms, Summer remained in the softly lit kitchen. Even then, she and B.J. and Vance skirted the question they had no answers for. Would this be their last time together?

B.J. sat at the kitchen table with Carrie on her lap. Vance also sat there, playing silly games with Carrie.

Yes, Summer thought, she liked Vance. Liked him a lot.

When Ryder breezed in, he cocked a brow at her but spoke to them all. "Nice tricks my brother teaches her, huh?"

"I'm sure you guys know all kinds of neat stuff you'll be more than happy to share with her."

B.J. piped up. "You can count on that. I don't know where little boys pick up the icky things they do, but they're always willing to share."

Vance glanced at Ryder. "Got everything?"

"Yeah, ready to go."

"Fill your tank?"

"Man, do you sound like a big brother."

The pair smiled at each other, but once again, it was a poignant exchange.

Getting to her feet, B.J. gave Carrie a tight squeeze. Then Vance did, too. "See ya, Boop," Vance said, handing the child to Ryder.

Summer realized that no matter what Ryder decided, he'd already committed to Carrie. And that meant B.J. and Vance would also be involved in her daughter's life to some extent. But as for Summer, well, she was obviously to be the casualty if—

If what?

She couldn't consider it. She'd been abandoned once in her life by the father she'd hardly known.

"So," Ryder said, "we're on our way."

Vance and B.J. drifted out onto the driveway, observing while Ryder secured Carrie in her car seat. At the last minute, B.J. grabbed Summer into a tearful hug. "Be careful," she said. "I'm sure it's going to be all right," she added into Summer's ear. "He's such a good guy."

Although Vance didn't say any more, he dropped a kiss on Summer's cheek before closing her car door. She heard Ryder say something to his brother and

B.J.—something about giving the boys a hug for him. Then he, too, got in the car. Vance and B.J. stood waving until Summer couldn't see them anymore.

Glancing at Ryder, she knew his emotions swamped him, and she relaxed into her seat. As much as she wanted to, she couldn't open any serious conversation now.

As if understanding some of her muddle, Ryder reached over and squeezed her hand. He kept his eyes to the road, but she thought that had he looked at her, she would have seen the same bittersweet expression.

Unbelievably, the next thing Summer knew they were pulling into the driveway at the Flamingo Resort. She'd obviously slept through the drive home.

"Sleepyhead," he said to her with a sideways glance and a soft smile.

"I can't believe I fell asleep."

"I can. Palm Beach was a hard haul. If I'd known, I wouldn't have taken you." He forced a dismissive smile. "Carrie slept all the way, too. She'll be fit for bear when she wakes up."

They both looked at their sleeping child, then at each other.

"Can't we talk about this?" Summer had to ask.

"I don't see what good it'll do."

"Your mother—"

"My mother has always known how to make me feel two inches tall. I'm as used to that as I'll ever get."

"Surely her opinions shouldn't matter to you so much anymore."

"Hell, I thought I was doing better. I thought she was unbending enough just to lay off you and Carrie."

"In the end, though, what counts is what we have, not whether she approves."

"God, I know that much."

"Then, why...?"

"Don't you see?" Ryder, who was usually patient with her and Carrie, grew impatient. Probably more with the subject and himself than with her.

"I don't want you living with that. With what Rochelle dragged out in the open again. And believe me, it's a matter of living with it. Every time I'm introduced to someone, I know there's a chance they've heard about me or read about me in the papers. I wonder if they're weighing my innocence, my guilt. Now that I'll never clear my name without damaging Rochelle, I'll have to go on living with that. And I can't ask you and Carrie to live with that, too. The innuendos are subtle, and I'm sure they'll fade more and more with time, but I don't want you facing that."

"What if I choose to? It's my choice."

"You don't choose. I do."

"Well, that sounds like we have a solid partnership going for us here."

"Yeah, well, I know what I'm talking about and you don't."

Both impatiently and apologetically he shrugged. "Come on. I'll help with your things."

Before Summer could say more, he opened the door and climbed out of the car. She had no option but to do the same. But then, after waking Carrie and getting their stuff inside the bungalow, Summer refocused on Ryder.

He observed Carrie's ongoing movements, her happy burble, with such remorse in his eyes that Summer spoke gently. Although she was determined, she couldn't hurt him. He was hurting enough.

"Ry."

He turned to her so quickly, scooped her to him so fiercely that it caught her off balance.

"Maybe," he said, his voice raspy and soft, "it's right I go on paying in shame. You have to remember that two people died as a result of my behavior. Bunny and my dad. Frankly, I feel lucky for what redemption I'll have through loving you and Carrie. And believe me," he pledged, his eyes revealing his soul, "I'll always belong to you and Carrie, no matter what."

"But, Ry, nobody died as a result of your behavior. That's—"

"No," he said, interrupting her statement and making his own through a tight throat. "That day, when I saved you out there in the gulf, I said you'd always belong to me. But it's the other way around. No matter what you do, I'll be out there, belonging to you. I'll always be wanting you and what we shared last night. That was the best I've ever known." He smiled at her softly, anchored a curl over her ear. "I know you understand. I can't discipline Boop, knowing I'm a sham."

"But you'll tell her what you've told me. When she's older, you'll show her how much you've paid for your mistakes. You can talk to her from your own experience and she'll listen. She'll love you, and—"

"And I'll do all that, anyway." He passed a finger down her cheek. "Look, Calder owes me some time, and I'm taking *Spare a Dime* up the coast for a while."

There. That was that, and Summer knew it. Oddly, instead of weeping, she felt stung. She stepped out of Ryder's arms. She faced him with all the heated resistance building inside her. He offered no phone number, no mention of a time element or a return. He didn't seem to consider their shared responsibility for Carrie.

"You know what?" she said. "You're right. You can't change the past, and you can't seem to let it go. You can't bring back Bunny and your dad. You can't get your mother to approve of you, much less to love you. You can't remember what happened in Vermont, and you can't clear your name."

She swung a hand, she didn't know where. "But look around you, Ry. I'll bet that most of those people who remember your past are willing to give you a second chance. Look at anyone—except for your mother. Look at what Rochelle Waller did in trying to help you yesterday. And at Calder Parks, who's helped you for over two years. Then, look at Vance and B.J. and Poppy and Irma. And look at me, Ry. As far as I can tell, you're the only one who isn't giving you a second chance."

She felt the fire in her eyes and stance. But when he stroked his finger down her cheek again, he couldn't have stunned her more if he'd struck her.

He wouldn't fight back.

"Hey, I love you and Carrie. I'll always do what I can to help."

Even with what they'd shared last night still in his eyes, he turned away from her. He left the bungalow, closing the door firmly behind him.

Summer knew he loved them. She also knew he'd be back. But, oh, God, what would he have decided by then? How much damage would he have done to himself? What she'd feared all along would happen now. Ryder would talk himself out of being with them.

"FRED?"

Irma entered the kitchen, and sure enough, she saw Fred at the sink doing the morning dishes. He kept a neat house, the man did. *Their* little rooms had never shone so brightly.

And Fred sure did look as cute as heck in that apron he had tied around his waist. He'd brought it from home, so it wasn't frilly. It was worn, a faded yellowish green color. A reminder of old times when every good housekeeper had worn an apron.

He glanced up from the last of the dishes he set in the rack.

She straightened her back.

She hated upsetting the apple cart. They were so happy together here of late. But—

"Fred?"

He eyed her.

"I'm sure you've noticed how unhappy Summer's been."

"She's been movin'. Bound to be tired."

"Yes, but that's not it, and you know it."

He held his ground.

She repeated herself. "Summer's unhappy."

"I'm stayin' out of it."

"You mean, you and Ryder are doing your *men thing.*"

"What in hell?"

Irma hadn't heard cuss words for some time now. Fred felt cornered. She backed him in further.

"Your *men thing.* You and Ryder. I've seen you do it before, you know. You two put your heads together and decide you can do Summer's thinking for her."

"The hell we do."

"You think you're protecting her or something."

"The hell we do."

"I can't know what Ryder's up to, but he's gone and Summer's unhappy." Walking over to him, she caged her temper. She even smiled a bit teasingly.

"I won't interfere."

"It won't be interfering to give her a phone number. An address. Then she can decide."

Fred sailed past her on his way out of the kitchen.

"Fred," she called after him.

He stopped.

Smiling at him, she sauntered over and untugged the apron strings.

"Okay, okay," he said, still grumbly. "I'm goin'."

When he turned away again, she called again. "Fred?"

He stopped.

She smiled, closed the distance between them. "Kiss me."

Fred strong-armed Irma into a fast embrace and kissed her soundly. Just that quickly he released her, and she let him escape from the kitchen.

SUMMER FOLDED the last carton shut, then stood with it against her hip. The empty bungalow reinforced her own sense of loneliness.

It was Friday, and Sunday would mark two weeks since Ryder had left to take *Spare a Dime* somewhere up the coast.

He'd left her, and he could still leave her permanently.

It seemed ironic that just as she felt herself gaining her feet and feeling comfortable with her looks, he was running away again. The oldest battles seemed to be the hardest to win, and she forced herself to face the fact that he might not come back.

With one last look at the empty living room, Summer stepped onto the porch. The sidewalks between the bungalows and the rest of the resort's facilities were drifted in sand. Automatically she scanned the horizon in the hope of seeing *Spare a Dime*.

Well, that was foolish and she knew it. What she did see was the same—the ever-changing waters that always drew and seldom frightened her. Way out, storm clouds built. From here they looked innocuous enough. But she knew they would close in on the old resort, then sweep off and let the sun shine again.

She would miss the wild, changeable weather terribly.

After putting the last boxes in her van, she turned in surprise. Poppy came toward her in his old beat-up station wagon. She couldn't help her pleasure at seeing him, but she wondered why he was here.

For weeks, he had been living with Irma, and they'd be married on the weekend following this one. A doubly happy occasion, they'd said, because they'd also celebrate Carrie's second birthday.

Summer especially avoided thinking about whether Ryder would return for those events. Instead, she concentrated on Poppy's scowl.

Jerking to a stop, he pulled his lanky frame from the old car.

"Is everything all right?" she asked, her primary thought for Carrie.

"She's still nappin'. She's fine with Irma."

When Fred shifted uncomfortably, Summer kept her thoughts from careening on.

"Wanna take a last walk?" he asked, nodding toward the beach.

Since Summer thought that was a good idea, she agreed, and they headed for the strip of sand, for that joining of land and sea that was as familiar to them as the patterns of their lives.

Finally, looking at the gathering storm clouds, Fred mustered the courage to say what was on his mind.

"You know, this ain't a good thing for Carrie, this business with Ryder. I mean, I don't have any room to preach. Your grandma left me shortly after your mama turned four, and then your daddy left you about the same time. But this business with Ry doin' the same..."

He shook his head, keeping his eyes on the glorious confusion of storm and sun. "I don't have a good record with women. Only you and Carrie have gotten me to try this deal with Irma." Exasperated, he slipped his hands into the back pockets of his slacks and forced himself on. "Oh, I guess I've cared for Irma for years, and was just plain scared to try."

"I know what you're saying, Poppy. And though I'm happy for you and Irma, Ryder and I are a different story. I can't explain it now, but if I could change things, I would." Summer's heart wrenched. "Besides, it's Ryder who's left me. If I knew where he was, I honestly think I'd go after him and make him see sense."

Poppy eyed her. "I'm tellin' you, girl," he said with a jabbing finger, "this goes against my very grain, but..."

"But what?"

"Well, hell, Irma says we're doin' our *men thing,* and that ain't fair, either."

Before Summer could inquire into this *men thing,* he cut her off.

"I think Ry is wrong, dead wrong, but it's up to him. Still, if I go home to Irma and she hears... Hell's bells," he muttered. "Women."

So Fred told Summer where she could find Ryder.

SUMMER MANEUVERED the van as carefully as she could. Beyond the road weaving along the shoreline, the gulf blazed with the brilliance of a summer day.

"It has to be along here," she kept telling herself.

Along here, boats wallowed in their slips, cut through the water, dotted the open sea. This was a boater's, surely a fisherman's paradise. Where else would she find Ryder?

"Now, remember, Carrie," she said, catching Carrie's concentrated stare from behind her, "we want to go fishing. Go fishing."

"Go 'ishin'," her daughter said, well rehearsed, if totally clueless.

Summer was pulling out all the stops. Every advantage she had would be exploited to the hilt. And that included Carrie. As Irma had said on wishing her good luck, scruples didn't count in nabbing your man.

Summer noticed then that a sign on what had to be a large boat-rental facility was being hauled down with ropes and ladders. *Crane's Full-Service Boat Rentals*. The rusted sign hung askew above a glaring white parking lot. An additional collection of buildings and docks baked in the late-afternoon sun.

"This has to be it."

But why were they taking down the sign?

Poppy had told her only an address, only the name of a place. Considering herself lucky for that much, she hadn't asked for more. She had no idea whether Ryder simply rented a slip here, or what.

Summer pulled into the parking lot. Almost ramming into a green Volvo in a hurry, she stomped on the brakes.

Ryder.

And then, surely he saw the logo for Dining In on her van.

Guiding the van around him, she parked in the lot.

"Remember now, Carrie," she said, "we're going fishing."

Carrie grinned her candyland smile. Stopping meant getting out. "Go 'ishin'," she parroted.

By then, Ryder approached the door of Summer's van, and she rolled down the window.

"I can't believe this," he said. "I was literally on my way to get you. I was—well, I was hoping..." Evidently, his enthusiasm got crowded out by uncertainty. "I mean, I was hoping to talk you into, uh...come on, get out," he added, going to Carrie's door.

But just as he reached for the handle, the two men who'd been shifting the old boat-rental sign down called to get Ryder's attention.

He seemed flustered, disappointed. "Just a minute," he said to Summer, walking over to the pair.

The large sign now slanted across the facade of the main building, and Summer noticed a second sign, obviously waiting to go in its place. Since it was turned away from her, she couldn't read the new sign, and so she concentrated on getting out of the van.

She'd had only yesterday, Saturday, to arrange her plans. As usual, Dee had been supportive, and Summer was wearing the smallest bikini she'd been able to find on such short notice.

The pebble-pattern metallic gold lamé suit of a scant three patches and straps was overlaid by her filmy, thigh-length cover-up. Sandals and sunglasses and her hair done in a studied disarray completed her outfit. Carrie also wore a gold lamé bikini and a flimsy cover-up. Sandals and big-rimmed Daisy Duck sunglasses made her a picture.

Summer had indeed pulled out whatever stops she could. Ignoring the three males who ground to a halt at the sight of her—the fourth tripped coming out of the rental place to find his car—she took Carrie from her car seat and set her on her small gold-sandaled feet.

"Go 'ishin'," Carrie repeated happily.

But then, catching sight of Ryder, she began to squeal.

Coming back to them, Ryder seemed torn between a grin and keeping his eyes in his head.

"We thought we'd see if you could take us out fishing for a while."

Ryder bent to press a deep kiss on her lips. "You look like you're ready for an X-rated movie, not for fishing."

Carrie, who wove around their legs, picked up on the new term. "Go 'ishin'," she insisted, reaching for Ryder. "Go 'ishin'."

He picked her up. "Yeah, yeah, go fishin'," he said. "But look up there, Boop," he added, redirecting Carrie's gaze to the sign. "They've just about got the second sign ready to go up, and there, there," he said, as the sign swung around, "it goes!"

Second Chance Rentals.

Summer's eyes met Ryder's.

"Yeah, I've bought the place, lock, stock and barrel. That's why I was coming to get you. I've been pushing to get the sign up so I could surprise you. And you're right," he said, "I've needed to give myself a second chance, and here it is. Now that you've seen the sign, I'll show you the rest of the operation."

Coaxing them forward, with Carrie still on his arms, Ryder guided them to the docks. "It's sort of outdated. I mean, the buildings and all. But I've got plans. Man, have I got plans."

He went on to explain his plans, and Summer saw that he wanted her approval. He also touched on the obvious chance he'd taken in deciding what he had without her. But he'd obviously needed this place that much.

Still, Summer was the most taken with that quick smile of his appearing so easily. Ryder seemed energized, renewed. He wore a softly constructed shirt and slacks in slate gray shades. This was apparently casual attire and yet suitable for the new owner of the premises. He was browner, sexier, more good-looking than ever. If that was possible.

Summer's hopes began to build. After all, he'd said he'd been on his way to get them.

"Yeah," he said, as if reading her thoughts, "I've been wanting to call, or even to come down. I mean, we're less than forty-five minutes apart. But I've been so busy getting the—well, no, that's not it, either. I wanted to make sure I could swing the deal, really make a place for us. A place you might consider sharing. I don't want to pressure you into doing something you don't want to do, but, oh, God, Summer," he said, stopping them short on the dock. "I want you to be here with me. I hope you don't mind the way I did this, but I just had to prove—"

"I understand. And no, I don't mind at all. I've been praying we'd end up someplace like this."

Summer noticed *Spare a Dime,* still looking spiffy, nearby. Nothing could be more like home, like Ryder, than *Spare a Dime.* The boat would remain a full-fledged reminder of that first time on that first day, a reminder of how far they'd come.

"Well, I suppose," she said with a wry grin, "I can manage the commute. But we won't have to live on *Spare a Dime,* will we?"

"No, no." He was so anxious to please her that he was endearing. "I've been looking for someplace nearby, and we'll talk about that next. Just as long as you're okay with this."

When a family moved by them on the dock—obviously pleased with an afternoon of fishing—Summer smiled and nodded along with Ryder.

"It's some operation," Ryder said, "but I know I can make it now. That was the most important thing I had to know before I called you. I mean, aside from admitting to myself that you were right in something else. No one died because of me. Not really."

Summer glimpsed the mist in Ryder's green eyes. But before she could tell him how glad she was for him, how wonderful he was, he plunged ahead.

"This place is no fantasy. This is hard work. This second chance of mine will be my clean sweep, but it'll also test me. Do you . . . ?"

"Yes, yes, I understand."

"Go 'ishin'," Carrie said, wanting some of Ryder's attention.

"Yeah, sweet pea, go fishing. All the time. You'll love it, grow up with it."

With that, Carrie grinned a pirate's grin to match her father's. When she planted a big sloppy kiss on his cheek, Ryder's gaze widened with surprise.

Summer saw his delight. But then, when he smiled at Carrie, when his eyes misted again and he kissed his child back, Summer knew he could hardly go higher.

"Say you love me, Carrie," he coaxed. He'd attained one goal. Now he pushed for the last.

But Carrie would be Carrie. "No," she said, condescending only to another smack of a kiss.

Ryder's gaze caressed Summer's. "I suppose that's enough for now," he admitted, swiping the heel of his hand across his eyes. Indeed, pulling Summer into a loose hug with Carrie and himself, he spoke just for them. "I love you both so much. Now that I see you here, I know we can make it."

"I know we can, too."

"I just can't quite believe it yet."

"But that's exactly it, Ry. You have to start believing you deserve good things for all the good things you do."

"Go 'ishin'," Carrie insisted, demanding her part in the conversation. This phrase worked wonders.

"Yeah, yeah," Ryder said. "I'll take you fishing, just as long as I get to be Mommy's catch."

Summer's smile was also wry. "Just remember, since I have to move again, you have to make it worth my while."

This time, Ryder smiled the smoldering smile of the sea bum. "How soon can I start, Aphrodite?"

HARLEQUIN SUPERROMANCE®

HARLEQUIN SUPERROMANCE WANTS TO INTRODUCE YOU TO A DARING NEW CONCEPT IN ROMANCE...

WOMEN WHO DARE!
Bright, bold, beautiful...
Brave and caring, strong and passionate...
They're women who know their own minds
and will dare anything...for love!

One title per month in 1993, written by popular Superromance authors, will highlight our special heroines as they face unusual, challenging and sometimes dangerous situations.

The lady doctor and the sheriff are heading for a showdown in
#574 DOC WYOMING by Sharon Brondos

Available in December wherever Harlequin Superromance novels are sold.

MEN MADE IN AMERICA

Fifty red-blooded, white-hot, true-blue hunks
from every State in the Union!

Look for MEN MADE IN AMERICA! Written by some
of our most poplar authors, these stories feature fifty of
the strongest, sexiest men, each from a different state in
the union!

Two titles available every other month at your favorite
retail outlet.

In November, look for:

STRAIGHT FROM THE HEART by Barbara Delinsky
(Connecticut)
AUTHOR'S CHOICE by Elizabeth August (Delaware)

In January, look for:

DREAM COME TRUE by Ann Major (Florida)
WAY OF THE WILLOW by Linda Shaw (Georgia)

You won't be able to resist MEN MADE IN AMERICA!

1993 Keepsake

CHRISTMAS

Stories

Capture the spirit and romance of Christmas with KEEPSAKE CHRISTMAS STORIES, a collection of three stories by favorite historical authors. The perfect Christmas gift!

Don't miss these heartwarming stories, available in November wherever Harlequin books are sold:

ONCE UPON A CHRISTMAS by Curtiss Ann Matlock
A FAIRYTALE SEASON by Marianne Willman
TIDINGS OF JOY by Victoria Pade

ADD A TOUCH OF ROMANCE TO YOUR HOLIDAY SEASON WITH KEEPSAKE CHRISTMAS STORIES!

HX93